Alexander McCall Smith is the author of over eighty books on a wide array of subjects. For many years he was Professor of Medical Law at the University of Edinburgh and served on national and international bioethics bodies. Then in 1999 he achieved global recognition for his award-winning series The No. 1 Ladies' Detective Agency, and thereafter has devoted his time to the writing of fiction, including the 44 Scotland Street series and the Isabel Dalhousie novels. His books have been translated into forty-six languages. He lives in Edinburgh with his wife Elizabeth, a doctor.

Praise for the 44 Scotland Street series

'Perfect escapist fiction'   *The Times*

'Simple, elegantly written and gently insightful'   *Good Book Guide*

'A joyous, charming portrait of city life and human foibles, which moves beyond its setting to deal with deep moral issues and love, desire and friendship'   *Sunday Express*

'Does for Edinburgh what Armistead Maupin did for San Francisco: seeks to capture the city's rhythms by focusing on a small, emblematic corner ... A light-hearted, genial soap opera'
Financial Times Magazine

By Alexander McCall Smith

ALEXANDER McCALL SMITH

BERTIE'S GUIDE TO LIFE AND MOTHERS

A 44 Scotland Street novel

Illustrations by
IAIN McINTOSH

ABACUS

First published in Great Britain in 2013 by Polygon,
an imprint of Birlinn Ltd
This paperback edition published in 2014 by Abacus

A CIP catalogue record for this book
is available from the British Library.

ISBN 978-0-349-14006-3

Printed and bound in Great Britain by
Clays Ltd, St Ives plc

Papers used by Abacus are from well-managed forests
and other responsible sources.

MIX
Paper from
responsible sources
FSC® C104740

Abacus
An imprint of
Little, Brown Book Group
100 Victoria Embankment
London EC4Y 0DY

An Hachette UK Company
www.hachette.co.uk

www.littlebrown.co.uk

This book is for David Robinson, friend and editor

BERTIE'S GUIDE TO
LIFE AND MOTHERS

1. Knives and Chromosomes

Bertie Pollock (6) was the son of Irene Pollock (37) and Stuart Pollock (40), and older brother of Ulysses Colquhoun Pollock (1). Ulysses was also the son of Irene but possibly not of Stuart, the small boy bearing a remarkable resemblance to Bertie's psychotherapist, recently self-removed from Edinburgh to a university chair in Aberdeen. Stuart, too, had been promoted, having recently been moved up three rungs on the civil service ladder after incurring the gratitude of a government minister. This had happened after Stuart, in a moment of sheer frustration, had submitted the numbers from *The Scotsman*'s Sudoku puzzle to the minister, representing them as likely North Sea oil production volumes. He had immediately felt guilty about this adolescent gesture – *homo ludens*, playful man, might be appreciated in the arts but not in the civil service – and had he been able to retract the figures he would have done so. But it was too late; the minister was delighted with the encouraging projection, with the result that any confession by Stuart would have been a career-terminating event. So he remained silent, and was immensely relieved to discover later that the real figures, once unearthed, were so close to his Sudoku numbers as to make no difference. His conscience was saved by coincidence, but never again, he said to himself.

Irene had no interest in statistics and always adopted a glazed expression at any mention of the subject. 'I can accept that what you do is very important, Stuart,' she said, in a pinched, rather pained tone, 'but frankly it leaves me cold. No offence, of course.'

Her own interests were focused on psychology – she had a keen interest in the writings of Melanie Klein – and the raising of children. Bertie's education, in particular, was a matter of great concern to her, and she had already written an article for the journal *Progressive Motherhood*, in which she had set out the objectives of what she described as 'the Bertie Project'.

'The emphasis,' she wrote, 'must always be on the flourishing of the child's own personality. Yet this overriding goal is not incompatible with the provision of a programme of interest-enhancement in the child herself' (Irene was not one to use the male pronoun when a feminine form existed). 'In the case of Bertie, I constructed a broad and fulfilling programme of intellectual stimulation introducing him at a very early stage (four months) to the possibilities of theatre, music and the plastic arts. The inability of the very small infant to articulate a response to the theatre, for example, is not an indication of lack of appreciation – far from it, in fact. Bertie was at the age of four months taken to a performance by the Contemporary Theatre of Krakow at the Edinburgh Festival and reacted very positively to the rapid changes of light on the stage. There are many other examples. His response to

Klee, for instance, was noticeable when he was barely three, and by the age of four he was quite capable of distinguishing Peploe from Matisse.'

Some of these claims had some truth to them. Bertie was, in fact, extremely talented, and had read way beyond what one might expect to find in a six-year-old. Most six-year-olds, if they can read at all, are restricted to the doings of Spot the Dog and other relatively unsubtle characters; Bertie, by contrast, had already consumed not only the complete works of Roald Dahl for children, but also half of Norman Lebrecht's book on Mahler and almost seventy pages of Miranda Carter's biography of the late Anthony Blunt. His choice of this reading, which was prodigious on any view, was dependent on what he happened to find lying about on his parents' bookshelves, and this was, of course, the reason why he had also dipped into several volumes of Melanie Klein and was acquainted too with a number of Freud's accounts of his famous cases, especially those of Little Hans and the Wolf Man.

Little Hans struck Bertie as being an entirely reasonable boy, who had just as little need of analysis as he himself had.

'I think Dr Freud shouldn't have worried about that boy Hans,' Bertie remarked to his mother, as they made their way one afternoon to the consulting rooms of Bertie's psychotherapist in Queen Street. 'I don't think there was anything wrong with him, Mummy, I really don't.'

'That's a matter of opinion, Bertie,' answered Irene. 'And actually it's Professor Freud, not Dr Freud.'

'Well,' said Bertie. 'Professor Freud then. Why does he

keep going on about …' He lowered his voice, and then became silent.

'About what, Bertie?' asked Irene. 'What do you think Professor Freud goes on about?'

Bertie slowed his pace. He was looking down at the ground with studious intensity. 'About bo …' he half-whispered. Modesty prevented his completing the sentence.

'About what, Bertie?' prompted Irene. 'We mustn't mumble, *carissimo*. We must speak clearly so that others can understand what we have to say.'

Bertie looked anxiously about him. He decided to change the subject. 'What about my birthday, Mummy?' he said.

Irene looked down at her son. 'Yes, it's coming up very soon, Bertie. Next week, in fact. Are you excited?'

Bertie nodded. He had waited so long for this birthday – his seventh – that he found it difficult to believe that it was now about to arrive. It seemed to him that it had been years since the last one, and he had almost given up on the thought of turning seven, let alone eighteen, which he knew was the age at which one could leave one's mother. That was the real goal – a distant, impossibly exciting, shimmering objective. Freedom.

'Will I get any presents?' he asked.

Irene smiled. 'Of course you will, Bertie.'

'I'd like a Swiss Army penknife,' he half-whispered. 'Or a fishing rod.'

Irene said nothing.

'Other boys have these things,' Bertie pleaded.

Irene pursed her lips. 'Other boys? Do you mean Tofu?'

Bertie nodded miserably.

'Well the less said about him the better,' said Irene. She sighed. Why did men – and little boys too – have to hanker after weapons when they already had their . . . She shook her head in exasperation. What was the point of all this effort if, after years of striving to protect Bertie from gender stereotypes, he came up with a request for a knife? It was a question of the number of chromosomes, she thought: therein lay the core of the problem.

2. *Essex Girls et al*

From Bertie's point of view his approaching birthday was the cause of immense excitement. Not only was there the issue of presents – although he was virtually reconciled to not getting what he wanted, as his mother had on previous birthdays always been careful to choose gender-neutral gifts – there was also the question of the party Irene had promised him. This was something to which Bertie looked forward with keen anticipation, although he knew that here, too, there would be snares and pitfalls that would require very careful evasive action on his part.

The greatest problem, of course, was the list of those to be invited. If Bertie had his way, the guests would all be boys, as that would mean that they would be able to play the games they wanted without having to take into account the wishes of any girls. Bertie had once been to a party where the guests had played British Bulldog, and he had enjoyed that every bit as much as that other game of rough and tumble, Chase the Dentist. Girls, he had learned, liked neither of these games, on the grounds that the boys, being rougher and more inclined to push and shove, had a natural advantage over them.

But the list, he knew, could not be an all-boy one, as Irene had made it very clear that she expected an equal number of boy and girl guests.

'There are plenty of nice girls who'd love to come to your party, Bertie,' she assured him. 'There's Olive, obviously, and Olive's friend Pansy. Then there's that pleasant girl Chardonnay, although heaven knows why her parents should saddle her with such a name . . .'

'It sounds rather nice,' said Bertie. 'I think she likes it. And she's got a little sister called Shiraz. That's a nice name too, I think.'

Irene rolled her eyes upwards. 'Such names are . . . well, they're rather closely linked with . . . well, Bertie, I'm sorry to say they are rather closely associated with Essex.'

'Essex?' said Bertie. 'Isn't Essex a place in England, Mummy?'

'Yes it is,' said Irene. 'Unfortunately.'

'What do you mean, Mummy? Are there lots of girls called Chardonnay in Essex, but not in Edinburgh?'

Irene suppressed a smile. 'You could say that, Bertie. Chardonnay is not really an Edinburgh name. But Essex, you see, is a bit . . . It's a bit . . . well, let's not worry about Essex, Bertie. Chardonnay can't help her unfortunate name, and I'm sure that she'll love to come to your party.'

'And there'll be boys too,' said Bertie quickly.

Irene nodded. 'I'm sure that Ranald will be very happy to come.'

'And Tofu.'

Irene made a non-committal noise. 'I thought you found Tofu a bit difficult, Bertie.'

Bertie nodded. 'Yes, he is, Mummy. But I have to invite him. He'd hear about the party and if I didn't invite him, there'd be trouble.'

The conversation about guests continued for some time, but Bertie's mind was not really on it. He was now remembering the party he had attended several weeks earlier, which had been to celebrate Olive's seventh birthday. Bertie had been reluctant to go to this but had been obliged by his mother to accept the invitation. 'You'll enjoy yourself once you're there, Bertie,' she had said. 'I often find that myself when Mummy and Daddy have to go out. We may not be in the mood to begin with, but then we find that we enjoy ourselves quite a lot once we're there. Daddy often finds that.'

Bertie thought about this. 'Is that because he gets drunk, Mummy?'

Irene looked shocked. 'Bertie, you mustn't say things like that. Daddy doesn't get drunk at cocktail parties. Anyway, the point is this: you'll enjoy Olive's party once you're there – you mark my words.'

Bertie did not enjoy himself. When he arrived at Olive's house in the Braids, his heart sank as he saw the cluster of pink balloons tied to the gatepost at the end of the short drive. And it sank even further when he realised that of the twelve guests invited by Olive, he was the only boy.

'Isn't Ranald coming?' he asked Olive as he handed over her present.

'Certainly not,' said Olive. 'Ranald Braveheart Macpherson has not been invited to my house and never will be, with those stupid thin legs of his! No, Bertie, you are the only boy who is privileged to join us today, and you should be jolly grateful for that.'

'Yes,' said Pansy, shaking her finger at him. 'You should know just how lucky you are, Bertie.'

Bertie did not argue. He was outnumbered in every way, and he had long ago learned that arguing with Olive got one nowhere. So he busied himself with a sausage roll and a slice of pizza and waited for events to take their natural course.

After tea, Olive had clapped her hands and announced that it was time for games. 'We're going to play a game now,' she said. 'A really good one.'

'Houses?' asked Pansy. 'Could we play houses, Olive?'

Olive appeared to give this request full consideration before she shook her head. 'No, we shall not play houses, Pansy. Houses is a very yesterday game. We're going to play Jane Austen!'

There were squeals of pleasure and excitement from several of the girls. 'Yes!' enthused Pansy. 'Jane Austen!' And then she asked, 'How do you play that?'

'I'm going to be Lizzie,' said Olive. 'She's a girl with lots of sisters. Pansy, you can be her Mummy, who is very stupid, and Lakshmi, you can be her sister Jane. And Bertie ...'

Bertie looked away. It was only three o'clock and the party was due to go on until five. Two hours of Jane Austen stretched ahead of him.

'And you, Bertie,' said Olive decisively, 'you can be Mr Darcy.'

'How do I do that?' whispered Bertie. 'I don't know how to play Jane Austen, Olive.'

'You just stand there and be handsome,' said Olive. 'That's all you have to do. And when one of the sisters asks you to dance, then you have to bow and say, "Madam, I would be most honoured, truly I would." That's all. You don't have to say anything else.'

'How long do I have to do that for?' asked Bertie.

'An hour or so,' said Olive. 'Then we're going to play another game. Royal Weddings!'

There were further squeals of excitement, but from Bertie there came only a sigh. Royal Weddings, he felt, was a game that adults played – not children.

3. A Psychiatrist's Daughter

For Pat Macgregor, the mother issue had been of a very different complexion. If Bertie might have been expected to wish to see rather less of his mother, then Pat would have liked to see rather more. Unfortunately, this did not happen, as Pat's mother was vague about most things, including the dates on which she and her daughter would meet. After a long history of absenteeism, Maureen Macgregor had eventually drifted out of her marriage by the simple expedient of moving to a village in Perthshire from which she made increasingly infrequent forays into Edinburgh. Her departure from the matrimonial home had not been in any way acrimonious: Dr Macgregor was a tolerant man, who understood that as life progresses we lose interest in some things and develop an interest in others.

In Maureen Macgregor's case, her interest in plants, which had not been present when she lived in the Macgregors' inconspicuous villa in the Grange, had become an abiding passion. Originally self-taught in the subject, she had eventually enrolled in a botanical course in Dundee, which she had completed with distinction. That had been followed by the purchase of a late-eighteenth-century walled garden in Perthshire – a garden that, though once sufficiently distinguished to be the subject of a book, had become derelict and overrun with giant hogweed. Maureen had seen its possibilities, and had acquired the garden and its adjoining cottage for a very small sum in return for a promise to restore it to its previous splendour. The giant hogweed had been slain, the rich earth below tilled, sifted, and raked into submission, and an ambitious physic garden had been planted.

In this task, Maureen had been assisted by a friend whom she had met on the botanical course in Dundee, a woman who, although a good few years younger, seemed to enjoy her company. They had become close friends and had ended up sharing the cottage – an arrangement that suited both of them and, most importantly, made them happy. Dr Macgregor had understood perfectly well and bore no resentment against the friend who had replaced him in his wife's life. He knew that people could drift apart, and he felt that there was no real point in trying to prevent it. In his professional practice, which was devoted to helping people in their unhappiness and distress, he had seen many cases of people trying to be something that they were not. One should not fight these things, he felt.

Pat had accepted the situation with similar equanimity. If her mother was happy, then the somewhat distant, slightly distracted air she had about her was something she could live with. When her father announced that on a busy morning in Perth Sheriff Court the marriage's legal existence had quietly and without fuss been brought to an end, she had experienced none of the disappointment and hurt that such a development can bring. Her mother and father loved her in their very different ways – she knew that, and felt the security that such knowledge brings – and both parents still seemed fond of each other. It could have been far worse, she decided, and for many, of course, it was.

'We stumble,' said Dr Macgregor. 'We try our best in this life, but we stumble. Then we pick ourselves up again, and the dance continues.'

That rather pithy remark resonated in Pat's mind that evening as she made her way from her flat in Marchmont to her father's house in the Grange, where they were due to have dinner together. Pat went for these meals every other

Saturday, although occasionally the routine would vary and they would go out to a restaurant instead. The conversation was always good; Pat's father took a close interest in the doings of Pat's friends, and she took a similar interest in the reported activities of her father's colleagues and the members of the book group to which he belonged. This book group was a serious-minded one that set itself books that could sometimes take months to discuss. Antony Beevor's history of the Second World War had recently taken them four months to deal with, with the discussion becoming bogged down in the North African campaign just as had Rommel's tanks in the sands of the desert. There had also been a heated debate on the qualities of the leaders of the time, with adverse comparisons being made between those politicians and current examples of the breed.

'The real difference,' Dr Macgregor said, 'is that politicians today won't tell people what they need to know. They spend all their time telling them what they think they want to hear.'

'Oh yes?' said Pat.

'Yes. Look at Churchill. What did he say to people? "I have nothing to offer but blood, toil, tears and sweat. We have before us an ordeal of the most grievous kind. We have before us many, many long months of struggle and of suffering." Imagine a politician today saying that! What do ours say? They say: everything's going to be fine, just fine. And it's not, you know.'

'Then why do they say it?' asked Pat.

'Because they know that if you offer people sweat and tears – let alone blood, and struggle and suffering, for that matter – they won't vote for you. They'll vote for anybody who offers them free sandwiches instead.'

Pat digested that. 'So you tell them . . .'

'You tell them that they can have what they want – which is more of everything. You don't tell them that we must all work harder. You don't tell them that we must all try to behave a bit better towards each other. You don't tell them that they must drink less and eat less fatty food. You act as if they must never, ever in any circumstances be offended, and if you inadvertently offend them – by telling the truth, perhaps – you must immediately apologise.'

Pat smiled. She did not think that her father should eat so many chips, for which he had a weakness; perhaps she should tell him, and then, of course, apologise.

'It's infantilisation,' continued Dr Macgregor. 'We have become thoroughly infantilised.'

Pat raised an eyebrow. 'Us? You and I?'

Dr Macgregor laughed. 'No, not us. Theories never apply to us, my dear. I meant the electorate.'

4. A Memory of Lavender

Now, from ancient habit, she reached into the waving forest of lavender and plucked a head. She sniffed it: the smell brought so much back, almost as powerfully as had Proust's madeleine cakes: she saw herself sitting at her desk; she saw her mother rearranging sheets of music on top of the family piano; and there was her friend Anna crouched behind the tree at the other end of the garden while she counted to one hundred, peeking illegally through the spaces between her fingers to see where her playmate was hiding. She felt a sudden pang of regret: life had been so comfortable and assured back then, whereas now ...

Final examinations were looming and her essay on Ridolfo Ghirlandaio had stalled. She was considering the influence of Raphael on his work, and was having difficulty with the topic. Did it matter? All that she was doing was jumping through a hoop to prove to the world that she merited a degree in the history of art. But was the world remotely interested in that fact? Would it make any difference to a prospective employer – if one could be found – that she knew that Raphael influenced Ridolfo Ghirlandaio? There were so many graduates working in coffee bars – one of these establishments in Morningside Road was staffed entirely by classicists, she had read, and there would surely be places where art historians would be welcome. Perhaps she could engage the customers in conversation, mentioning the Florentine renaissance as she handed them their low-fat lattes or their double americanos, or whatever it was they wanted.

She tucked the lavender into a pocket. One never really grows up, she thought; not really. She looked up; her father must have spotted her coming, as he had opened the front door and was standing on the doorstep, silhouetted against the light of the hall. 'I saw you, darling,' he said. 'I saw you picking some lavender.'

She kissed him lightly on the cheek. He smelt of father.

'I love lavender. I always have.'

'Yes,' he said. 'It's your protection, isn't it?'

She looked at him in surprise. 'My protection?'

'I saw you do the same thing every day. You always stopped and picked a few heads of lavender. It was obviously one of those childhood rituals.'

She nodded. 'Yes. I thought I had to do it to stop something terrible happening.'

Dr Macgregor smiled. 'We all do that, in one way or another. I suppose we haven't stopped believing in the gods. We need to placate the gods, although we'd never put it that way these days.'

They made their way into the drawing room, where Dr Macgregor poured his daughter a sherry. 'I know it's desperately uncool to pour people a sherry,' he said. 'But I feel that if I don't do it, something will go wrong.'

'You're not serious . . .'

'No, not really.'

They sat down and talked about what each had been doing. Pat told her father about her essay and he suggested that she cut it short. 'Tell them that it's on the short side because you don't have anything more to say. There's no point in verbiage for verbiage's sake.'

'But they told us it has to be five thousand words. At the moment, it's only two and a half.'

Dr Macgregor made a dismissive gesture. 'What about those PhD theses in mathematics? Some are only, what, twenty pages?'

'That's mathematics,' said Pat. 'Mathematicians don't have much to say – or they can say what they need to say in a few lines.'

'Maybe,' said Dr Macgregor. 'There are some charming and articulate mathematicians, but they can be – how shall I put it – terse. And some mathematicians are certainly on the spectrum.'

'What spectrum?'

'Social inadequacy. When I was at university there was a mathematician who had never been heard to speak – at all. He was regarded as very brilliant, of course, but he never uttered a word. And then, at the opposite end of the spectrum, there was a mathematician who was regarded as being very outgoing because at least he looked at your shoes when he spoke to you.'

'That's cruel,' said Pat.

'But rather funny, I'm afraid,' retorted Dr Macgregor. 'Funny things are very often cruel.'

They sat in silence for a moment. Pat looked at her sherry glass. Then she looked at her father. There was something different about him. Had he had a haircut?

'Your hair,' she said.

He answered quickly. 'I have a new barber.'

'Oh, has Jimmy retired? What's the new one called?'

'No, Jimmy hasn't retired, and the new one is called Angie.'

Pat raised an eyebrow. 'A woman?'

Dr Macgregor nodded. 'Yes, a woman.'

Pat laughed. 'I never thought I'd see the day. You always used to go on about how Jimmy was good enough for you with his gardening shears or whatever he used. You said that male barbers understood men.'

'I still believe that to be true. However, one must move with the times, and now I go to a unisex salon in Bruntsfield.'

'A unisex salon!' exclaimed Pat. 'Daddy, are you all right?'

The question was posed in a tone of amusement. But the concern that underlay it was serious. Pat had long been worried that her father would do something peculiar, and had been ready for signs of this. Abandoning Jimmy was aberrant: men did not change their barbers – at least not men like Dr Macgregor. And as for moving with the times, any middle-aged man who said that he must move with the times was signalling something just as clearly as if he were using an Aldis lamp.

5. Rob Roy as Flawed Hero

They went through to the dining room. In most places people move into rooms rather than through to rooms, but not in Edinburgh where they move through, just as they go through to Glasgow while Glasgow people go across to Edinburgh. People in Scotland go down to London, and Londoners go up to Scotland, which is not surprising, bearing in mind the way the map looks (when held the right way up). The English, of course, think of Edinburgh as being in the north, which it most certainly is not. It's in their north, but not our north; in Scotland, Edinburgh is in the southeast, more or less, or possibly in the central belt, although there are some in Edinburgh who think that particular belt starts slightly further west, but not in the west, which starts a bit further north.

The Macgregor house was not of a sufficient size to justify the use of compass points to describe rooms. It had two storeys, the ground floor consisting of a hall, kitchen, drawing

room, dining room, scullery, and what the property depart-
ments of solicitors' firms used coyly to describe as the usual
offices. These usual offices contained something called, in the
same descriptive tradition, a vanitory unit. The word vanitory
appears only on sufferance in dictionaries and possibly came
into existence through the tendency of plumbers installing
such things to add the occasional syllable, as a courtesy. The
term stuck, and summed up, rather neatly some felt, the aspirational quality of such an item. This was no mere vanity unit,
no everyday basin for the washing of hands; this was a large,
avocado-coloured ceramic construction with ornate taps and
a substantial mirror into which the vain might peer – hence
vanitory. The first floor consisted of three bedrooms and a
large, draughty bathroom in which there was no vanitory unit
at all, but only an uncomfortable bath and a meagre basin.

The dining room that Pat and her father now entered was
furnished comfortably, with a large red Turkish carpet on the
floor, a sideboard on which a seldom-used decanter stood
along with a silver coffee pot and an empty Mason's Ironstone
fruit bowl, a three-leaved mahogany table, and a set of six
ladder-backed chairs the seats of which were covered with
now somewhat threadbare tapestry work. On the walls were
the usual views of Perth in mezzotint, and a large Victorian
painting of a hillside in the Trossachs. While such pictures
might normally be expected to have a small herd of Highland
cattle in the foreground, or perhaps a stag or two, this painting was distinguished by a group of kilted figures engaging in
vigorous disagreement with a detachment of soldiers. The soldiers were on the losing side: the Highlanders having floored
several of them were now clearly on the point of putting the

rest to flight. At the bottom of the gilded frame, a small tablet gave the name and dates of the artist and the title of the picture, Rob Roy Macgregor Defeats the Duke of Montrose's Men.

Pat had lived with the painting and with her father's claim that he – and therefore she – stood in a direct line of descent from the famous outlaw. She had never liked the painting, though, which she felt was too partisan, rather like one of those works of discredited Soviet Realism that left little doubt as to the artist's sympathies, simulated or genuine. Now, coming into the room for dinner, she glanced up at it as she sat down and her father began to serve the cold quiche that he had prepared.

'I always thought that if Rob Roy were the hero he's made out to be he would have been kinder to those poor soldiers,' said Pat.

Dr Macgregor looked up at the painting. 'Artistic licence,' he said. 'The artist romanticised him, as just about everybody did. He's made to look like a tall, handsome Highlander. In fact he had terribly long arms. They went down almost to his knees – he looked a bit like an orang-utan, I suppose.'

Pat laughed. 'National heroes very rarely look like orang-utans.'

Dr Macgregor smiled. 'Exactly. Not at all fitting.' He paused. 'He was probably also a psychopath – not that anybody mentions that openly.'

'Really?'

Dr Macgregor slipped a large slice of quiche onto his daughter's plate. 'Yes. Psychopathic personality disorder as we used to call it. There are fancy new names for it these days –

sociopathy, anti-social personality disorder and so on – but what we're talking about is good, old-fashioned psychopathy.'

Pat looked up at the figure of Rob Roy, surrounded by his Highlanders, his claymore raised above his head. The arms were quite long, she realised. A long-armed psychopath of orang-utanlike appearance . . . It sounded so iconoclastic . . .

'He showed all the signs,' Dr Macgregor continued. 'He lied. He cheated. He stole livestock as if cattle were going out of fashion. He pretended to be a Jacobite and all the time he was passing information on to the Duke of Atholl and the like.'

'He was a traitor to his cause?'

Dr Macgregor shrugged. 'It doesn't make me particularly proud to be a Macgregor, but yes, he was. The only real cause that Rob Roy cared about was his own interests. He was an informer.' He paused. 'Mind you, just about everybody at that time was every bit as bad. There were plenty of others who switched sides. Gordon of Glenbucket, for instance.'

'Glenbucket?' Was there really somebody called Glenbucket?

'Yes. It makes one think of Oor Wullie and his bucket, doesn't it? But Glenbucket did exist, and he changed sides too.'

'What an awful place Scotland must have been in those days,' said Pat.

'My dear,' said Dr Macgregor, 'everywhere was awful, and, in a sense, everywhere still is awful. The world, I'm afraid, is a vale of tears and always has been. But Scotland suffered from particularly unpleasant nobles – a dreadful bunch in every respect. The nobles, after all, were simply the more successful thieves. That's what made them noble.'

Pat shook her head. 'Isn't it odd that we actually accepted all that?'

'Not everybody did,' said Dr Macgregor. 'Remember what Burns said in "A Man's A Man For A' That". Remember that?'

'Yes,' said Pat. 'Of course I do.'

'Well,' said Dr Macgregor, 'what Burns says is what we, as a nation, want at heart.'

6. *Socks Bought by Somebody Else*

Dr Macgregor served them coffee in the drawing room, using the chipped cylindrical coffee cups – coffee cans as he called them – that had belonged to an aunt of his wife's. These might have ended up in Perthshire, he thought, but his wife had taken little from the house, out of awkwardness or guilt, or perhaps because the cottage in Perthshire was not the place for such dreary china. He had been in that kitchen once, and had seen that everything was bright and modern: a red fridge, a framed Hockney print, retro mugs that said *Keep Calm and Carry On*; there was no place for fuddyduddy Wedgwood there, he thought, and no place for him either. Sometimes, he reflected, a spouse or partner simply becomes aesthetically unsuitable and has to be scrapped. That happened to women, of course, when their husbands began to notice the effect of gravity and the years, the sagging, the desiccation, the wrinkling, and started to pay attention, as men did, to younger women. He, of course, would not have cared about such things, and would have adhered, as his lawyer had put it, but she had decided otherwise, and, well, he could understand why.

But then there had been that article in the copy of *Gentleman's Quarterly* that he had read in the dentist's waiting room, and it had occurred to him that he might be able to do something about himself and have the makeover the magazine suggested. 'Nobody is beyond the help of a looks-and-style assessment,' the article advised. 'Everybody can be helped to get the woman he deserves.' This wording had intrigued him. Did we deserve emotional or sexual satisfaction? Was that now something that we were somehow owed by some external dispenser of such things, some Cupid or Eros, the god of mortal doting envisaged by Auden in his *Bucolics*? Was that what people now expected?

Over her full coffee can – and the coffee's cold, she thought; poor Daddy – Pat looked at her father and noticed, now that he was sitting down and had crossed his legs, that he was wearing striped socks. He had never worn anything but black socks before, even on holiday in Spain when she, as a teenager, had experienced burning, mortifying embarrassment at her father's holiday garb that had included those black socks. This settled the matter: something had happened. At what age did men have their mid-life crisis? And did it matter all that much? There were presumably many men who had their mid-life crisis quietly and with such consideration that nobody, not even their wives, noticed it – the Grange must be full of such people, she felt. Of course there were those who had vivid and disruptive mid-life crises, and behaved, as a result, like Italian prime ministers. Some men, perhaps, even had fatal mid-life crises: she imagined those obituaries that stated the cause of death – these would say, discreetly, *Died, of a sudden and unexpected mid-life crisis* ...

Dr Macgregor looked at his watch, and she noticed.

'Yes,' she said. 'It's late and I must get back to the flat. That essay ...'

He nodded. 'I'll walk you back.'

'No need, Daddy. It's not really dark yet.'

He glanced out of the window. The Scottish summer made the sky still light, even at this hour. 'No, I'd like the walk anyway.'

In your new socks, she thought.

'Those socks,' she said. 'They're very nice. Bright. Where did you buy them?'

He opened his mouth to speak, but nothing came, and she realised, in a moment of insight, that when somebody can't say where their socks come from then that can only mean one thing: somebody else had bought them.

'I find it really difficult to get good socks,' she said quickly. 'I found a mohair pair the other day.'

He seemed relieved not to have to answer her question. 'Mohair,' he said, rising from his chair. 'Thank heavens for mohair. Where would we be without it, I wonder.'

'Where indeed?'

They left the house and made their way to the Marchmont street on which Pat lived. At the front door of her common stair, Pat said goodbye to her father, kissing him on the cheek. Aftershave? Cologne?

'You're wearing . . .' She stopped herself. She was going to say 'You're wearing something' but then she realised that she should not; she did not want to embarrass her father. And so she said, 'You're wearing nice socks.'

He smiled, and nodded. 'Maybe I should look for some mohair socks – like you.'

He turned away with a wave and she went up to her flat. Once in, she made her way to the sitting room window that overlooked the street. From there she looked down and saw her father walk back along the way they had come, only to stop suddenly, look over his shoulder, and then turn in the opposite direction.

Pat acted impulsively. On sober reflection she would never have entertained the thought of following her father, but at that moment it seemed to her to be the only thing to do.

She went out into the street. Dr Macgregor was now some distance away, walking fairly quickly, and had arrived at the end of Spottiswoode Road. When he turned that corner, Pat accelerated her pace, although she was careful to keep sufficiently far away from him so that if he turned and looked back he might not spot her.

They reached the Meadows, and Pat watched from the

cover of the trees as Dr Macgregor began to walk down one of the transverse paths that led down towards Tollcross. Then, satisfied that he would not be able to see her, she continued to follow him.

In Brougham Place, he lingered briefly outside the window of a still-open grocery store but did not enter it. Pat watched as he went further down the road. There were more people about now – a group of students heading to a party, a man walking a couple of elderly dogs, a few couples coming out of restaurants – and she felt more confident about not being seen. And if the worst came to the worst and she was spotted, then here she could at least claim to be going off to meet a friend in one of the nearby bars, having decided that the essay would not progress that night.

Then she stopped. Dr Macgregor had paused outside a doorway in a tenement of flats. Then he pressed a button on an intercom, leaned forward to announce himself, and disappeared inside.

7. *The Declaration of Arbroath*

From her flat on the top floor of 44 Scotland Street, Domenica Macdonald looked out at the windows on the opposite side of the road. The view was one that would have been much appreciated by anybody with a close interest in the affairs of neighbours, but Domenica had always resolutely averted her gaze when anything unduly personal began to unfold before her eyes. This seemed to her to be the minimally decent thing to do, but she knew that this forbearance had not been shared by her former neighbour, Antonia, who had been unable to resist the temptation to look.

'You'll never guess what I've just seen,' she had remarked to Domenica one evening on the common landing. 'You'd think that people would draw their curtains.'

Domenica was silent.

'That young woman opposite, the one from Stornoway ...'

Domenica smiled. 'Ah yes, such a nice girl ...'

Antonia smirked; she knew better than that. 'She was having a flaming row with that boyfriend of hers. You should have seen the saucepans flying ...'

Domenica pursed her lips. 'I'm sure she thought she was having it in private – one does make that assumption, you know, that what one does in one's own space is free from the gaze of outside eyes. And we all throw saucepans from time to time ...' she stared at Antonia before continuing, 'believing ourselves, perhaps naïvely, to be throwing them in privacy ...'

Antonia's nosiness was only one of the reasons for strained relations between the two women; there had also been the vexed affair of the blue Spode cup Domenica had been convinced had been stolen from her flat by her neighbour. She repatriated the cup, only to discover later on that the original cup had been in her flat all along, meaning that she, not Antonia, stood accused – in a metaphorical sense – of the wrongful taking of blue Spode.

Now, of course, everything had changed, including, Domenica imagined, Antonia herself, who was now some sort of lay associate of an order of nuns in Tuscany. These nuns had offered Antonia hospitality during her convalescence from the sudden attack of Stendhal Syndrome that had struck her in the

Uffizi Gallery, and the spiritual peace of their rural convent had so impressed itself upon their guest that she had decided to remain there on a permanent basis.

This decision to stay in the Italian convent had been accompanied by an offer to sell Domenica her flat at a very attractive price – an offer that Domenica had agonised over at some length before eventually reaching the conclusion that she should buy it. Antonia's flat was contiguous with her own, and could be joined to it with minimal structural alteration: a door inserted into a shared wall would easily and appropriately add a further four rooms to Domenica's five, and all without months of building works. That had been done shortly before Domenica's wedding to Angus, with the result that they now each had a separate study and a bathroom, and Cyril, who had been accustomed to sleeping in a large dog basket in Angus's kitchen, now had the luxury of sleeping in a room exclusively given over to his use.

Cyril had originally been confused by these new arrangements. He understood that his place was with his master – wherever Angus might be – but he could not fathom the reason why, instead of walking back round the corner to Drummond Place at the end of a visit, as they always had done, they should stay for such long periods in Scotland Street. And then there was Domenica to contend with: Cyril had been aware of her disapproval, at least in the early days of their relationship, but had been pleased when she began to show first acceptance and then affection. If she was prepared to move emotionally, then so was he, and by the time of the merging of the households he regarded her as being every bit as much his responsibility as Angus was.

Angus and Domenica themselves had adjustments to make – both had been accustomed to living alone, even if Domenica had been married before. For Angus, having somebody else in the house all the time was an entirely delightful feeling, so much more satisfactory than the isolation at the heart of his previous domestic arrangements. He had had no idea how lonely he was – singularity had seemed a natural state for him – and it was only now, with Domenica's reassuring presence constantly at hand, that he realised the length and depth and breadth of his previous loneliness. How had he tolerated it? How had he endured those empty evenings when the flat was silent and the hours of darkness stretched out ahead? One answer had been the Cumberland Bar, where he went several nights a week, or the Scottish Arts Club, where he met his artist friends and, from time to time, that sociable dentist who, after a party, had inserted Cyril's gold tooth. Another answer was that he had resorted to engaging himself in solitary conversation, a habit that he had now been obliged to break.

'You do realise, I take it,' Domenica pointed out to him, 'that you speak to yourself?'

He had blushed. 'I shall try not to. Living alone, you know, one gets into these habits.'

She laughed. 'No, I wasn't referring to remarks you address to yourself during the day. We all do that – mutter away if we think nobody's listening. No, it's what you say in your sleep that interests me.'

Angus froze. 'In my sleep?'

'Yes. You can be quite articulate – sometimes. At other times it's difficult to work out what you're saying.'

Angus looked away. He had no idea he spoke in his sleep and the thought appalled him. 'What sort of thing do I say?' he asked. His voice had a faltering tone.

'Well, last night you said something about Creative Scotland. And then there was something about the Declaration of Arbroath. That was the night before.'

Angus felt a degree of relief. That was nothing too embarrassing – there must be plenty of people muttering about the Declaration of Arbroath in their sleep.

'And then the other night there was something that surprised me.'

Angus looked at Domenica anxiously. He hardly dared ask.

'You said, "They're getting my vote all right."'

'Who? Who's getting my vote?'

Domenica shrugged. 'You didn't say. I must confess I was rather interested, and so I gave you the gentlest shake and asked you who was getting your vote, but you just mumbled something unintelligible and then became quite uncommunicative.'

8. Narrow Ledger

It was bad enough for Angus to hear that he was talking in his sleep about his political intentions, but what Domenica now went on to disclose was even more unsettling.

'Do you know you got up the other night?'

Angus frowned. 'To go to the bathroom?'

'No, not that. You sat up in bed, bolt upright, as if you'd suddenly had some sort of brilliant idea.'

Angus's frown deepened. He had no recollection of this; brilliant ideas were few and far between and one should surely remember them when they occur. 'Are you sure?'

'Am I sure? Of course I'm sure.'

'And?'

Domenica continued, speaking cautiously, as if particularly concerned to get the details right. 'I woke up and saw you sitting there, and then you got out of bed and put on your dressing gown. You took it off the peg on the back of the door, wrapped it round you, and then padded off in the direction of the kitchen.'

Angus looked down at the floor. I'm a somnambulist, he thought, feeling oddly ashamed. And then he thought: what was the title of that opera, and who wrote it? *The Somnambulist*. And what happened in it?

Domenica sensed that Angus was embarrassed, and she reached out gently to place a hand on his forearm. 'You shouldn't worry,' she said, adding, 'too much.'

'I don't remember any of this,' Angus stuttered. 'I ... I ...'

'I decided to follow you,' Domenica continued. 'You went into the kitchen, you see, and then you started to open and close the drawers. You didn't take anything out of them. You just opened and closed them.'

'Oh,' said Angus.

'I asked you what you were doing and you said something about ...' She began to smile. 'I know it sounds ridiculous. I know that ...'

'Tell me,' muttered Angus.

'It was something about the Declaration of Arbroath.'

Angus looked at her in astonishment. 'The Declaration ...'

'Yes,' said Domenica, continuing to smile. 'It was as if you ... well, it was as if you were looking for the Declaration of Arbroath in one of the kitchen drawers.'

Angus shook his head in bewilderment. 'I find this almost unbelievable. Why on earth would I go on about the Declaration of Arbroath while opening the kitchen drawers? It just doesn't make sense.' He paused. 'You didn't dream all this, Domenica?'

Domenica was quick to deny the possibility. 'Of course not! I remember it all quite well and I assure you I was not dreaming.'

'You see,' said Angus, 'it's possible that you don't remember that it was a dream. Sometimes that happens, doesn't it? People think that something happened and it didn't – not really. The mind can play all sorts of tricks on you.'

Domenica was not to be shifted. 'I'm sorry, Angus,' she said firmly. 'I've looked the subject up and I know what I'm talking about. What you did was classic somnambulistic activity. Somnambulists perform banal actions – opening and closing drawers, for instance – that's exactly the sort of thing they do.'

Angus was silent. If this revealing conversation was an instance of the necessary intimacy of marriage, then perhaps he could understand why people remained single.

Domenica looked at him doubtfully. 'I wasn't certain that I should raise this with you. But I decided that I should.'

'Why?' He sounded resentful – he did not intend that, but that was how his question emerged.

She chose her words carefully. 'Sometimes somnambulists can harm themselves ... or others.'

The last two words were uttered softly, and Angus had to strain to hear them. He stared at Domenica mutely, wondering

31

whether she thought him dangerous. The idea was an appalling one.

'Really?'

Domenica nodded. 'It's relatively uncommon,' she went on. 'But I read that sometimes somnambulists can walk along narrow ledges – that sort of thing.'

'We haven't got any narrow ledges,' said Angus.

'You know what I mean,' said Domenica. 'There are plenty of ways of harming yourself. What if ...' She hesitated. 'What if you took a knife out of one of the drawers and cut yourself?'

'But I didn't. You said that I just opened and closed them – as if I were looking for the Declaration of Arbroath.'

'Yes, but there have been cases ...' She did not finish her sentence.

'What cases?'

'Cases where somnambulists have hurt others.'

It's out in the open now, he thought. At least she has said it.

'Look,' Angus said. 'Are you worried about this? Is this something I should be worried about?'

She took a few moments to consider his question. 'I'm not sure,' she began. 'I've made it my business to read up about it, but I'm no expert. Most of what I've read is quite reassuring, but there are one or two cases that people write about that might make one a bit more worried.' She paused, as if judging the effect of her words. 'I think that it might be an idea to see somebody. Just for general reassurance. And there's somebody in Edinburgh, apparently.'

He realised that she must have spoken to somebody to find that out. 'Did you speak to our own doctor?' he asked.

Domenica said that she had. 'He says that he can arrange an appointment for you with a sleep expert. He said you should come and see him first, and then he can refer you. There's somebody at the Royal Ed.'

Angus bit his lip. The Royal Edinburgh was the local psychiatric hospital.

'The loony bin?' he asked.

Domenica looked disapproving. 'Angus! You mustn't call it that! Nobody uses that term any more.'

He shrugged his shoulders. 'But that's what it is. And that's what you seem to be arranging for me – an appointment at the loony bin.'

Domenica shook her finger at him. 'I don't like that expression. Far be it from me to be PC – heaven forfend that possibility, but I really think there are things you shouldn't say.'

'All right,' said Angus. 'I won't say them.'

'Good,' said Domenica. 'It's very childish to talk about loony bins – or funny farms, for that matter. It stigmatises.'

Angus was looking at his hands. 'I'm really upset,' he muttered.

Domenica moved forward to comfort him. Placing an arm about his shoulder, she pulled him to her. 'I'm sorry, Angus,' she whispered. 'I'm so sorry. It's only because I care about you. You're very precious to me. I don't want you ... '

'Walking along any narrow ledges?' he supplied.

'Of course not.'

'I don't see what this doctor – whoever he is – will be able to do for me,' he said.

'Well, I think he might be a big help,' said Domenica.

'He's a shrink?' asked Angus.

'Yes,' said Domenica. 'He's a shrink.'

'What's he called?'

Domenica made an effort to remember. 'Dr Macgregor,' she answered. 'I think.'

9. In the Cumberland Bar

A dog will always sense when its owner's spirits are low. With that uncanny canine ability to detect distress, Cyril crawled up to Angus like a soldier making his way through a minefield. It was his apologetic gait – belly hugging the floor, paws akimbo – the gait that a dog will use when guilt makes it want to keep its profile low, or, as in this case, when it hesitates to intrude upon its owner's feelings of dejection.

Angus looked down at Cyril, at the dog's wide, imploring eyes. 'You know something's wrong, don't you?' he said.

Cyril whimpered, and inched forward.

'You wouldn't understand, old boy,' said Angus. 'If I'm looking a bit down it's because Domenica has just booked me into the loon– the Royal Ed. That's why.'

Cyril, now at Angus's feet, nuzzled at his master's right hand. The feel of the dog's tongue moist and raspy against his skin, the warmth of his breath, the unmistakable and unconditional sympathy from the animal, lifted his spirits. If the world misunderstands us, as it sometimes does, or is indifferent to our sorrows, as it often is, then the loyalty of a dog may remind us that at least in one heart are we loved and admired without question and without thought of reward or advantage. For Angus, this reminder was timeous, and looking down on Cyril he stroked the dog's head gently. 'All right, Cyril, I shall avoid self-pity. There's nothing more unattractive than self-pity, is there?'

Aware that he was being asked a question, but unsure of what it was or of what answer was expected of him, Cyril shook his head vigorously and then modulated the movement into a nod. At the same time he smiled, allowing his single gold tooth to catch the light and send out a little signal of warmth.

'Cumberland Bar?' asked Angus, glancing at his watch.

Now this was something that Cyril understood, along with a small list of key words and phrases: walk, lead, stick, Turner Prize (at the mention of which he would give a growl and lift his leg in vulgar protest), stay, quiet, bad dog, good dog, Valvona & Crolla, and biscuits. At the mention of the bar at the corner of Cumberland and Dundonald Streets, Cyril leapt to his feet, uttered an enthusiastic bark, and went to fetch the lead from its new position – hanging on the back of the kitchen door.

It was a short walk to the Cumberland Bar but by the time he reached it Angus already felt more cheerful. It had been a shock to discover that he was a somnambulist, but now that he had had the opportunity to reflect on the information, he had begun to feel that of all the discoveries one might make about oneself, this one was perhaps not too bad. And it was not unusual, he thought, to find out something about oneself that one did not know. People found out things about their ancestry, for example, that could completely change their sense of who they were. Who, he asked himself, was that man in Australia who discovered that if the rules of succession had been properly applied – in so far as they discriminated against the illegitimate – then he would have been the rightful claimant to the throne. He had apparently been unaffected by this information, and had continued to lead his modest suburban life without affectation. Of course there were worse things to discover about oneself than that one was a Plantagenet.

He reached the door of the Cumberland Bar and released Cyril from his leash. The dog required no further command nor encouragement. Pawing at the bottom of the door, he succeeded in opening it and sauntered in with all the confidence of a regular entering his local bar.

The barman, seeing Cyril, immediately reached for the

dog's dish kept under the bar and held it under the Guinness tap.

'The usual, Cyril?' he asked.

Cyril wagged his tail in response and looked over his shoulder for Angus, who had followed him into the bar. Angus now ordered his own drink and then took that, together with Cyril's dish, to a table in the corner. Several other customers, recognising Angus and Cyril, gave a nod in their direction, and one or two uttered words of greeting. Cyril was a popular dog, and had a wide circle of acquaintances who knew his name and would stop to ruffle his coat if they met him in the street. The story of his gold tooth was well known too, and regular customers at the Cumberland Bar would point it out to visitors or newcomers.

Angus sat down at his table. Down at his feet, Cyril slurped thirstily at his dish of beer, licking the plate once he had drunk it all. Then he settled down at his master's feet, dozing off, but keeping half an eye on the door in case anybody he knew should come in.

And somebody did. This was Matthew, who had just locked up his gallery in Dundas Street and had decided to spend half an hour or so in the Cumberland Bar before returning to the flat in India Street. When one is the father of triplets, as Matthew was, the prospect of returning after bath-time, rather than before it, was an attractive one. Not that he did not enjoy the company of his three young sons, Tobermory, Rognvald and Fergus; it was just that Elspeth seemed to be so much better at bathing the boys than he was and whenever he bundled them up in their nappies they seemed to wet them almost immediately, and they would cry when he started all over again. On balance, he thought, the Cumberland Bar was perhaps rather more congenial than India Street at six in the evening.

He swallowed, feeling a sudden surge of guilt. That was the trouble with being the father of triplets: there was no relief from the sheer burden of having three tiny lives dependent on one. That, of course, was what being a parent was all about – being the author of another life. Most people became accustomed to that, and managed it quite well when the duties were staggered, but suddenly to be responsible for three young children all at once was three times as onerous, thought Matthew. Entering a bar was never the solution to a problem, of course, but it could at least put it off, as any anodyne does, for a while.

10. *Definite Articles, et cetera*

Matthew sat down beside Angus. Reaching down, he gave Cyril a pat on the head, which Cyril acknowledged with something between a sigh and a grunt. He liked Matthew, and the young man's ankles, which had been such a temptation to him before, and, in a moment of weakness, he had eventually nipped, he could now face with equanimity – the benefit, perhaps, of that sagacity that comes to most of us, even to dogs, with the passage of the years.

'I can't stay too long,' said Matthew, glancing at his watch. 'Elspeth ...'

Angus Lordie grinned. 'Ah,' he said. 'The wife.'

Matthew looked at him sideways. What was Angus

doing talking about wives in that way, when he had been married for months rather than years? And should one ever say the wife? It was such an old-fashioned expression, redolent of every cliché of the married state: the shrew of a wife, the wife who kept her husband on a short leash, the husband who is sair hodden-doon. Matthew thought of a friend of his father's, a man in his early fifties who, having always referred to the wife, after his divorce started to refer to the girlfriend. Definite articles could be complimentary, as in the Chairman, or the Earl of Auchtermuchty, or the Pope, but they could also be sarcastic or derogatory, as in 'There he is with the friend', there being no doubt but that the friend is not a good influence or has no right to be there.

'Does Domenica disapprove of the Cumberland Bar?' he asked.

Angus looked surprised. 'No. Not as far as I know.'

'It's just that sometimes wives don't like their husbands going off to the pub,' said Matthew. 'Avoiding the children's bath-time, and ... ' He looked away guiltily.

Angus took a sip of his beer. 'I don't think that Domenica resents my having friends. Surely Elspeth doesn't, does she?'

Matthew shook his head. 'No.' He looked up at the ceiling of the bar, and thought. What exactly was Elspeth's attitude to his friends? And, come to think of it, who were his friends anyway?

'Of course there are some women who won't tolerate them, you know,' Angus continued.

'Their husbands' friends?'

Angus nodded. 'Particularly if the friends are women.'

Matthew frowned. 'But that's different. A wife feels threatened if her husband has women friends. And you can see why.'

Angus was reluctant to exclude the possibility of a man's having women friends. He was friendly with Big Lou, for instance, and with ... He paused. Did he have any other women friends? There were women in the Scottish Arts Club, but did they count as friends or were they simply people he occasionally met in the Scottish Arts Club? It was difficult to decide. 'I think it's sad,' he said. 'Why shouldn't we have friends of the opposite sex?'

'It's because of what's lurking in the background,' Matthew said. 'It's always there in relationships between men and women, whether you like it or not. There's always the possibility of a romantic dimension, no matter how unlikely it is in the particular circumstances. And both parties know it. But there's no problem if you're gay. Then you can have bags of women friends. They'll like you because anything other than friendship isn't on offer.'

Angus thought about that. It was true. And it was unfair. 'How many women friends have you got, Matthew?' he asked, adding, 'Other than Big Lou.'

Matthew smiled. 'I don't see why we should exclude Big Lou, but in answer to your question ... ' He looked up at the ceiling. Then he said, 'None, really.'

Angus was moderately surprised by this. 'Pat Macgregor?'

Matthew conceded that Pat was a friend. 'I wasn't thinking of her. She's been an employee, you see, and ... '

'But you were in love with her, weren't you? Once.'

Matthew glanced at Angus, and then looked away. 'Maybe. But yes, she's a friend. And then there are a couple of girls who were in my year at school. Well, in my year in the sixth form, because the Academy only took girls for the last two years in those days. They had been at St George's. And then there were some women friends from St Andrews, and . . .'

'So you have lots of female friends,' interrupted Angus.

'Whom I never see. Never.' He felt a sudden sadness as he spoke. He was losing contact with his friends, he thought, and that was why he had so quickly said he had none. He had been wrong, but he had been right – as we often are, he thought. He looked down at the floor.

'May I give Cyril some of my beer?' he asked.

Angus glanced at Matthew's glass. 'He normally drinks stout, but you could try him on lager. Not too much, though. He only has a very little bit.'

Matthew bent down and poured some of the beer from his glass into Cyril's dish. The dog, surprised at this sudden largesse, rose to his feet, his tail wagging enthusiastically.

'He's very pleased,' said Matthew.

'It's been a rather frustrating day for him,' said Angus. 'He saw several particularly smug-looking cats in Drummond Place today. He would have liked to have sorted them out, but he was on his lead at the time. Unfinished business. He probably feels he needs a drink.'

Matthew had intended to pour only a small quantity of beer into Cyril's dish but had inadvertently filled it with what amounted to half a pint. Cyril, unaccustomed to such a large amount of beer, and rather taking to the unfamiliar taste of Matthew's lager, lost no time in lapping up what was before him. Then he sat down, looked up at Matthew, and uttered a loud bark of joy.

'Rather vocal,' said Angus. 'I think he liked that.'

'I might have given him a bit too much,' said Matthew. 'I didn't mean to.'

'He'll be all right,' said Angus. 'He'll quieten down.' He looked sternly at Cyril. 'No barking in the Cumberland Bar,' he said. 'It calls attention to the fact that you're a dog.'

Matthew said nothing. He was watching Cyril, who was now beginning to execute what appeared to be a small dance. And then there was another bark – this time even louder than the previous one. Then Cyril sat down and looked about him, grinning, his tongue hanging out of his mouth, his gold tooth catching the light.

'I think he's drunk,' said Matthew. He turned to Angus. 'Look, Angus, I'm very sorry. I've made your dog drunk.'

11. *Cyril Draws Attention to Himself*

Angus understood, of course.

'You didn't mean to,' he said. 'And it's my fault, really. I told you that you could give him more beer. It's my fault.'

Matthew was watching Cyril. The dog, who had been sitting, was now back on his feet and appeared to be dancing some sort of Irish jig. He did this for a moment, then, after a brief pause, began to chase his tail. That did not last long, and the jig was resumed.

By now one or two of the other customers in the bar were looking on with interest. There were smiles, not to say similes.

'See that dog,' said one of the regulars. 'Angus gives him a dish of beer. He's had too much. He's fu'!'

'Drunk as a dog,' said his friend. 'Isn't that what they say?'

'No, sick as a dog. Drunk as a lord,' corrected the other. 'Sober as a judge, but drunk as a lord.'

'Great metaphors.'

'You mean analogies.'

'Perhaps.' But this was followed by a pause. 'A metaphor is a sort of analogy.'

'Yes it is. But a metaphor says that something is something else. An analogy says that something is like something else.'

Angus decided that it was time to remove Cyril. The Cumberland Bar was a respectable bar, and the spontaneous dancing of an Irish jig was not conduct that would be viewed with favour. Irish jigs were all very well in their place, which was in Ireland, but not in an Edinburgh bar. Indeed Angus was of the view that Irish dancing, in general, was to be

43

discouraged, along with faux Irish bars called Donohue's or McGinty's and decorated outside with shamrocks and copious quantities of green paint. And now here was Cyril, on whom faux Irishdom might have been expected to have no real cultural impact, descending to the performance of an Irish jig. He would have to remove him before matters became even more embarrassing.

'We're going to have to get Cyril out of here,' he said, gesturing to the dog. 'A couple of brisk circuits of Drummond Place might sober him up.' He turned to Matthew. 'Fancy a walk?'

Matthew glanced at his watch. It was turning into a guilty evening: guilt over his avoiding the triplets' bath-time and guilt over getting his friend's dog drunk. 'I should get back,' he began, but then faltered. No. Cyril's intoxicated state was his fault and he should keep Angus company while he tried to sober the dog up. He would give his explanations to Elspeth when he returned to India Street and of course she would understand. Elspeth always understood. 'I'll come with you,' he said. 'Who knows what a drunk dog might do. Two people may be needed.'

Angus did not think there was any real likelihood of Cyril's proving difficult. Intoxication, in his experience, disclosed a person's true nature. Nice people were nice when they had taken too much to drink; nasty people were nasty. What had Domenica said about Auden? Hadn't she said something about his views on the weather that could be applied here? He racked his brains and yes, that was it: nice weather is what nice people were nice about and nasty weather was what nasty people were nasty about. It was such a peculiar thing to say – at least at first blush – and yet it was, Angus decided, so true. People giving to moaning about things in general moaned about the weather; people not giving to moaning took an optimistic view of a darkening sky. Darkening skies could – and did – lighten. Rain fell, but then stopped falling; wind gusted, but also petered out.

'Cyril will not be difficult,' Angus said confidently. 'His true nature will reveal itself. *In vino veritas.* He's a good dog, you see.'

Matthew picked up his coat, which he had deposited on the back of his chair. Although it was a fine summer evening, there had been a chill in the air that morning when he had left the flat, and he had taken a lightweight coat to work. 'I still feel rather bad about this,' he muttered to Angus.

Angus assured him that an apology was not necessary. 'Who amongst us has never made a dog drunk?' he asked.

'Virtually everyone,' said Matthew, smiling.

Angus reattached Cyril's lead to the dog's collar, and the three of them began to make their way out of the bar, Cyril walking somewhat unsteadily, his tail wagging preternaturally fast. As they approached the door, a man who had been watching Cyril's antics with interest slipped off his stool and approached them.

'Excuse me.'

Angus stopped and looked at the stranger. 'Yes?'

'May I have a word with you? Outside?'

Angus looked down at Cyril. 'I can't linger, I'm afraid. My dog's a bit under the weather. But yes, if you wish . . . '

They left the bar. Outside the cloudless evening sky was still filled with midsummer light. A jet trail intersected the blue – a line of white, wispy at the edges, stretched back towards Norway.

The stranger introduced himself, showing Angus a small identity card that he extracted from his wallet. 'I'm an animal welfare inspector,' he said. 'And I'm sorry to say I take a very dim view of how your dog is being treated.'

Angus stared at the man. 'What do you mean?' he stuttered. 'I love my dog. He's very well looked after.'

Matthew, frowning, chose to intervene. 'Yes,' he said.

'I can vouch for that. This dog is one of the most . . . ' He searched for the right word. '. . . most appreciated dogs in Edinburgh. Everybody knows that.'

The inspector appeared not to hear what Matthew said. He continued to address Angus. 'Giving alcoholic drinks to a dog constitutes ill-treatment, I'm afraid.'

'But it's only beer,' protested Angus. 'It's not as if I'm giving him whisky, for heaven's sake!'

The inspector shook his head. 'Anything with alcohol in it is bad for a dog.'

'But all sorts of things are bad for us,' said Angus, looking briefly to Matthew for support. 'Too much red meat. Too much chocolate. You name it; it's bad for us.'

'I'm sorry,' said the inspector. 'I'm not prepared to argue with you. Your name and address, please – I'm going to have to file a report with a view to taking this dog into care.'

12. The Hinterland

Big Lou, proprietrix of the Morning After coffee bar in Dundas Street, allowed her thoughts to wander as she polished the stainless steel surface of the counter. This was the place from which she dispensed cups of latte and cappuccino from eight in the morning until six at night, hours that were on the generous side: hardly anybody came into the coffee bar before half past nine, and it would have made no dent in Big Lou's turnover if she were not to open until then. But an early start to the day was deeply ingrained in Big Lou's nature: she had never stayed in bed beyond six in the morning, summer and winter, and saw no reason to change.

Those robust attitudes had been instilled in Lou by her mother, Agnes Pittendreich, who came from rural Aberdeenshire, where the early start is enshrined in the culture. The beginning of the day in Scotland is staggered: breakfast in Edinburgh may be at eight, but in the East Neuk of Fife it is at seven-thirty, at seven in Arbroath, at six-thirty in Aberdeen, while in the rolling hinterland of the granite city it is at five-thirty, or even five.

Agnes had known nothing but the agricultural life. She had been raised on the farm Cauld Hillock, just outside the well-set market town of Turriff, and had left Turriff only once she had married Big Lou's father, who was, of course, also a farmer, but from Angus rather than Aberdeenshire. Agnes's mother, Big Lou's grandmother, or Grandmother Fraser, struggled with the stony soil of Cauld Hillock but in spite of this her farm remained in Big Lou's mind a sort of Eden – a land of lost content, a place of warmth and security to which she was sent on the first day of every school holiday, only to return on the day before school was due to begin.

While the sending away of children for such long periods might raise an eyebrow – not to say questions as to whether the parents were avoiding their child's company – this was certainly not the case here. If the choice had been theirs, Big Lou's parents would have had her remain with them during the school holidays, as there was a great deal of useful work a child could do in the busy growing season. But their daughter had made it clear to them that she wanted to spend time with her grandmother and they had acquiesced. So at the end of each school term Lou was duly placed in the train in Arbroath, entrusted to the care of the train's guard, carrying her battered leather suitcase to which she had tied a home-made label reading *Passenger from Arbroath to Aberdeen*. She was proud of that label, and indeed it was still attached to that suitcase, although half of it had fallen off making it say, enigmatically, *Passenger from*.

Grandmother Fraser doted on Lou, who reminded her of the daughter – Agnes's sister – whom she had lost to a disease of childhood, now conquered. She had a predilection, as many in those parts did, for speech diminutives, adding ie if not to every noun, then at least to a good number of them. And while in some cases this might become annoying, it was not with her, its effect being only to impart a feeling of benignity and affection. And for the rest, her Doric was entirely natural: the patterns of rural speech in Aberdeenshire, unchanged for centuries, meant that the language fitted the land as a glove might fit the hand. She called Lou her quine, the word for a girl in that part of Scotland. Boys were loons, of course, which somehow seemed to suit them every bit as well as quine was right for a girl. Lou, to her grandmother, was her wee quine, or, in a moment of particular fondness, her wee quinikie.

Grandmother Fraser's husband, Neil, was a farmer of the old school. Except on Sundays, when he donned for the kirk a starched white shirt and a carefully pressed black suit – his gweed claes, as he called that outfit – Lou had never seen him wear anything but his working clothes. These consisted of a pair of stout trousers, his breeks, a shirt with no collar, but fastened at the top by a brass stud, a pair of heavy boots, and, if the day were colder than usual, an ancient green jacket. A particular feature of his dress was his Nicky Tams, a garter-like arrangement wound round the lower leg that prevented cold, or even mice, from making their way up the trousers to the warmer regions above.

Grandmother Fraser baked girdle scones for Lou and served them with jam of her own making. She also made kailkenny, a dish of cabbage and potatoes, and skirlie, Big

Lou's favourite, which consisted of oatmeal cooked with onions and suet.

'Naebody ever got thin eating skirlie,' announced Grandmother Fraser, a statement that might have been so obvious as not to require making in the first place, but was somehow invested with wisdom when spoken in the accents of rural Aberdeenshire. The Scots language can do that – can effortlessly transform the mundane into the poetic, giving the dignity of profound truth to the most banal of observations, making even a weather report sound dramatic. Grandmother Fraser may have said nothing of real importance, but that was not the impression she gave, and Lou found herself recording her grandmother's observations in the diary she had kept since the age of seven.

Even now, she took her old diaries out from time to time and read of those days at Cauld Hillock. On this morning in late June, as she polished the counter in her coffee bar, she thought of the entry she had seen the previous evening, for this very day, thirty-one years ago, when she had recorded the visit for lunch of the minister, the Reverend George Garioch. Her grandparents were so proud of him, and they had told Lou that as a young man he had graduated with a doctorate in divinity from Heidelberg. 'Just think,' said Grandmother Fraser, 'that this is just an ordinary parish and we have such learning at our disposal. Just think.'

Big Lou had sat bolt upright, on her best behaviour, watching the minister as he raised his cup of tea to his lips and smiled at her, to all intents and purposes as human and as sympathetic as those who had no doctorate in divinity from Heidelberg, or anywhere else.

13. Matthew and Big Lou Ponder Reincarnation

Matthew, who was first in that morning, interrupted Big Lou's thoughts, which were just on the point of returning to skirlie as the memory of the Reverend George Garioch and his Heidelberg D.D. faded. He had left the gallery in Pat's charge – it was a Thursday morning, and since she had no lectures on that day she could work all day if required. This was not really necessary, as Thursday was a quiet day for the gallery too, but Matthew liked having somebody around, even if there was not much to do.

Big Lou glanced up from her task of cleaning the stainless-steel counter.

'So, Lou,' said Matthew cheerfully. 'Thursday again.'

Big Lou folded her cloth. 'Happens once a week, Matthew. Regular as clockwork.'

'In this universe at least, Lou. There's always the possibility that there are parallel universes in which things may be quite different. No Thursdays, for instance.'

'Or just a whole succession of Thursdays,' said Lou, reaching for a cup from below the counter. 'Do you believe in reincarnation, Matthew?'

Matthew frowned. 'Why do you ask, Lou?'

'You mentioned parallel universes – isn't it possible that we go from one into the other after we die? Hence the conviction that people have always had that there's another world – the other side, heaven, whatever you want to call it. People believe that, don't they?'

'Because they've got some memory of it? Somewhere in the collective unconscious?'

Big Lou nodded. Of the many books she had acquired when she had bought the bookshop – and its stock – that had previously occupied her coffee bar's premises, several had been by Jung, and by Jungians. The idea of a collective unconscious seemed entirely plausible to her, although its precise location was problematic.

She pressed the button on the gleaming Italian coffee maker that would, with subterranean grindings and gur-glings, make Matthew an almost perfect cappuccino. This machine, which had laboured without complaint or inci-dent since its purchase some years previously, was called the Magnifica, an entirely suitable name, she thought. 'Of course, the idea of reincarnation is that we come back right here, into this world,' said Lou. 'We don't find ourselves in a parallel universe, we find ourselves in the same place we were before.'

Matthew thought this unlikely. The little he had read of reincarnation suggested that one might return in very differ-ent circumstances, and sometimes with a gap of centuries in between appearances. Who was that woman in Edinburgh who claimed to be James IV and had written a book about her earlier existence, including a moving account of her demise at the Battle of Flodden?

'Exactly the same place?' he asked. 'Surely not?'

'No,' agreed Big Lou. 'Not exactly the same. This world, of course, but not always the same bit. It depends on your karma, doesn't it? If you believe in it all, of course. But if you do, then the state of your karma will determine where you come back.'

Matthew sniffed at the coffee. It was his favourite smell –

ranking above the smell of new shirts or the leather interior of a new car, or truffle oil, or the smell of gorse in blossom on an Argyll shore. If he came back, then he hoped it would be into a situation where coffee still existed.

'Of course,' he said. 'Karma. So if your karma's bad you might be sent somewhere worse than where you are now?'

Big Lou nodded. 'So they say.'

As Big Lou applied the milky foam to the top of his coffee, Matthew explored the implications. To be living in Edinburgh was undoubtedly a great privilege, and if one's karma was bad – through the doing of bad deeds – then one might expect to be demoted in the next life to somewhere less desirable. For a moment he felt a twinge of anxiety. Glasgow?

He voiced his doubts to Lou. 'We might not get Edinburgh, then, Lou? If our karma's bad?'

Big Lou thought for a moment. 'Yes, you might go some-where else. Or you may just get sent to a worse part of Edinburgh than you're in at the moment.' She fixed Matthew with a gaze that struck him as being almost evaluative. 'You're in India Street, aren't you? That's obviously because you've done good things in a previous life. India Street is for people with good karma, and if they improve this time round they can get Heriot Row. People who live in Heriot Row aren't there by accident, Matthew. They're there because they've done good things in a previous life.'

Matthew smiled. 'I'd never thought of that. Of course, it's all wishful thinking, isn't it? There's nothing else, you know, Lou. It's just this time, and that's it.'

Big Lou looked at him dismissively. 'Hamlet?' she said. 'You remember what Hamlet says? No, maybe you don't. There are more things in heaven and earth, Horatio, than are dreamt of in your philosophy.'

'But you don't really believe in all that stuff, Lou,' said Matthew, wiping away the milky moustache with which his cappuccino had endowed him.

'What about that wee boy?' asked Lou. 'The one they made the film about? Cameron Macauley. He was a wee boy who lived in Glasgow and he was convinced that he had had another family. He kept speaking about it.'

'Children fantasise,' said Matthew.

'You think so? Maybe they do, but this wee boy des-cribed a place on Barra in some detail. So they took him over and they found the house and it was just as he said it would be. And what's more, he had given the name of the family who owned it. And after a lot of research, they discovered that the house had been owned by a family of that name.'

'This happened?'

'Yes, it did. And they brought this important American psychology professor over from Virginia or wherever it was and he looked into it and made sure there was no cheating.'

Matthew shivered. 'Creepy.'

'Yes,' said Big Lou. 'It is.'

'Yet vaguely reassuring,' Matthew went on. 'And . . . and if reincarnation, and perhaps more importantly this karma business, were to be true, then it would give the world a sense of justice. Evil people would get their just deserts in the next life.' He paused. 'You know, Lou, I find that helps quite a lot.'

Lou thought for a moment. She thought he was right: there might be no ultimate assertion of justice, but we had to behave as if there were. The problem of human evil was not so simple as we might blandly assume, she felt, and removing the eschatological dimension had only made it even harder.

14. Matthew's Lack of Tact

The discussion about reincarnation, unexpected at that hour of the morning, when most of us are concerned with the immediate challenges of this life, rather than those that might be encountered in the next, or, *a fortiori*, in the life beyond that – this intimate discussion prompted Matthew to ask Big Lou how matters stood with her farmer friend, Alex. He would not normally have asked her this, as Big Lou's love life seemed to him to be an area of disappointment that was perhaps best not talked about too much. Somehow, though, the moment seemed right.

'So, Lou, how's Alex?' he asked. 'Is that going well?'

Big Lou had been bending down to pick up a cloth that had fallen from the counter. She stopped, mid-way, arrested by what had been said. For his part, noticing the effect of his question, Matthew became flustered.

'Maybe I shouldn't ask ... sorry ...'

Big Lou retrieved the cloth. She did not face Matthew, but looked away when she replied.

'He's fine. He's still coming to the Farmers' Market. But ... well, you know how it is.'

Matthew hesitated. 'Over, Lou? It's over?'

She nodded, and his heart went out to her. This strong, resourceful woman from Arbroath; this representative of a whole Scotland that people who lived in places like Edinburgh sometimes never saw; this woman whom they all rather took for granted, was suffering.

'I'm sorry, Lou,' he mumbled. 'It must be hard. Men can be so ...'

She turned to face him. 'You think he broke it off?'

Matthew blushed. 'I assumed ... I mean, I thought ...'

Big Lou sighed. 'It was me, Matthew. I know you think I'm the one who'll always be given the heave-ho, but it was me this time.'

Matthew felt slightly better. He had, of course, assumed that Lou had been abandoned because that was the way it had always been. That seedy chef, that ridiculous Jacobite with that half-mad Belgian pretender of his, that Elvis impersonator who took her to Crieff Hydro for the Elvis conference and paid no attention to her once there, immersed as he was in Elvis matters ... Every one of Big Lou's men had ended the relationship rather than the other way round. But now that she had herself brought an affair to its end, his intrusive question seemed less tactless.

'What went wrong, Lou?' Matthew ventured. 'It seemed so suitable, what with you both coming from Aberdeen ...'

'Angus,' corrected Big Lou sharply. 'Alex came from Mains of Mochle. That's just outside Arbroath.'

'Yes, Arbroath. So you both had a similar background. You could both talk about ... Arbroath and ... well, farming and things. Cattle. You know.'

Big Lou corrected him. 'Alex has pigs. They always had pigs at Mains of Mochle.'

'Of course,' said Matthew quickly. 'Mains of Mochle. But you did have a lot in common, didn't you? More than you had in common with that Elvis chap. You said he could only talk about Elvis and how he'd been to Memphis once. You told me that. Remember?'

'Yes. And Alex was definitely better than that. And yes, we could talk, but it may surprise you, Matthew, that I don't always want to talk about pigs and tatties and things like that. Not any more.'

Matthew was quick to agree. He knew that Big Lou had not had the advantages of the education he had himself had, but he knew, too, that she had done a great deal to remedy that through reading.

'Of course, Lou. Of course. You've got all those interests of yours now. I assume Alex wasn't much of a reader.'

She shook her head. 'No. Just the *Courier*. Not that

there's anything wrong with the *Courier*, but after a while . . . '

'After a while you might want broader fare?'

'Yes.'

Matthew made a gesture of acceptance. 'Well, perhaps you're best out of it, Lou. But it's a pity because I thought that you and Alex might . . . well, I thought maybe you might like to have children some day, Lou. I thought . . . ' He stopped. He had not intended to bring that subject up; it had somehow slipped out. And now that he thought of it, he realised that he had no idea of Lou's age. Thirty-eight? Forty? Was she too old to have a family, or was it possible nowadays? There were plenty of women having children in their early forties, weren't there?

Big Lou reached out to refill his cup. 'Me? Have children?'

'Well, lots of people want that, Lou. Look at us. We've got three. Just like that.'

'Aye, you have, but I'm getting on a bit, Matthew, and . . . and I don't have a man, do I?'

Again Matthew did not think before he spoke. 'But you don't need a man these days, Lou.'

Big Lou pressed the button on her coffee machine. 'Oh yes? Having been brought up on a farm, Matthew, I learned at a very early age that men have their role in all this.'

Matthew laughed. 'Oh, of course. But what I meant was that you don't have to have a husband. Lots of women these days have children by a . . . well, by an obliging friend or by going to a clinic and getting them to arrange things.'

The coffee maker hissed and gurgled; so much noise, Matthew thought, for a little dribble of dark black liquid and white foam. But that was what the world was like; we battered and bashed and poured out clouds of smoke and chemicals and particles of every description to bring forth our little objects of desire, our baubles.

Big Lou handed him his second cup of coffee. 'You offering, Matthew?'

There was complete silence. For a moment there was no traffic noise; no purring from the fridge; no sound at all.

Matthew looked down at the surface of his cappuccino. Was she asking him? He looked up. Big Lou was watching him, her face quite impassive. It was as if she had asked me the time, thought Matthew. That simple. You offering?

'I'm a married man, Lou. I couldn't . . .'

Big Lou smiled. 'I wouldn't expect that. There are ways, though, Matthew.'

Matthew broke into a nervous laugh. 'Of course, yes. Yes, I understand. But . . .'

He did not finish.

'I'm not serious, Matthew. Thanks anyway for thinking about it.'

'You could adopt, Lou.'

She shrugged. 'There aren't many babies, Matthew.'

'We've got three,' he said.

15. I Know What I Don't Mean

Matthew's wife, Elspeth, had spent that day in the way in which she now spent every day – coping. She was not given to bemoaning her situation, and did not do so, but having

59

triplets, all boys, who were just at the point of crawling energetically would have given anybody an entire litany of possible complaints against a Fate that had dealt her this particular set of reproductive cards.

Of course there were people who were considerably worse off than her; Elspeth had become an avid devourer of the literature on multiple births, and had read of a Texan woman who, in the space of some twenty-two years, had given birth to one set of quintuplets, one of quadruplets, three sets of triplets, and five sets of twins. Not content with that, she was also the mother of nine children who were born singly. Of course there was a lot of room in Texas, and Elspeth assumed that this woman had not lived on the top floor of whatever building she occupied and had not had to struggle to get baby buggies down several flights of stairs.

Elspeth had Anna to help her, and that made a major difference. The Danish au pair had very quickly made herself indispensable, making it possible for Elspeth to get the occasional chance to read the paper, attend to household bills, or snatch a half-hour of the sleep that had become so precious to her, and so elusive too: the boys invariably chose different times at which to wake up during the night.

'I don't know what I'd do without you,' Elspeth once said to Anna. 'If you went back to Copenhagen ...' She left the sentence, and its awful speculation, unfinished.

'They're getting on perfectly well over there without me,' Anna assured her. 'Your need is much greater.'

Elspeth looked at her in sheer gratitude. She would do anything to keep Anna, even to the extent of getting an au pair for her au pair.

When she had gone so far as to make that offer, Anna had simply laughed. 'I don't need an au pair,' she said. 'I am the au pair.'

'But we can get you one,' Elspeth insisted. 'She could be your assistant.'

Anna had looked thoughtful. 'You mean I could tell her what to do? She'd work for me, rather than for you?'

'Yes,' said Elspeth. 'We'd pay her, but she'd report to you. Anything you like.'

'And she can be Danish?' asked Anna.

'Yes, she can be Danish.'

On hearing about this, Matthew had at first been incredulous. 'Hold on,' he said. 'You mean you're getting an au pair for Anna? Is that what you mean to do?'

Elspeth nodded. 'You have no idea, Matthew,' she said. 'You come home and see the boys all neat and tidy, but have you got any idea – any idea – of how difficult it is to run them? Just getting them dressed in the morning is a major battle – three writhing little boys resisting your efforts. And then feeding them involves the sort of effort that a military field kitchen must have to make in the midst of battle. They throw things now, you know. Boiled egg, porridge, bowlfuls of that ghastly prune stuff – everything is a missile, Matthew. These boys have never even heard of the Geneva Convention, you know.'

He did not argue, sensing that he was on weak ground. The addition of another au pair would mean that he would have to give up the room that he used as a study, as the au pair would have to be given somewhere to sleep. But he sensed that Elspeth had made up her mind and that the matter was not open for discussion. So the agency that had sent them Anna was contacted and invited to send somebody as similar to her as possible. And that person – the au pair's au pair – was due to arrive in little over a week.

But now, it was just Elspeth and Anna who had to keep the boys fed, dry, and amused. That was a more or less full-time job for both of them, and tiring as well. So when Matthew came home that night, Elspeth was exhausted, as she always was at the end of a day spent with Tobermory, Rognvald, and Fergus. Matthew began to help with the boys and it was not until they were safely in bed and their light turned out that he and Elspeth were able to talk to one another.

'I can tell you've had a demanding day,' Matthew said. His tone was apologetic, as he knew that his own day would sound positively leisurely in comparison with Elspeth's.

Elspeth shrugged. 'The usual,' she said. 'Nappies. Feeding. Sick. Nappies. Feeding. Sick.'

Matthew smiled. 'It won't go on forever,' he said. 'They'll grow up.'

'I don't want them to grow up too quickly,' said Elspeth. 'It's just that I wish there weren't ...' She hesitated. 'I wish there weren't quite so many of them.'

Matthew looked down at the floor. 'I had a conversation with Big Lou today.'

'Oh yes?'

'Yes. We talked about whether she would ever want to have children.'

Elspeth thought for a moment. 'She'd make a wonderful mother. I can just imagine it. But it's a bit late, isn't it?'

'Possibly. And she hasn't got a man, anyway.'

He explained about Alex, and Elspeth said that she could well sympathise with Big Lou and her disinclination to talk about pigs and potatoes forever. 'We move on,' she said.

'We discussed adoption,' said Matthew.

'What did she think?'

Matthew told her that Big Lou was well aware of the scarcity of babies for adoption. Then he said: 'I suggested she could have one of ours. I didn't say that in so many words, though – I suppose I implied it.'

Elspeth stared at him. 'You what?'

'I was just thinking aloud,' Matthew said. 'I wondered if it would be easier for you to have just two, rather than three. And we'd see the other one at Big Lou's. He'd have an excellent upbringing – you know what she's like.'

Elspeth was silent. For a while she did nothing, but simply stared unflinchingly at Matthew. Then she said: 'I can't believe what I've just heard.'

Matthew paled. 'I ... I was just speculating,' he said. 'I wasn't serious about it.'

'You were,' said Elspeth, through clenched teeth.

'But you just said you wished that there were fewer of them. You said it. I heard you.'

'I'm not talking about me,' Elspeth shot back. 'I'm talking about you. I know what I don't mean.'

16. Bertie's Party: Social Issues

Word had got out at the Steiner School that Bertie would be celebrating his seventh birthday with a party in Scotland Street. Bertie knew how this had happened; it was Olive who had been responsible for spreading the news, even if he had been as guarded as he possibly could when she had started to question him.

'So you'll be turning seven quite soon, Bertie,' Olive remarked casually one morning. 'And about time too, in my view. One can't be a Peter Pan forever, you know.'

'I don't know what you're talking about, Olive,' said Bertie. 'What's this got to do with Peter Pan?'

Olive laughed. She had a very particular laugh she employed when she was keen to imply that something glaringly obvious had not been sensed by the person to whom she was speaking.

'Poor you, Bertie,' she said. 'You're so naïve. Peter Pan never grew up. He wanted to be a little boy forever. But you can't do that, I'm sorry to tell you. You have to grow up, Bertie. You just have to.'

'But I do want to grow up, Olive,' said Bertie. 'I want to be eighteen.'

Olive laughed again. 'Eighteen is a long way ahead, Bertie.' She paused. 'Of course that will be more or less when we announce our engagement, so perhaps we'd better start getting ready.'

Bertie looked away in embarrassment.

'You can't deny it,' said Olive. 'You promised ages ago that we'd be getting married when we were twenty. I've got it in writing, Bertie Pollock, and if you think you can just ignore something like that, then you've got another think coming. What do you imagine happens to people who break their promises, Bertie? Their pants go on fire. It happens all the time.'

'I never said ...' Bertie began, but Olive cut him short.

'That's just by the way,' she said. 'The real question is your party, Bertie. I know you're having one.'

Bertie tried again. 'I never said ...'

'You never said anything about a party?' interrupted Olive. 'You don't have to say it, you know. Of course you're having a party. Why wouldn't you?'

Bertie sighed. 'Some people don't have parties,' he said.

'Oh yes?' challenged Olive. 'I can't think of any, Bertie. Even Tofu had a party, I believe – not that anybody wanted to go.' She paused to take breath. 'So your party, Bertie – who's going to be invited, apart from me?'

'I haven't decided,' mumbled Bertie.

'So you are having a party,' crowed Olive. 'I knew it, Bertie! My mother says men are really hopeless liars, and she's right!'

After that, the news soon spread, and it was later that day that Tofu raised the subject with Bertie.

'This party of yours,' said Tofu. 'Thanks, I'm coming.'

Bertie bit his lip. He knew that he would have had no alternative but to invite Tofu, but he did not like the other boy's assumption.

'Well ...' he began.

'Yeah,' said Tofu. 'Just as well you're inviting me. Who else? Can I bring Larch?'

Bertie's heart sank. He had not intended to invite Larch, who was well known for his tendency to hit those with whom he disagreed – and occasions of disagreement with Larch were frequent.

'I'm not sure if Larch will want to come,' he said mildly.

'No, he will,' said Tofu. 'I've already asked him, you see, and he says that he's coming.'

'I see.'

'Yes,' said Tofu. 'And he wants to bring his cousin Eck. He doesn't go to Steiner's. In fact, I don't think he goes to any school.'

Bertie looked puzzled. 'But everybody has to go to school. It's against the law not to go to school.'

'Not if you're a tinker,' said Tofu. 'Tinkers don't go to school. Eck lives in a caravan, except in the summer, when he lives in a tent.'

Bertie frowned. 'I'm not sure that you're meant to call them tinkers,' he said. 'My mummy says that you should call them travelling people. She says it's rude to call them tinkers.'

Tofu made a face. 'But that's what they are,' he said. 'And Eck pinches things.'

Bertie looked shocked. 'But my mummy says that you must never say things like that.'

'But what if he does?' asked Tofu. 'Eck's got four watches that he's pinched. He wears them all the way up his arm. I've seen him.'

'How do you know they're pinched?' asked Bertie.

'Because he told me,' said Tofu. 'He said, "Look at all the watches I've pinched." That's what he said. And then he tried to pinch mine, but I held on to it until Larch came and hit him.'

Bertie was silent. He had nothing against travellers, and no time for unkind talk like that – indeed it seemed to him that it would be rather fun to live in a caravan, and even in a tent if it was not raining too heavily – but he was appalled at the thought that both Larch and Eck were proposing to come to his party uninvited. Tofu had no right to go around inviting people; it was not his party, and the only person who had the right to invite anybody was him, Bertie.

'I don't think I want them to come to my party,' he said. 'We haven't got enough chairs in our flat. Sorry about that.'

Tofu made a dismissive gesture. 'That doesn't matter. Larch and Eck don't need to sit down. They're quite happy to stand if necessary. They told me that.'

And that was just the beginning of it. Later that day, Bertie was approached by Olive's friend and lieutenant, Pansy, who had a small diary in her hand, pencil poised at the ready.

'What's the date, Bertie?' she asked.

Bertie affected ignorance. 'What date?'

Pansy smiled. 'Come on, Bertie! I know you know. It's the date of the party of the year – the party they're all talking about. Your party: what date will it be? Next Saturday? Don't say it's next Saturday because I won't be able to come, and nor will my friend Hyacinth.'

'Who's Hyacinth?' asked Bertie.

'Just a girl,' said Pansy. 'I don't think you know her, but that doesn't matter. She always comes to parties with me. She's learning salsa. I've texted her about this.'

Bertie drew in his breath sharply. Mobile phones and texting were not allowed at school, but Pansy was noted for her care-free attitude towards regulations – except when they suited her purposes, when she would become their stoutest defender.

It was all too much for Bertie, and he suddenly found himself in tears. The sight of this brought Olive running to his side. 'Oh, poor Bertie,' she said, putting a comforting arm about him. 'I so understand; I really do. It's stress. Parties are such stressful things. I sooo understand.'

17. *Tintin Issues*

Bertie's mother, Irene Pollock, had not given much thought to Bertie's party after that initial, and rather brief, conversation about it that they had on their way to the psychotherapist's consulting rooms in Queen Street. That discussion had been cut short by Bertie's disclosure of his wish list for his birthday (a Swiss Army penknife and a fishing rod), and that had given rise to an anxious and inconclusive discussion with Dr St Clair as to why it was that boys yearned after penknives. Now, sitting at her writing desk in the Pollock living room in Scotland Street, Irene gazed at the blank sheet of paper before her. Her husband, Stuart, was watching a football game on the television, with the sound turned off in response to Irene's request for the quiet that she needed to think, while Bertie was in his room reading. Ulysses had already been put to bed, and it would be Bertie's bedtime, too, in forty minutes or so.

'What's Bertie up to?' asked Stuart, in a lull in the action from Celtic Park.

'Reading,' answered Irene. 'And has that ridiculous tribal encounter finished yet?'

'It's football, actually,' said Stuart.

'Exactly,' said Irene.

Stuart ignored the taunt. 'Reading what?'

Irene sighed. 'Tintin. I've done my best to discourage it, but he gets hold of it from the library. You'd think they'd know better than to display such books – if you can call them that – in the children's section, of all places.'

'I don't know,' said Stuart mildly. 'I rather liked Tintin. It's pretty harmless stuff, I would have thought.'

Irene turned round to glare at Stuart. 'Harmless? Are we talking about the same books?'

'I imagine so,' said Stuart. 'That young Belgian detective. The boy in plus-fours.'

'Boy?' snorted Irene. 'He's utterly sexless. Androgynous.'

'Well . . .' began Stuart.

'And as for the violence,' continued Irene, 'I've come across a very interesting analysis of that. Do you realise the sheer amount of head trauma in those books, Stuart? Tintin himself loses consciousness at least fifty times in twenty-three volumes. Fifty times! Mostly from being hit over the head with a blunt instrument.'

Stuart could not repress a laugh. 'But that's always happened in that sort of thing. Remember westerns? Remember how often everybody was knocked out? Losing consciousness is essential to the plot.'

Irene's eyes narrowed. 'I don't think you should make light of it, Stuart. Those books are about anger, you know. Look at that ridiculous Captain Haddock. There's an immense amount of anger there – manifesting itself in swearing, Stuart. Yes, swearing. He rants and raves all the time, expressing intense inner anger. Is that a suitable role model for boys?'

Stuart shrugged. 'I honestly don't think anybody sees Captain Haddock as a role model. Bertie certainly won't. The good captain is more of a joke than anything else, and as for swearing, it happens, doesn't it? Look at contemporary Scottish literature. Some of it consists entirely of expletives.'

'That,' said Irene scornfully, 'is social realism. That's swearing as an expression of outrage. That's different.'

Stuart turned back to face the screen. At Celtic Park, the police had finished making their arrests and the game had resumed. 'Well,' he said, 'we can talk about that later perhaps. I'd better watch. Hearts are having a tough time.'

Irene returned to the contemplation of her blank sheet of paper. Her conversation with her husband had been apposite to the task in hand, which was to prepare a talk for the next meeting of her book club. This club, which met every month in a flat in Great King Street, was composed of eight like-minded readers, all interested in psychological issues. It had emerged from the ruins of a previous book club founded by Irene, which had been devoted to the critique of the works of Melanie Klein, but had deteriorated into rebarbative arguments after there had

70

been some fairly fundamental differences of opinion. Irene had picked up the pieces and re-formed the group, excluding those members who had disagreed with her. Now, she felt, reason prevailed, and the meetings of the group had become a much-anticipated fixture in the members' diaries.

The meetings always took the same form. The evening would begin with a short talk by one of the members – often Irene – on a subject of literary interest, and this would be followed by a lively discussion of the ideas presented in the talk. Then there would be coffee and shortbread, after which the book chosen for that month would be introduced by the member who had picked it – often, also, Irene.

At the next meeting, Irene was due to give a short talk on the subject of hidden meanings in children's literature – hence her recent reading of Tintin and 'Colleagues Go to the Doctor', an article from the *American Journal of Neuroradiology* that she had downloaded from the web. Much else had been revealed in her trawl of the literature on the subject, including a ground-breaking psychiatric study of *Winnie the Pooh* that she intended to address in some detail in her talk. There was, she had found, so much to be said from the Freudian and Lacanian points of view about children's literature that it was difficult to know where to start – and that was why her piece of paper remained stubbornly virginal.

She decided to start with Milne. The author was the father to the book, and if one wanted to understand just what was going on in *Winnie the Pooh* – and there was a great deal going on beneath the surface – then it would be necessary to start with the man who created this strange menagerie of stunted and unhappy stuffed animals. So she picked up her pen, and deliberately ignoring the muffled sounds of cheers from Stuart's football game she began with an observation on the transparency of the authorial act.

'All authors come from somewhere,' she wrote, pleased with the turn of phrase which had, she felt, the necessary authority for a first sentence. 'And so when we confront that strange and rather sinister world that is the world of Winnie the Pooh and Christopher Robin we must ask ourselves not only who was A. A. Milne but also why was A. A. Milne.

'Milne,' she wrote, 'was the product of a typically repressed and authoritarian Edwardian household. His childhood was unhappy, as all childhoods are where an authoritarian figure forces children into a world in which they do not want to be. Later in life, the child may remember the unhappiness, but still seek to idealise the whole idea of a childhood that he never had.'

She put down her pen, and for a moment allowed herself to be satisfied with the acuity of her insight. Then she picked up her pen and wrote: 'So, all authors are unhappy as children. All authors suffer, and that is why they write. They are calling for help. Listen! Can you hear them?'

18. A Serious Case of Male Fright

Irene was getting into her stride. A few more paragraphs were devoted to Milne and his desire to create an Arcadia by constructing a world of childhood that was secure and timeless. In the books, she decided, Christopher Robin was not subjected to what Milne suffered at school – bullying, threats and violence. These staples of English private education – Scotland had its own particular problems – had produced generations of repressed and unhappy boys, taken from their mothers and their homes and put into a world in which the denial of feeling was the norm. Coerced into submission, these boys were ideal material to staff the sprawling enterprise that was the British Empire. Who else could bear the isolation of distant postings, the deprivation of female companionship that was the lot of colonial officials and army officers, the acceptance of authority and hardship? But some of these boys would, as adults, pick up a pen and then ... and then it all came out. Kipling. Maugham. Dahl.

'So,' wrote Irene, 'Milne created an Arcadia, but in this Arcadia he was destined, by virtue of his early experience, to reveal the pathologies that had blighted his own childhood and childhoods like his. Consequently in the characters who are Christopher Robin's companions – that stuffed bear and so on – we see embodied all the sequelae of the emotional deprivation and repression of the author's own childhood.

'Take Pooh for instance. He is described, and depicted by the artist, as physically battered. This is because physical abuse at the hands of all-powerful adults was the lot of Edwardian children. The bear is now reduced to pathetic dependence on the boy, and must accept the boy's authority in all matters. This is the continued infantilisation that results from a childhood spent in fear of authority figures.'

There was more, and by the time that Stuart's football game was finished Irene had covered both sides of an A4 sheet of paper with her dissection of Milne and of the problems of the Hundred Acre Wood. She was pleased with what she had written: parts of it might be slightly abstruse, but that would serve

73

to inspire other members of the book club to raise the intellectual level of their own contributions which was, almost without exception, considerably below that of Irene's observations. That was the problem with book groups, thought Irene: one had to put up with people who simply were not up to one's own standards. She sighed. The trouble with living in society was society … If only one did not have to put up with the weaker brethren who could be so … so trying. Still, she resolved, those to whom the gift of insight is given have to shoulder the burden as best we can and take a lead. There should be more of us in the Scottish Parliament, of course, thought Irene; the trouble with that body is that we aren't there in sufficient numbers to guide them in their deliberations.

With the encounter at Celtic Park over – resolved in favour of the west of Scotland rather than the east – Stuart rose from his chair and came to peer over Irene's shoulder.

'Writing?' he asked.

Irene glanced down at her satisfactorily filled paper. 'Yes. Some remarks for the book group.'

Stuart nodded. 'Perhaps I should join a book group.'

Irene raised an eyebrow. 'I don't think there are many for men. At least not round here.'

'Odd, that,' mused Stuart. 'I wonder why?'

Irene knew the answer. 'Male fright,' she said.

Stuart frowned. 'Male fright?'

Irene explained. 'Men are fearful of intellectual intimacy,' she explained. 'They're more comfortable when they are making a series of statements or propositions – putting them out to people. They don't really talk to one another – not in the way that women do.'

'I see,' said Stuart.

'Yes,' said Irene. 'And that's something I really want Bertie to avoid. I want him to be able to talk to others as a woman can.'

Stuart said nothing. He was staring at his wife.

'So,' continued Irene, 'I'm keen for him to be able to see the world through female eyes.'

Stuart tensed. 'I'm surprised you don't make him wear a dress.'

Irene shot him a withering glance. 'There's no need to be facetious, Stuart. It ill becomes you.'

'I'm not being facetious,' he countered. 'I'm deadly serious.' Stuart hesitated before continuing. 'Do you want him to grow up rejecting masculine identity?'

Irene spun round. 'That,' she said, 'is a typically shallow and, if I may say so, offensive comment. But now that you ask, the answer is: what is wrong with a rejection of masculinity? Is there anything intrinsically good in being masculine?'

After this, for a moment neither said anything. Then Stuart spoke. 'There's a difference, surely, between accepting something and setting out to ensure that it happens. I would always accept Bertie however he turned out. But that is a very long way from setting out to put him off being masculine. You shouldn't set out to manipulate these things.'

Irene rose to her feet. 'Oh no? And what do you think society does at the moment? Do you think there's no pressure, no manipulating of people to conform to a created notion of masculinity when it comes to these things? What planet are you on, Stuart?'

Stuart moved away, struggling to control himself. He stared out of the window as he replied. 'I suggest we don't let this argument go nuclear. I'm sorry if I spoke out of turn. Let's not fight.'

'All right,' said Irene. 'I have no desire to quarrel with you, Stuart. All I ask is that you don't make offensive remarks. I have Bertie's best interests at heart, as you well know. All that I am trying to do is to make sure that our son grows up adapted to the gender-neutral world that is being constructed around us. That means that a lot of old-fashioned ideas are going to have to be scrapped. That's all. Just don't stand in the way of that – that's all I ask.'

Stuart decided to change the subject. 'His birthday – he's very excited about it.'

'Yes.'

'What shall we get him?'

Irene folded the piece of paper on which she had written her speech. 'I've already bought him his present,' she said. Then, raising a finger, she continued, 'And I don't want any backtalk from you when I show it to you.'

19. *Antonia Writes from Italy*

While the increasingly acrimonious exchange between Irene and Stuart was raging, upstairs at 44 Scotland Street, in their now-shared flat, Domenica Macdonald and her new husband, Angus Lordie, were talking about something that had every bit as much unsettling potential as the topic being discussed below. This was the arrival that morning of a letter from their erstwhile neighbour, Antonia Collie, announcing that she would shortly be arriving from Italy and proposing that she stay with them for a couple of weeks.

'Read me her letter again, Angus,' said Domenica. 'I really have to savour the nuances. One gets so few letters with nuances these days.'

Angus retrieved the envelope from its place on the kitchen dresser.

'She has such peculiar writing,' he began, glancing at the face of the envelope. 'A graphologist would have a field day with her.'

'Graphology's nonsense,' said Domenica. 'It's pop psychology at its worst.'

'Her writing slopes all over the place,' said Angus. 'And Antonia herself is all over the place, isn't she?'

'Possibly. But we must not be uncharitable, Angus. We must bear in mind that Antonia is a new person since she joined that convent. I'm sure that the old Adam is well and truly put in his place by now.'

'Or Eve,' said Angus.

'No, I never felt that Eve had a fair trial. But let's not get bogged down in such minor details. The letter – read it to me.'

Angus took the letter from the envelope. It was written on two thin sheets of paper – paper of the sort that used to be employed for the airmail edition of *The Times*.

'My dear friends,' he began.

'Stop there,' said Domenica. 'Note the tone, Angus. Who addresses people as "my dear friends"? Who does she think she is? The Pope, now that she's so cosy with Rome?'

'I think she's being friendly,' said Angus.

'Perhaps,' said Domenica. 'Although it would have been more natural to say "Dear Domenica and Angus". Or even "Dear Angus and Domenica".'

Angus looked thoughtful. 'That raises an interesting question,' he said. 'Are we Angus and Domenica or are we Domenica and Angus?'

'Interesting,' said Domenica. 'I suppose a couple's names do tend to find their order, so to speak. Interesting.'

'You put the more forceful, more outgoing person first,' said Angus, thinking, as he spoke, in that case, it's Domenica and Angus, definitely.

Domenica thought the same thing, and then thought that she would make an effort to sign cards from Angus and Domenica. A man might well feel destabilised if he saw his name taking second place all the time.

'Perhaps that's why she wrote dear friends,' said Angus. 'It meant that there was no issue as to whose name went first.'

'Read on,' said Domenica.

'Dear friends,' read Angus. 'At the moment we are having gorgeous weather here in Tuscany – so different from the dreary weather you are no doubt having in Scotland, poor you.'

'Well!' exclaimed Domenica. 'How rude! You should never crow over somebody else's weather.'

'Even if what you say is true?'

'Especially if what you say is true,' emphasised Domenica. 'You do not remind somebody of their geographical misfortunes – or indeed any other misfortune. But carry on.'

'And here at the convent we are busy with so many things that need to be done – the sorts of tasks that I never even thought about when I lived in Edinburgh – clearing paths, tending vegetables, gathering wood for the fire.'

'Listen to that!' exclaimed Domenica. 'She implies that we have no paths to clear.'

'We don't.'

'Nor wood to gather for the fire.'

'And we don't have that either,' said Angus.

'Carry on.'

Angus looked down at the letter. 'How I envy the two of you your leisure,' he continued.

'So we have nothing to do,' said Domenica. 'Sitting here idly. Read on.'

'Being busy, though, is such a privilege, as I can offer up all my works to my Creator and know that they are good in His sight.'

'So she hopes,' said Domenica. 'Although frankly I doubt whether the Supreme Being is all that interested in her path clearing and wood gathering. He has bigger fish to fry, no doubt. Carry on, Angus.'

'Now we get to the interesting part,' said Angus. He returned to the letter. 'I hope that you don't mind if I come to Edinburgh for a few weeks, as I have some work to do in the National Library in connection with my Scottish Saints book. I am so looking forward to staying in my flat – it will be just like old days, looking out of my window onto Scotland Street again!'

'That's the bit,' said Domenica. 'My flat. She should say "my former or erstwhile flat". I don't like to stand on ownership, but there are occasions when people make remarks as if they had no regard at all for what the Registers of Scotland have to say to us on these matters. Her flat is now our flat, Angus. She is not entitled to use the term "my flat". She has no flat at all. She is quite without a flat. That's not to say that she doesn't have many other things in this life – she has her path clearing and wood collecting, for instance – but she does not have a flat.' She paused. 'Nor does she have a window. My window. Where, one might ask, is this window? I know of no window in Edinburgh out of which Antonia is entitled to look and think, contemporaneously, I am looking out of my window. I just don't.'

Angus gazed at Domenica in sheer admiration. In his eyes, she was like a galleon in full sail, a fully rigged vessel prepared for engagement on the highest of high seas. Before such opposition, what chance did somebody like Antonia, an ill-equipped minor ship of the line, have? None, he thought.

'I'd be perfectly prepared to have Antonia to stay,' he said. 'But I do think it's a bit much proposing yourself on somebody for, what is it? Three weeks. And ...'

Domenica completed his sentence. 'And to bring somebody with you. Finish the letter, Angus.'

'And I do hope,' Angus went on, 'you won't mind if I have one of the sisters with me. She won't take up much space – she's very small – and she eats like a bird. You'll love her, and never having set foot outside Italy, poor dear, she can't wait to see Scozia, as she charmingly calls it. I know you won't mind, because I know that at heart you both have a very strong sense of your moral duty.'

'That's the bit!' Domenica exclaimed. 'That's the bit that takes the shortbread.'

20. *Art, Resolution, and St Ninian*

Whatever surprise they felt over the sheer presumption of Antonia's letter, Angus and Domenica nonetheless realised that they could hardly turn down their former neighbour's request. It would have been possible, of course, to claim that they were going to be away, but there were several objections to that, not the least of which was that it would be a lie. Both of them had a strong objection to lying – something that, in a way that was becoming increasingly rare, they regarded as impermissible.

'There are so many people,' Domenica had remarked a few days earlier, 'who seem to think that the truth is whatever you want it to be. I once read a novel with that message. It didn't commit to a definitive version of the story – it said: you decide what you like. You choose what was true.'

Angus thought about this. 'You mean that the author didn't tell you what really happened?'

'Exactly. Two possible explanations were given. Then the reader was invited to decide which was preferable.'

'Which was more likely?'

Domenica shook her head. 'No, which was the one you liked more. There's a difference.'

Angus was not sure that he liked that. 'But the author himself knew?'

'Yes, he did. The omniscient author idea. We do, I suppose, expect rather a lot of an author. We expect him or her to know the inmost thoughts of his characters – to know what goes on behind closed doors. And we expect him to tell us all this precisely because he's omniscient.' She paused. 'We also expect resolution, and if we don't get it – if things are left up in the air – we complain vociferously.'

Angus smiled. 'But life . . .'

Domenica knew what was coming. '. . . isn't like that. No, it isn't. We have all sorts of unresolved issues in our lives – friendships we give up on, letters we forget to answer, things we meant to do but never get round to, and so on. A lot. But art . . .'

'Art's different,' said Angus.

'Exactly. Art observes our need for resolution – or should do. Musicians know that, of course. Chords need to resolve, don't they? Otherwise the tune just sounds wrong. And pictures too.'

'Yes, much the same thing applies in painting,' said Angus. 'If something is missing from a picture, it's pretty obvious.

The thing isn't whole. You're left waiting for something that just isn't there. You end up dissatisfied because your quest for beauty is frustrated.'

Domenica liked the notion of a quest for beauty. It was true, she thought; that was what our lives were – a quest for beauty. We might not know it – we might never actually express it that way – but that was what we were doing. We yearned after beauty, which we could find in so many different ways, not just in the obvious ones.

And now, faced with the need to respond to Antonia's annoying letter, she knew that she could not do anything but offer the other woman, and her companion, their hospitality for the full three weeks that had been proposed. To put Antonia off with a lie would be to sully herself with falsehood; would be to negate the moral dimension of that quest for beauty. It would be, quite simply, messy.

'I'll try to make the room as attractive as possible for her,' Domenica said at last. 'We wouldn't want her to be uncomfortable.'

Angus looked at his wife in admiration. He was inspired by her example, and put out of his mind the thought that it would be rather a good idea to make Antonia uncomfortable, with a view to her deciding that her visit should be shorter. But he could not say that, of course, now that the high moral tone had been struck by Domenica.

'Three weeks will go quite quickly,' he said.

Domenica was not convinced. 'I doubt it,' she said. 'But let's not think too much about that. I'm not sure how I shall be able to deal with Antonia going on about early Scottish saints. I'm not sure I want to hear about St Ninian for a full three weeks.'

'He was an interesting man,' said Angus. 'I read John MacQueen's book about him. He performed some amazing miracles, we're told, including giving the power of speech to babies.'

'Only one baby,' corrected Domenica. 'He made it possible for a newly born infant to make a pronouncement about somebody's innocence.' She paused. 'The infant baby identified its real father. It was quite remarkable.'

Angus laughed. 'Do you think Antonia believes all that?'

'Not literally. She's not that credulous.'

Angus looked out of the window. 'What do you think a baby would say if given the power of speech?'

Domenica smiled at the thought. 'Complain about the food? Baby food is so dull, don't you think? All those squashed peas and so on.'

'Maybe. But I have a very different image, now that I come to think about it.'

'Oh yes?'

He transferred his gaze away from the window. Now he looked at her. A conversation, begun light-heartedly, can change so quickly, he thought.

'I suppose that we shouldn't be all superior about those early saints. They were really up against it, weren't they? The world was a dark and violent place. Scotland was particularly so.'

She nodded. Can still be, she thought, for some.

'I can see it,' said Angus. 'I can see the scene.'

She was quiet for a moment. 'Tell me, Angus.'

He closed his eyes. 'Ninian comes into a room and there's a baby there, you see. The mother is somewhere nearby, and some other people. And Ninian has this ... well, he has this air of peacefulness about him. He isn't frightening the baby. The baby just looks at him and then suddenly stands up. Babies do, in early pictures, you know. The Veneto-Cretan school, for instance. They sometimes stand up.'

She waited.

He spoke carefully, as one who has witnessed something important and wishes to convey what he has seen as accurately as possible. 'And then the baby turns to his mother and he speaks. A tiny voice. Just the voice you'd expect a baby to have. Like a breathing of the wind.'

She watched him.

'And the baby speaks.' He hesitated, looking at her. '"Mother, is it true that men are cruel?"'

Domenica gasped. 'Is that what the baby says?'

'Yes,' he said. 'Just that.'

21. Bruce Goes to the Waxing Studio, for Waxing

Bruce was on his way to a session at the waxing studio. He had telephoned the day before to make the appointment and had spoken to the owner, Arlene, who announced that she would be his personal therapist. 'Beauty therapist, that is,' she explained, 'although men sometimes prefer it if I call myself a grooming adviser. Sensitivities, you see. Same thing, though.'

They had then very briefly discussed what Arlene called his 'personal depilation programme'. 'Face, arms, and whatever,' she intoned. 'We can sort all that out when I see you.'

'Whatever,' said Bruce, and laughed. He liked the sound of Arlene, and he was confident that she would like the sound – and sight – of him. He was probably going to concentrate on face and chest, as it happened, as it was in these regions that he felt he needed a little attention. Not much, of course, but just a little bit of tidying up; a few stray hairs here and there. Women, he knew, loved nothing more than the sight of a male chest devoid of hair – he had it on good authority that they went wild over that – and he was happy to oblige, although of course no woman had ever actually complained to him about the very modest chest hair he sported.

It would be his first waxing, and he felt slightly anxious. He had watched a video about the process and had noticed that the man being waxed wore an expression of remarkable, almost transcendental serenity throughout the whole procedure. It was an expression similar to that seen on the faces of Buddhist monks reciting mantras in the Himalayas, an expression of indifference to the annoyances of this world. It did not seem that in this clearly trancelike state he was experiencing the slightest discomfort, but surely, Bruce thought, there must be some degree of pain when those white strips were eventually pulled off. Even a Buddhist monk might be expected at least to wince if you put a depilatory strip on his arm and then pulled it off, or if you waxed his chest and tore the wax away.

One must be willing to make sacrifices, though, Bruce told himself; one must be prepared for a small measure of discomfort if one is going to get results. Physical perfection – in the quest for which he had always had such a head start over others – only came with the right attitude, with the right commitment. One could so easily ruin a fine physique through over-indulgence of one sort or another; one could so easily go to seed if one failed to take exercise and let one's abs go flabby, as so many did. Not me, thought Bruce, not my abs, nor any part of me come to think of it; those hours in the gym, that extra effort in finding just the right hairdresser, that particular care taken in applying facial moisturiser: people could sneer at all that – and there were such people – but what did they see when they looked in the mirror? Enough said.

It would be good to lose a little hair from the right places, thought Bruce. His eyebrows, for example, could benefit from a bit of attention, and waxing was so much easier than plucking. He had once had a girlfriend who had plucked his eyebrows for him – she loved doing it – but he had found it slightly uncomfortable. Estelle, or Arlene, or whatever she called herself could presumably do that so much more easily, and it would be a bit of a treat for her to work on a face like mine, he thought.

It must be awful being really hairy, he thought as he made his way along Hamilton Place to the waxing studio in Stockbridge. Who was that boy in his year at Morrison's Academy – that excessively hirsute one? What was he called? Something-or-other McTaggart, and his nickname was Yeti McTaggart. Hah! That was so apt, as these nicknames often are, thought Bruce. Poor Yeti – he was covered in thick body hair from the age of ten or so; it was awful, just awful. And when they went swimming they stood around and watched as he got changed, marvelling at how hairy he was – rather like an ape, actually – hence the witty nickname.

There had been that occasion when Bruce had taken Yeti's school jotter and drawn hair all over the cover. How they had laughed, and Yeti had turned red with anger, though you could scarcely see the red underneath all the facial hair, Bruce remembered, with a smile. Waxing would have sorted Yeti McTaggart out, although you would need great tubs of wax to get all the hair off him.

What happened to him? Bruce wondered. He had seen him years later, when they both must have been nineteen or so, and Bruce had been back in Crieff and had spotted Yeti in the High Street. Bruce, who had been driving along with a girlfriend, had slowed, wound down the window and called out 'Yeti!' and Yeti had been stand-offish and had turned away. He never had much of a sense of humour, of course, and there wasn't much one could do about that. Still, you'd think that he would have at least acknowledged me, thought Bruce. After all, we had been friends since the age of ten or whatever it was. Some people had no sense of loyalty, of course; they turned their backs on the people they had grown up with. They turned their hairy backs on them.

He crossed the bridge and made his way down towards Raeburn Place. The waxing studio was in a small cul-de-sac off the main shopping street, on the ground floor of a tenement stair with flats above. It was quite discreet – a modest sign announcing its presence and giving the name of the owner: Arlene Porteous, Member of the Institute of Waxology. Bruce read the sign and smiled. Waxology! Well, at least it showed that she knew what she was doing. One would not want to put oneself at the mercy of somebody who was professionally unqualified – heaven knows what might be pulled off by mistake.

He rang the bell and waited for the door to be opened.

'Bruce?'

He nodded and smiled. 'Yes, that's me.'

Arlene returned the smile. 'Good to meet you, Bruce. Come right in.'

He followed her into a small room in which there was a high, plastic-covered couch over which a towel was draped.

'Just my face and chest today,' said Bruce quickly.

'Whatever,' said Arlene.

22. *Arlene Talks About Her Ex and Pulls Hairs Out*

'Where do you stay, Bruce?' asked Arlene as Bruce lay back on the plastic-covered couch.

Bruce, his shirt removed, felt at a disadvantage, as anybody might on lying prostrate before one who would at any moment start pulling one's hair out by its roots.

'I live in Albany Street,' he said. 'Do you know it?'

Arlene touched his chest gently, pulling up a single hair as if to test its resilience.

'By yourself?' she asked, peering down at him.

Bruce looked up into the waxer's face. She was attractive, he thought, but not his type. He would resist any moves she made, if she fancied him, which was more than likely.

'Yes,' he said. 'Just me.'

'Nice,' she said. 'Nice to have a flat all to yourself.'

'Yes,' said Bruce. 'It is. And you?'

'Liberton,' she said. 'I've got a wee boy who's in primary school there.'

'Oh yes.'

'Yes. I'm divorced. My ex lives in Aberdeen. He works on the rigs. He's good with the wee boy – you have to hand him that.'

'Good,' said Bruce.

'Yes. You see, nobody's all bad, know what I mean? Most people have got some good in them if you look hard enough. That's what I've found out, anyway.'

She focused a light on his face; it was disconcerting, and he closed his eyes against the glare.

'You've got some nasal hairs, Bruce. Let me count them. One, two, three, four, five – five hairs coming out of your left nostril and ... let me see, one, two, three, four, five, six coming out of the other one. Eleven hairs altogether, Bruce.'

Bruce frowned. He had not been aware of having any nasal hair.

'Nasal hair is a real turn-off, Bruce,' Arlene went on. 'In fact, I think there's nothing worse than getting up close to somebody and seeing they have nasal hair.'

Bruce's voice was strained. 'Yes?'

'Yes. You know something, Bruce? I've had people in here who've been divorced because of nasal hair. Yes, I'm not making it up. There was this man who was something really senior in the Royal Bank of Scotland, but you know what his problem was? I'll tell you: nasal hair. His wife couldn't bear it. She left him for some guy in the Clydesdale Bank. That's what nasal hair can do.'

Bruce was still smarting at the discovery that he belonged in the ranks of those thus troubled.

'Mind you,' said Arlene. 'You show me anybody – anybody – who hasn't got at least some nasal hair. Everybody has it.'

Bruce felt relieved. 'Oh well . . . '

'But not as much as you,' said Arlene. 'You're at the extreme end of the spectrum. You could have really prolific nasal hair in a few years' time – unless you do something about it, that is.'

Bruce said nothing. He was beginning to regret the consultation, although he felt that he could not get out of it now. But this tactless woman would be lucky if he returned, he decided.

'So we'll tackle that, shall we?' continued Arlene. 'But first we'll look at some of your other areas.' She stared at his chest. 'Interesting,' she said.

Bruce frowned again. 'What's interesting?'

'I think this is a wart,' said Arlene. 'See over here. Well, it looks like one of those warts that people sometimes get. I blame swimming pools, you know. I say that warts are transmitted in the changing rooms. You get all those people walking around barefoot, and naturally the spores that cause warts get passed on. Did you know that warts are caused by spores, Bruce? Like mushroom spores. They float around.'

Bruce made a non-committal sound.

'Anyway,' continued Arlene. 'I suggest a general waxing for the whole chest area, except for that bit where the wart is. And then I think I need to do something about your eye-brows – a reduction on either side. It'll look good. Agree?'

Bruce nodded. 'Do what you think you need to do,' he said.

'Right,' said Arlene. 'Do you want any music? Some people like music. Music to depilate to – that's what I call it. What do you think? Abba, Bruce? You like Abba?'

Bruce shook his head.

'You don't like Abba?' asked Arlene. 'I thought everybody liked Abba.'

'Whatever,' muttered Bruce. 'You choose.'

'Abba, then. It calms my nerves.' Arlene reached across and turned on the music. Then, after busying herself with a dish that had been sitting on a heating apparatus, she extracted a long white strip, rather like a bandage, and placed it across Bruce's chest.

'I don't mind telling you something, Bruce,' she offered.

He looked at her, but said nothing.

'No, I don't mind telling you,' she continued, 'I've been through a bad time. Lawyers.' She rolled her eyes. 'My ex has been a bit difficult about the mortgage payments and I had to get the lawyer to deal with him. And then I've had a legal case against me that's been really upsetting. I've had two lawyers involved in that. Two, Bruce! Two lawyers. And it wasn't my fault in the first place. It was an accident.'

Bruce's eyes followed her as she spoke. 'An accident.'

'Yes. Human error.'

She reached forward, and with a swift movement of her wrist tore off the strip of material across his chest. Bruce felt an odd sensation – a prickling – but it was hardly pain.

'See?' she said, showing him the results. 'See all the hair? Gross, isn't it?'

He nodded. 'This accident? What happened? Was it in the car?'

She tossed the strip into a bin and returned with a fresh one. 'No. Here. It was a professional accident.'

He took a moment to digest this.

'The wax was a bit too hot,' she said. 'It wasn't my fault.'

'I see.'

The pace of the music suddenly seemed to increase. 'I love this one,' said Arlene. 'I'm not sure what the words are, but I love it. I think it might be Swedish.'

A further strip was removed, and several more after that. Then it was time to turn to Bruce's eyebrows. A small strip was placed above Bruce's right eye, and then, with a further deft movement, torn off. This time he felt pain.

'Look out,' he muttered involuntarily.

'Oops,' said Arlene. And then, 'Oh!'

Abba continued in the background, unaffected by the unfolding waxing mishap.

'What?' exclaimed Bruce, sitting up and reaching to feel the place where, until very recently, his right eyebrow had been.

23. In the Elephant House

Pat Macgregor had at last finished her essay on the influence of Raphael on the work of Ridolfo Ghirlandaio. It was four hundred words short of the required length – five thousand words – but she had been able to add three hundred words by expanding the bibliography to include several articles with lengthy titles and of joint or multiple authorship. This was a subject once discussed with her by her father, who had described to her the importance of the position of names in scientific articles by more than one author.

'Never just cite something by X et al,' he said. 'Because X will be pleased to see his name mentioned, but what about W, Z and Y who were his co-authors? How are they going to feel about being described as "et al"? It's a quick way to make enemies.'

'But somebody has to be et al,' Pat pointed out. 'We call them randoms.'

Dr Macgregor laughed. 'I've noticed that. Who are these randoms?'

'People you don't know particularly well. People of no importance.'

'I see.' He paused. 'Except to themselves.'

'Of course.'

It was true, he thought. The world of each of us was

composed of those who meant something to us, and those who did not: passers-by, strangers, people we saw in the street who were as unknown to us and as transient as the extras in a film. He occasionally entertained himself by looking at these background people in a film scene – the anonymous extras – and studying their expressions and movements. For the most part they were good at what they did, and appeared unaware both of the camera and of the fortunate few with speaking parts, but on occasion you could see past the casual saunter, the studied indifference, and glimpse the agony, the look-at-me desperation of the person who wants to be noticed, who wants to be something. Just as it is in life, he thought.

But now the completed essay was in Pat's hand as she entered the offices of the Department of History of Art in Chambers Street. She knew that her efforts would be read by the Watson Gordon Professor himself, but what were her chances of making him sit up at any of her observations? The other essays all looked so much more impressive; so much more memorable. Her own thoughts on the subject were quite forgettable, she thought, and would surely be eclipsed by the clever insights of the other students.

She sighed as she left the office. In a short time, no more than a month or two, she would walk out of that building for the last time, her course – her education really – finally at an end. She would be, or about to be, a graduate of the University of Edinburgh, and would leave the world in which she had spent the last four years, a world of discussion and ideas, for a world of ... what? More discussion and ideas? Hardly. The real world, the world she was about to enter, was all about things;

about making things and moving things; about figures and money and trading one thing for another. That's what people did – they sold things and bought things, and paid one another for their attention, or labour, or for the things they possessed that others might want to acquire. That was all. Material needs and their satisfaction, just as Marx had said.

And so she would have to leave this world of ideas that her professors and lecturers had shared with her – this world in which there was time for the contemplation and analysis of beauty and for the finding of meaning. She thought of Professor Thomson's lectures and of how he had talked about the ideals of the Third Republic in France; of how beliefs in science and progress had found their expression in naturalism in art. She had sat there entranced, and inspired, and had thought about how her own life might be made to mean something. But now she was leaving that world where such meaning might be found, and was going to have to find a job buying and selling things, just as everybody else bought and sold things.

Feeling slightly flat, Pat decided that she would go to the Elephant House on George IV Bridge. This café, with its curious collection of carved elephants, was popular with students, and with people who remembered that they once were students, who sat at the pleasantly scattered tables and looked out over the roofs of the Old Town. She would find somebody to talk to, or could read a newspaper if there was nobody she knew, and thoughts of graduation and reality could be put off for just a little longer.

She bought herself a cup of coffee and, after a brief moment of conscience-induced hesitation, a large Danish pastry. In the back room, well placed for the window, was an empty table, at which Pat seated herself. The smell of coffee drifted up from her cup, and her spirits rose accordingly. There would still be time for coffee in the real, post-university world. There would still be the opportunity to think, even if one could no longer think for quite so long about Raphael or Poussin or the naturalism of the Third Republic.

'Do you mind?'

She looked up. The boy was holding a mug of coffee in one hand and a paperback book in the other. He had a bag slung over a shoulder and she noticed the top of a mobile phone protruding from a pocket in his jeans.

She could not help herself. She smiled, and it was a smile of amusement, rather than just a smile of welcome.

He raised an eyebrow. 'I could try somewhere else. It's just that all the tables ...'

'No,' she said quickly. 'I don't mind. Sure, sit down.'

She glanced at his face. Harmony. Perfect Renaissance proportions. He needed a shave, but only just.

'I'm sorry,' she said. 'I wasn't laughing at you. It's just that ...' He looked at her enquiringly. 'Yes?'

'It's just that you looked like an advertisement – a picture in an advertisement.' She hesitated. 'In a mag ... Those ads for ... Oh, I don't know what I'm trying to say.'

24. The Working of Wood

For a moment or two, neither of them said anything. Then the young man, resting one hand on the table and touching his mug of coffee with the other, as if testing its heat, said, 'I'm Michael.'

Pat said, 'I thought you might be.'

'That's funny,' he said.

'I don't know why I said it. I wasn't expecting a Michael ...'

'Who were you expecting?'

She shrugged. 'Nobody special. Sometimes friends come in. Often, in fact. But today ... they're somewhere else.'

'I come here a couple of times a week. I've seen you once before, I think. Maybe more. Twice, perhaps. You were sitting with a group of girls. One of them had red hair ...'

'Ellie.'

'Is that you, or the girl with the red hair?'

'Not me. My name's Pat, by the way.'

'I thought it might be.'

They both laughed again, but behind her laughter Pat was studying the young man seated before her. He had said that he had noticed her, but she had not noticed him, which puzzled her, as he would have stood out in any crowd; not for the way he was dressed, of course, which was how most other young men dressed, but for ... She found herself wondering about this. What was the quality that made him noticeable? How exactly does somebody become good-looking? It was probably a matter of mathematics, as so many things ultimately were: harmony of features could be reduced to mathematical ratios. If your eyes were just the right distance apart and this distance was just right for the distance between the top of your lips and the point of your chin, then you were, by the grace of harmony, good-looking or beautiful. And that simple fact could dictate the course of your life – could mean that you, rather than a person whose eyes were not quite in the right position, might be given the chances that led to success. It was as simple – and as unfair – as that. Beautiful poets were always published; ugly ones were not. A fine actor would never get very far unless the mathematics of facial structure were on his side.

Michael was holding his mug of coffee with both hands, as if he were warming them. She noticed that on his right hand there was a small scar running down from the knuckle of his middle finger. She glanced at his nails; boys' nails interested her. They were usually bitten, sometimes down to the quick, but every so often one encountered a boy with unbitten nails.

Michael noticed her glance. 'My hands,' he said. She looked away guiltily. 'My hands,' he said again. 'They might be knocked about a bit. I have to use them a lot.'

She looked at him inquisitively.

'Guess what I do,' he challenged.

She looked at the paperback he was holding, trying to read the title upside down. *The Lost Car* ... The final word was partly obscured by the strap of his satchel and she could not make it out. She looked at the author's name: David Esterly.

'You're studying engineering,' she ventured. 'Mechanical engineering?'

He shook his head. 'You were looking at my book.'

'Yes, it's something about cars.'

He smiled. 'Carving. Wood carving. *The Lost Carving*. David Esterly is a wood carver in America. He restored the Grinling Gibbons carvings in Hampton Court after the fire. You should see the work he does – it's unbelievable.' He opened the book and showed her one of the plates.

She looked at the picture in wonder. 'Is that carved in wood? It's so delicate. Like ... like lace.'

'Yes,' he said. 'That's what wood carving can be like.'

She looked at him. 'You're a wood carver, then. Right?'

He shook his head. 'No. I wish I were. I do work with wood, though. I make furniture. Tables. Chairs. You name it.'

She stared at him in admiration. 'You actually make them? You don't just design them?'

He laughed. 'It's odd, isn't it? We're so used to people not being able to make anything that we're surprised that anybody still can. What do you call that? The de-skilled society?'

'Yes. I thought nobody made anything any more. Furniture ... furniture comes from that big Swedish shop on the other side of the bypass. And everything else comes from China.'

He grinned. 'It seems like that sometimes. But there are people who make things. And I always wanted to be one. Right from when I was a wee boy.'

She asked him where he did it, and he told her that he had a small workshop on Candlemaker Row. 'It's just behind us. If you look out of that window, you can just see my skylight. I also have a workshop down near Haymarket – for bigger things. I make the smaller things in Candlemaker Row.'

She asked him to tell her more about what he made. 'Bespoke tables. If you need a special table, I can do it. I do inlaid work – you know, designs in the wood. It can be quite complex.' He paused. 'But what about you?'

'I'm just a student. Or I am at the moment. Finals are in a few weeks' time and then ... and then I'll be an ex-student. Out in the real world.'

He smiled. 'The real world isn't all that bad, you know. Once you take the plunge.'

'Is that what you did? You took the plunge?'

'Yes, I took the plunge. I left school when I was sixteen and did an apprenticeship as a joiner out near Ratho. I didn't like it very much because we had to do everything as cheaply as possible. Modern doors, for instance, are more or less made of cardboard. They're hollow in the middle and you can't screw anything into them. I wanted to work with oak and lime. But people who build houses don't use oak and lime any more.'

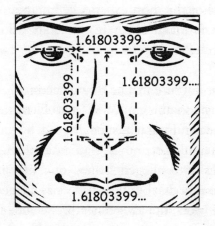

'So?'

'So, when I finished my apprenticeship, I said that I'd start my own business as a cabinet-maker. I hadn't done the right apprenticeship for that, but I taught myself. I started that three years ago.'

She did a quick calculation. Left school at sixteen; assuming the apprenticeship lasted four years he would have finished at twenty; three years in his own business; that made twenty-three.

A perfect age for him to be, thought Pat. Hers.

25. Bruntsfield Noir

Angus Lordie had left plenty of time to walk to his appointment in the outpatients department of the Royal Edinburgh Hospital. He had been referred there by his own doctor, who had assured him that the psychiatrist who would be seeing him was one of the most experienced practitioners of sleep medicine in Scotland. 'If there's anybody who can sort out this somnambulism problem of yours,' he said, 'then he's your man.'

Angus was not sure that he would necessarily have thought that his being a somnambulist was a problem, had it not been for Domenica's raising it as such. Indeed, he thought, I'm an alleged somnambulist rather than an actual somnambulist; not that the term alleged helped one very much. When people were described in newspapers as alleged burglars or alleged fraudsters, the alleged simply seemed to accentuate the noun rather than qualify it. 'Oh yes,' people would think. 'No smoke without an alleged fire!'

But even if he were a somnambulist – alleged or otherwise – he was not sure that this was something that required treatment. So far, Domenica had merely reported that he had opened and closed drawers, while apparently asleep, and muttered something about the Declaration of Arbroath. Well, there was nothing inherently dangerous in opening and closing drawers – people did that all the time in their waking hours, to no apparent detriment to themselves – and as for the Declaration of Arbroath, he failed to see what was wrong with muttering about that. Domenica had, of course, implied that he might fall out of a window or walk out on a ledge, as somnambulists were said to do from time to time, but there had been no sign of that and he did not consider it to be a real risk. So although Angus did not protest when the appointment was made for him, he did not feel that it was really necessary.

Now he was walking through Bruntsfield with at least an hour in hand before he was due to meet Dr Macgregor at his clinic. Looking at his watch, he realised that unless he wanted to be excessively early, he had a good half-hour to have a cup of coffee before walking the final few blocks to the hospital. This was not an area of town he knew particularly well, but he would not have too much trouble in finding a suitable place, given that every second doorway seemed to invite the passer-by in for a cup of coffee. After walking past several crowded coffee houses belonging to well-known chains, Angus went into a small French café, La Barantine, where he ordered a cup of coffee and a pistachio macaroon. Sitting at a seat in the window, he watched the people walking past on the pavement. They were an unexceptional mix of the people one might expect to encounter in that part of Edinburgh – students at Napier University, which was just round the corner; Morningside ladies on their way to the traditional butcher more or less next door; unkempt and glassy-eyed actors arriving early in Edinburgh for some obscure production on the Festival Fringe, and ... he stopped. A familiar-looking man was trudging past, a shopping bag in his hand, a rolled-up newspaper under his arm. He was wearing a black T-shirt and had a fashionable amount of stubble on his chin. Angus had seen him somewhere before, but where ...

Suddenly he remembered. This was Ian Rankin, the creator of Inspector John Rebus, an Edinburgh detective and habitué of the Oxford Bar. Angus looked at the passing writer with the expression of surprise that sometimes comes to the face when one sees somebody well known. It is a curious form of surprise – a slight astonishment that the person actually exists, perhaps, or a sense of good fortune in being given a glimpse of some *rara avis*.

The man outside stopped in his tracks, more or less directly opposite where Angus was sitting. It seemed as if he had forgotten something – some item on his list that he had left unpurchased – and for a moment he stood quite still. Then, turning slightly, he looked through the window of La Barantine, directly at Angus. The gaze of the two men met.

Angus gave a start. To be discovered staring at somebody can be embarrassing, but it was not so much embarrassment that he felt as a curious sense of meeting, or encounter. And for his part, Ian Rankin did not avert his gaze out of a corresponding embarrassment, but smiled at the man sitting within. Angus nodded and returned the smile. Then Ian Rankin gave a thumbs-up gesture – a gesture of encouragement, of fellow feeling, of understanding; a simple human gesture in which one person conveys to another a recognition of common humanity.

The writer continued on his journey, and Angus continued to sit in his seat in the window, his half-drunk cup of coffee before him, a crumb of pistachio macaroon on his lip, to be brushed away with a quick movement of the hand. He felt a curious sense of elation – an enhancement of the moment. He did not want the feeling to end, because it was so powerful, so moving. It was not just the fact that he had seen Ian Rankin that lent significance to the moment; it was the fact that he had shared with him an experience of common human feeling – a glimpse of that sentiment that links us one to the other if only we open ourselves to it, which we do rather too rarely. That this should happen between two strangers, and in such an unexpected way, struck Angus as extraordinary, and precious. Ian Rankin had no idea that he was looking through the plate glass at a man on his way to a hospital appointment, and yet his kind recognition of the other had reassured Angus in a time of anxiety. And as for the pistachio macaroon, how appropriate that a crumb should linger, and that this should happen in a French café, the owners of which would certainly have understood all about madeleine cakes and their Proustian associations, their Proustian echoes.

26. *Angus Lordie Meets Dr Macgregor*

Angus did not have long to wait in the waiting room before Dr Macgregor appeared at the doorway asking him to come in. Entering the psychiatrist's consulting room, he was invited to take a seat on the other side of the doctor's desk.

'No couch,' he remarked, as he sat down.

Dr Macgregor smiled. 'I have a couch at home,' he said.

'From which I watch television. Not that there's anything remotely worth watching these days.'

'The dumbing down of the culture,' said Angus.

'Exactly,' said Dr Macgregor. 'And that brief exchange between us establishes exactly who we are, wouldn't you say?'

Angus relaxed. He had taken to Dr Macgregor immediately. 'Yes, it does, I suppose. To say that one doesn't watch television is a real statement these days, isn't it?'

'It certainly is,' agreed Dr Macgregor. 'It means that one is, to an extent, alienated from the common herd.' He paused. 'Mind you, to use the expression common herd in itself reveals a great deal.' He looked at the letter before him, the single piece of paper in the file. 'Your GP doesn't say a great deal about you in his referral letter. Perhaps you would tell me a little bit about yourself before we get on to the somnambulism issue.'

Angus sat back in his chair. 'There's not much to say, really.'

Dr Macgregor interrupted him. 'But my dear Mr Lordie, there is a great deal to say about everyone – even the least of men. Everybody has the most fascinating story, you know. Everyone.'

Angus looked doubtful. 'Are you sure? Aren't there some frightfully dull people around?' As he spoke, he thought of poor Ramsey Dunbarton, WS, the Edinburgh lawyer whose sole distinction – indeed the highlight of his life – had been to play the Duke of Plaza-Toro in the Church Hill Theatre production of *The Gondoliers*. He had been terribly dull, poor man.

Dr Macgregor did not agree. 'Even an apparently dull story can be fascinating,' he said. 'The tiny details – the tedious things – have a certain grandeur to them, I find. And they also reveal the reasons for why we are what we are. So nothing is really unimportant.'

Angus shrugged. 'In that case, here goes. I was born in Perthshire. I went to school there at a place called Glenalmond.'

Dr Macgregor made a note on a pad of paper beside the file. 'Glenalmond. An interesting place. I went to their prize-giving day a couple of years ago, you know. The daughter of some friends was leaving school that year and they invited me to go up there with them. It was a rather moving occasion.'

'They can be,' said Angus.

'Well this one most certainly was,' continued Dr Macgregor. 'We had a picnic lunch out on the grass after we had sat through the actual prize-giving and the address, and then we went off to the quad and listened to the pipe band. That was the end of the day, and I watched the pupils saying goodbye to one another. Do you know something? They were in tears. Boys and girls – all in tears, embracing one another, saying goodbye to their friends. I must admit I had a lump in my throat too. It was very affecting. And it made me realise how happy a school it must be for the pupils to feel that way.'

Angus was silent. He remembered his last day at Glenalmond. It was just for boys in those days, and they had not cried; girls had made it possible for boys to cry. He had shaken hands with all the others in his year and had thought that he would never again have such a strong experience of friendship and belonging. And then he had been driven by his parents down the long drive into the outside world and his future, and had looked back, just once, to catch a glimpse of the buildings in which he had been so happy. And after that, everything had been harder, somehow, and less innocent, less hopeful.

'So, anyway,' Angus continued, 'I then went to the Edinburgh College of Art. I studied under Robin Philipson, just before he retired, and then I became a portrait painter. That's more or less it. Family? I have a dog – a rather remarkable creature called Cyril – and recently I got married. It's a late marriage, but I count myself very fortunate in having found a wonderful person, Domenica Macdonald. She's a cultural anthropologist – quite well known in her field. We live in Scotland Street.'

'And . . .' said Dr Macgregor.

'And it appears that I've been sleepwalking,' Angus supplied. 'Hence my presence here.'

Dr Macgregor nodded. 'Interesting. May I ask: did you have any sleep-related issues when you were a boy? Any sleepwalking, night terrors, anything of the sort?'

Angus shook his head. 'Nobody said anything about it, if I did. I used to have nightmares, though. I had quite bad nightmares for a while when I was at art college. I used to wake up shouting. My flatmates complained. I lived in a flat behind the King's Theatre.'

Dr Macgregor made another note. 'Do you recall the subject of the nightmares? Do you remember what you shouted?'

'No,' said Angus. 'But they told me. They said that I shouted out: they're going to stop teaching people how to draw! Very strange.'

'And prescient too,' said Dr Macgregor. 'A typical anxiety dream. We all have them. A lot of people dream about being out in public with no clothes on. Some people dream that they're writing an examination in ancient Greek or mathematics or whatever, and they have no knowledge of the subject. Anxiety dreams are almost universal.'

'So not being taught how to draw is what you'd expect an artist to dream about?' asked Angus.

'A real artist, yes,' said Dr Macgregor. 'But tell me: apart from those nightmares, have your sleep patterns been reasonably normal? Have you been getting your eight hours or so?'

Angus nodded. 'I sleep quite well. I never have any trouble getting to sleep, and I rarely wake up in the middle of the night.'

Dr Macgregor made a further note on his pad. 'Well, Mr Lordie, I suspect that these episodes of somnambulism are relatively minor things – they are what we call a parasomnia, but nothing too worrying. There's been no evidence of violence or aggression during the episodes your wife has witnessed, has there?'

'Not as far as I know,' said Angus. He looked enquiringly at the doctor. 'Can somnambulists be violent?'

'Oh yes,' said Dr Macgregor. 'Let me tell you about one or two cases that'll make your hair stand on end.' He corrected himself quickly. 'Not that I want to make your hair stand on end, of course.'

27. *Interesting Somnambulism Cases*

Dr Macgregor would not normally have allowed himself such an excursus with a patient, but he felt an essential rapport with Angus and so he spoke quite freely.

'The first thing I should say is this,' he began. 'The overwhelming majority of cases of somnambulistic activity give no cause for alarm. Sleepwalking is, in fact, quite common in childhood and it's something that people grow out of, rather like an appreciation of pop music – Abba, for instance – or any other childish aberration. But sometimes somnambulism continues into later life, or indeed first appears later on – as I suspect is the case with you. But whenever it first manifests itself, it tends to be pretty insignificant, and nothing needs to be done. However ...' He looked at Angus cautiously. 'However, there are cases – and I'm not sure if I should be bringing these up, as I don't want to alarm you.'

'Too late,' said Angus.

Dr Macgregor smiled. 'Yes, perhaps it is. Well, let me tell you about a couple of cases I know about – one of which I've had some personal involvement with. A couple of these cases are Scottish, interestingly enough – one of them quite a well-known one among the lawyers. That was the Simon Fraser case, back in the nineteenth century.'

The psychiatrist picked up his pen and doodled with it as he spoke, describing small arcs and circles on the pad in front of him.

'Simon Fraser killed his young son while he was, by all accounts, fast asleep. Fortunately for him, he did this just at the time that forensic psychiatry was getting going in Scotland – we were pretty much at the vanguard of it in those days – and there was some enlightened medical opinion available at his trial. He was dealt with humanely and allowed off as long as he promised to sleep in a locked room from then on – which he did. The alternative, of course, in those days would have been the end of a rope – so poor Mr Fraser was indeed fortunate.

'Then, much more recently – only a few decades ago – there was a curious case written up in the medical literature. A teenage boy in Edinburgh attacked his cousin at night with a knife and injured her. Fortunately, not too badly, but it was a knife attack and the authorities had to do something about it. The boy had a perfectly good relationship with the cousin – there was no reason for him to do what he did, and it was out of character too. It looked as if he had done it in his sleep. Again a humane result was achieved, as he was not convicted. Which goes to show that the law can be sympathetic when there's good supporting medical evidence.'

Angus shifted in his seat. There but for the grace of God, he thought ...

'But listen to this,' Dr Macgregor went on. 'The really astonishing case is a Canadian one. I had some involvement in that as I was one of the experts to whom the papers in the case were sent by the defence for comment. They consulted psychiatrists in a number of countries, as it was a rather important case. A man in Toronto was sitting about in his apartment. He had a couple of beers – nothing much – and then dropped off to sleep on the couch. Later that night he got up, went down to his car and drove quite a few miles – over twelve, I think – to his parents-in-law's place, negotiating, on the way, quite a few traffic lights. All of this, we were told, was done while he was sound asleep. Then he got out of the car, went into the parental-in-law apartment, and proceeded to attack his mother-in-law with a tyre lever. Psychiatric evidence was produced at the trial to the effect that all this was somnambulistic. The result was that he was acquitted.'

Angus raised an eyebrow. 'I suppose they had no alternative,' he said. 'The things you do in your sleep aren't voluntary, are they? You can't be blamed for things you don't intend to do.'

'Indeed you can't,' agreed Dr Macgregor. 'If you tap my knee and in reflex action my foot comes up and kicks you, that's automatism. I shouldn't be held responsible for the kick.'

'No, you shouldn't,' said Angus firmly. As a somnambulist, he felt that perhaps he had an interest in asserting the principle of non-responsibility for such acts.

'However, there is a public safety issue,' said Dr Macgregor, 'and that means that the law must have one or two tricks up its sleeve to ensure that dangerous somnambulists don't go round attacking their mothers-in-law. And there's another thing. There was a fascinating study in Montreal some years back that shows that even when we are asleep there are certain inhibitory mechanisms operating in the brain. So things done in the sleeping state might just be the object of moral evaluation.'

Angus looked at him expectantly. 'Yes?'

'There was a woman in Montreal,' Dr Macgregor said, 'who was obese. Now there are undoubtedly many women in Montreal who are obese, but this woman had an additional problem: she was a somnambulistic fridge-raider. She used to sleepwalk down to the fridge and tuck into various fattening snacks. And she had another problem: fear of snakes – ophidiophobia, to give it its full name. And this gave the doctors a chance to do a rather interesting experiment.'

Angus sat at the edge of his seat. 'What happened?' he asked.

'They got her each night to put a large rubber snake on the fridge,' he said. 'She did this just before she went to bed at night, and, would you believe it, it stopped her somnambulistic snacking – she was too frightened to go near the fridge.'

'Although she was asleep? So she was frightened in her sleep?'

'Yes,' said Dr Macgregor. 'But then one night she forgot to put the snake in position – and she somnambulistically snacked that particular night. So that shows ...'

'That we are aware of things while we are asleep?'

'Yes. And it means that somnambulistic acts are influenced by thoughts of consequences and implications.'

'Heavens!' said Angus, and thought: michty me!

28. Birthday Presents

Bertie had stayed awake much longer than usual on the night before his birthday. It was his last night, he reminded himself, of being six. His seventh year, it seemed to him, had lasted a remarkably long time and there were points at which he frankly wondered whether he would ever turn seven. But now it was the night before his birthday, and barring some cosmic disaster, the advent of some unexpected black hole into which the earth might be sucked, with the attendant reversal or suspension of time, in a very few hours he would be waking up to a world in which he was numbered among the seven-year-olds.

There was much to think about as he lay in bed waiting for sleep to embrace him. There was his party – that was to take place on a date yet to be fixed; there were the inscriptions in his books that would need to be changed (they currently read *Bertie Pollock (6)* and that would need to be changed to *Bertie Pollock (7)* as soon as possible); and of course there was the important question of presents. Bertie had spent some time calculating how many presents he might reasonably expect to receive. There would be his big present from his mother and father; there would be a present bought by his parents on behalf of his baby brother, Ulysses; there would be a present from his friend Ranald Braveheart Macpherson; and possibly a present from Olive. In due course, when his party took place he could expect as many presents as there were guests, but there were a certain number of imponderables in that respect that made any specific calculation a little difficult. Tofu always spoke about giving presents but almost always came up with some excuse for not doing so. And as for Larch, who was one of the worrying, uninvited guests on the party list, he tended to take presents from parties rather than bring them. Ranald, however, could be counted on to give a generous present. He bought these himself, using money that he was able to remove from his father's safe now that he had worked out the combination. 'It's OK with my dad,' Ranald had said. 'He has bags of money in that safe, Bertie – you should come and look at it some day. He doesn't mind.'

Bertie eventually drifted off to sleep and at six o'clock the next morning woke up a seven-year-old. When his eyes first opened on the important morning, he lay quite still, savouring the sheer pleasure of being seven. It was different; it most definitely was. He felt mature, responsible, filled with a sort of juvenile gravitas.

Getting out of bed, he dressed quickly and made his way

into his parents' room. His mother was already awake, and was sitting up in bed reading.

'Well, Bertie,' she said as he came into the room. 'Happy birthday, darling!'

Bertie went to his mother's side and allowed her to give him a birthday kiss. From inside the shower in the adjoining bathroom, he heard his father calling out, 'Happy birthday, old fellow!'

'How does it feel to be seven?' asked Irene. 'Different?'

Bertie nodded gravely. 'I feel a bit more grown-up, Mummy,' he said. 'I feel a bit more capable of making my own decisions.'

Irene smiled. 'So you should, Bertie. However, we don't want to run before we can walk, do we? Seven is still quite young, you know.'

'But now that I'm seven can't I decide for myself what I want to do, Mummy?'

Irene looked at him cautiously. 'Decide what sort of thing, *carissimo*?'

'Well, for example: yoga. Can't I decide not to go to yoga now?'

Irene laughed. 'Of course not, Bertie. Yoga's fun! You love yoga.'

'I don't,' said Bertie. 'I think it's silly twisting yourself like that. You could break your back doing yoga.'

'How amusing,' said Irene. 'No, Bertie, we mustn't give up on our yoga just yet.'

There was a brief silence, interrupted by Stuart's coming back into the room, wearing his tartan dressing-gown.

'Well done, wee chap,' he said, tousling Bertie's hair. 'Seven! What a thought!'

'Is it time for presents yet?' asked Bertie politely.

Irene nodded, and reached for two wrapped parcels by the side of her bed. 'Which would you like first, Bertie? Ulysses' present, or the present from Mummy and Daddy?'

Bertie looked uncertain, but after a moment or two opted to receive the present from Ulysses.

'Here we are,' said Irene, handing Bertie a large rectangular parcel. 'Open it up, Bertie, and let's see what little Ulysses has bought you.'

Bertie fumbled with the wrapping paper. A box was revealed. He turned it over so that he could read the inscription: *Junior UN Peacekeeping Kit*.

Bertie looked at his mother.

'Well, *carissimo*, open it up and tell us what you find inside.'

He took off the lid. Inside was an entire set of items

enabling children to play UN peacekeepers. On the front of the book of instructions was the following text: *A fine gift for those who wish to avoid militaristic play (Cowboys and Indians, soldiers etc.). Children become UN peacekeepers with these handy blue UN armbands, pacification leaflets, and pretend maps. Hours of constructive fun for children aged 5 to 10. No small parts.*

'Thank you,' said Bertie quietly. He had noticed that there was no Swiss Army penknife included.

'And now this is from Mummy and Daddy,' said Irene, handing him a smaller box wrapped in bright red paper.

Bertie took the box, his small hands shaking as he unwrapped it.

'It's a doll,' he said, his voice so small as to be almost inaudible.

'Not a doll, *carissimo*,' said Irene. 'It's a play figure.'

Bertie took the doll out of the box. She had long blonde hair and a sort of jumpsuit in green. Around her waist was a thick belt from which tiny spanners were hanging. He looked at the box and read: *This is Jo, our gender-neutral friend. Jo can do all sorts of things! Watch her fix that jeep (not supplied)! Watch her carry out mountain rescues! Watch her care for others! There's nothing that Jo cannot do!*

'You see,' said Irene. 'Jo can have all sorts of adventures, helping people. Isn't that nice, Bertie?'

Bertie nodded. 'Thank you, Mummy.'

He was thinking of where he could hide Jo so that nobody should see her. He was thinking about how he could cut her hair off so that she might just pass for a boy doll, like Ken.

'You can take her to school today if you like, Bertie,' said Irene.

He looked at his father, who was standing motionless at the end of the bed.

29. Today's News

Although Bertie had planned to say nothing about his birthday at school that day, the matter was brought up in a daily slot in the class timetable, Today's News. This was an opportunity for any member of the class to report on events of significance. Pansy, for example, had entertained the class the previous day with an account of her mother's purchase of a Maltese terrier, and the day before that Larch had reported on his victory at his boxing class. Boxing was not a sport appreciated at the Steiner School, and the teacher had listened in pained silence as Larch described the bloody nose that he had inflicted upon his opponent.

'There was blood everywhere,' Larch had said. 'On his face. On his shirt. Tons of blood.'

'Gross!' exclaimed Olive. 'You're disgusting!'

'You shut your face, Olive,' warned Larch.

Their new teacher, Mr Cowie, had intervened. 'We'll have none of that language, please, Larch. And I feel that Olive does have a point, even if her criticism was somewhat personal. I don't think boxing sounds a very nice sport, quite frankly.'

'No, it doesn't,' said Pansy. 'Olive's right.'

Tofu came in on Larch's side. 'Boxing builds character,' he said. 'That's what it's meant to do, isn't it, Larch? It also teaches you to look after yourself, so that if anybody comes up to you in the street and pushes you around you can break their nose.'

'Yes,' said Larch. 'That's why I do it. And there are lots of girls doing it now. There are three in my group at the sports centre.'

'Those are really sad girls,' pronounced Olive.

Pansy agreed. 'Nobody will marry girls like that,' she said. 'They're destined for lives of disappointment, Mr Cowie. Just like you. It's really sad.'

The discussion had proved inconclusive, and the topic had been abandoned. Now, however, a far less controversial matter was being mooted.

'There's some very important news today,' announced Mr Cowie. 'Today, girls and boys, is Bertie's birthday! Bertie Pollock is seven, and I suggest that we all give him a round of applause! All together now, clap clap!'

The class clapped, and Bertie looked down at the floor in embarrassment.

'Bertie,' said Mr Cowie, 'perhaps you'd like to say a few words.'

Bertie looked at the teacher. 'I haven't really got much to say, Mr Cowie. I'm just seven – that's all.'

The teacher smiled. 'Perhaps you'd tell us what it feels like to have a birthday. Do you feel any different, do you think, or is it pretty much the same? What difference does a birthday make, Bertie?'

The class looked at Bertie expectantly. 'I don't think I feel all that different,' he said. 'But I think it's better to be seven than to be six.'

'Now that's very interesting, Bertie,' said the teacher. 'Tell me: why is it better to be seven than to be six?'

Bertie thought. 'I think you feel a bit bigger inside,' he said. 'I think it sounds a bit more important to be seven than to be six.'

The teacher nodded. 'Very interesting, Bertie. Do you think that people will listen to you a bit more now that you're seven?'

'Yes,' said Bertie. 'I think they will.'

'You're probably right,' said the teacher. 'But tell us now, Bertie: did you get any presents this morning?'

Bertie froze. It was exactly the question that he had hoped would be avoided. For a moment he toyed with the idea of saying no, but he was a truthful child and he did not feel that he could lie. If he started to lie, he would be putting himself on the same level as Larch or Tofu, both of whom lied with enthusiasm, and at every opportunity. He would not do that.

'Maybe,' he muttered.

'Maybe?' said Mr Cowie. 'Does that mean yes or no? Surely you received some presents this morning, Bertie?'

Bertie bit his lip. 'My baby brother Ulysses gave me something,' he said.

'He's really only your half-brother,' said Olive in a loud stage-whisper.

Mr Cowie looked at Olive with disapproval.

'It's true,' she said.

'It isn't,' said Bertie. 'You've got no right, Olive ...'

'But it's true,' retorted Olive. 'My mummy said that Ulysses looks exactly like your old psychotherapist, Bertie. That stupid psychotherapist who ran away to Aberdeen. My mummy says that everyone knows that your mummy got the psychotherapist to help her make Ulysses. Everyone, Bertie. That means all of Edinburgh, and probably one or two people in Glasgow too. I think it was in the newspapers.'

Bertie stared at Olive with outrage. 'You mustn't say things like that, Olive,' he began.

He did not finish. 'Olive!' snapped Mr Cowie. 'That's very rude. And it's unkind. You mustn't say things like that.' He paused. 'Don't pay any attention to her, Bertie. Now tell us, what did Ulysses give you?'

'He gave me a Junior UN Peacekeeping Kit,' said Bertie.

'How very nice!' enthused Mr Cowie.

'What?' snorted Tofu scornfully. 'A UN Peacekeeping Kit? That's rubbish, Bertie. The UN's just rubbish.'

'The UN is not rubbish, Tofu,' said Mr Cowie. 'The UN is a great organisation – our only hope really. But let's not get bogged down in such matters – tell me, Bertie, what did you get from your parents? They must have given you a present.'

Bertie was aware that all eyes were on him. He looked out of the window. If only a hurricane would suddenly brew up; if only there were to be a major earthquake, or a bolt of lightning. If only something were to happen to distract attention from this awkward situation.

No natural disaster obliged.

'Well, Bertie?' pressed Mr Cowie. 'I'm sure they gave you something nice. What was it?'

He spoke so quietly they almost failed to hear him. 'An action figure,' he said.

'Cool!' said Larch. 'One of those superheroes?'

Bertie wondered whether Jo could by any stretch of the imagination be called a superhero.

'Maybe,' he said.

Tofu was looking at him strangely, as if trying to make sense of something.

'I think Bertie's fibbing,' he said. 'I think it was something else. His mum's really weird, you know. I bet she gave him a doll. Was it a doll, Bertie?'

Bertie stood quite still.

'I think that's quite enough,' said Mr Cowie. 'Thank you very much, Bertie, for sharing all that with us. And happy birthday from all of us!'

There were echoed calls of happy birthday from the various corners of the room. But Bertie did not really hear those; what he heard was the laughter of Tofu and Larch. What he

123

heard was Tofu whispering to Larch. 'Poor Bertie,' he said. 'A doll! Imagine getting a doll when you're a boy! How gay is that?'

30. A Walk with Father

Stuart could tell that something was wrong. He had come home early from work so that he could be there waiting for Bertie when he returned from school on his birthday. He had no particular plans in mind, but he thought that he and Bertie might go off on some sort of outing together. It was a Wednesday, and Bertie normally went to Italian and saxophone classes on that day, but Stuart felt that these could be missed on a special day such as this. Now, as he saw Bertie come into the flat with his mother and Ulysses, he immediately saw that Bertie looked crestfallen.

'Well, well,' said Stuart breezily. 'I bet you didn't expect to see me home so early!'

Bertie, whose eyes had been fixed on the floor, looked up at his father. 'No,' he said flatly. 'Hello.'

Irene took off her scarf and tossed it over a chair-back. 'Bertie's only got ten minutes or so before he'll need to leave for Italian,' she said. 'You'll have to hurry up and change, Bertie.'

Stuart frowned. 'But it's Bertie's birthday,' he protested. 'You don't do Italian on your birthday.'

Irene turned to stare at him. 'Of course you do. What's wrong with doing Italian on your birthday?'

Stuart made a gesture of despair. 'But birthdays are all

about fun! They're about doing the things you normally don't do.'

Irene sniffed. 'Are you suggesting Italian can't be fun?'

Stuart shook his head. 'I'm not saying that. Or, hold on, maybe I am. Maybe I am saying that Italian is no fun on your birthday.'

Hearing a sentiment with which he could thoroughly agree, Bertie looked hopefully at his father.

'Stuart,' warned Irene. 'Why don't you go back to the office? Bertie and I have our plans for this afternoon, and Italian is one of them, thank you very much, or *grazie tante*, should I say.'

'*Ma ... ma*,' began Bertie. '*Ma, non mi piace parlare italiano. Preferisco giocare che parlare italiano.*' (But I don't like speaking Italian. I prefer to play rather than to speak Italian.)

Irene glared at Stuart. 'You see?' she said. 'You've upset Bertie.'

'Me?' stuttered Stuart. 'I've upset Bertie? I beg your pardon, but ...'

Irene signalled to him to follow her through to the kitchen, but Stuart stood his ground. 'I think you should go and get ready, Bertie. We're going for an outing. And, as a special treat, Mr Lordie has lent us Cyril for the afternoon. He says we can collect him from upstairs when we're ready.'

Irene stopped in her tracks. 'That dog ...'

But she did not finish, as Stuart had already ushered Bertie through the door into the boy's bedroom and closed it behind him. A few minutes later, he and Bertie emerged and made their way purposefully through the hall. 'We'll be a couple of hours,' shouted out Stuart. 'Maybe three or four.

We might pick up something to eat afterwards. Fish and chips, or something like that. So don't bother to make any supper for us.'

They were gone before Irene had time to remonstrate further. Once outside, they went quickly upstairs and knocked on Angus and Domenica's front door. This door now had a neatly inscribed brass sign that read: *Macdonald-Lordie*.

Angus let them in. 'Cyril's waiting,' he said. 'He's delighted to be asked. Positively overjoyed at the thought of going out with Bertie.'

Hearing their voices, Cyril bounded into the hall, carrying his lead in his mouth. When he saw Bertie, he opened his mouth to utter a bark of joy, dropping the lead in the process. Bertie bent down and allowed Cyril to lick his face exuberantly.

'It's his way of saying happy birthday,' said Angus. He paused. 'I haven't given you a present yet, have I, Bertie?'

Bertie shook his head. 'But you don't have to, Mr Lordie,' he said.

'Well, I feel I'd like to,' said Angus, reaching into his pocket to extract a five pound note. 'Here we are, Bertie. A Royal Bank of Scotland five pound note, no less.'

Bertie's face broke into a broad grin as he received the present. The value of money is subjective, depending on age. At the age of one, one multiplies the actual sum by 145,000, making one pound seem like 145,000 pounds to a one-year-old. At seven – Bertie's age – the multiplier is 24, so that five pounds seems like 120 pounds. At the age of twenty-four, five pounds is five pounds; at forty-five it is divided by five, so that it seems like one pound and one pound seems like twenty pence. (All figures courtesy of Scottish Government Advice Leaflet: Handling your Money.)

They said goodbye to Angus and went out into Scotland Street.

'Where are we going?' Bertie asked his father.

Stuart shrugged. 'Out, in the first instance. Then it's up to us, Bertie. I thought we might walk down to Stockbridge and get an ice cream. Then perhaps we could go for a walk along the Water of Leith and throw stones into the river. We haven't done that for a long time, have we?'

Bertie consulted his memory. 'I don't think we've ever done it, Daddy,' he said. 'But I'd really love to throw stones into the Water of Leith.'

Stuart looked down at his son. 'I used to be able to skip stones, Bertie. Do you know what that is? You throw a stone along the surface of a loch and it bounces on the surface.'

'You'd think stones would sink, wouldn't you, Daddy?'

'Yes,' said Stuart.

They walked on.

'Daddy?' said Bertie hesitantly.

'Yes, Bertie?'

'You know that present I got this morning. You know that ... that play figure.'

Stuart winced. 'Mummy chose that for you, Bertie.'

Bertie nodded. 'I knew that. What I wanted to ask is this. Can I throw it away? Can I throw it into the Water of Leith?'

Stuart stopped. 'Are you sure you want to do that, Bertie?'

Bertie nodded. 'They made fun of me at school today because I got a ... a doll for my birthday. Tofu and Larch laughed at me. They said ...'

Stuart bent down to embrace his son. 'Listen, Bertie, we'll throw that awful doll away. Shall I go back and fetch it? Yes? All right, you stay here with Cyril and I'll run back.'

Bertie watched his father turn on his heels and walk swiftly down Scotland Street. A few minutes later Stuart returned with a plain brown paper bag in his hand.

'Mission accomplished,' he said to Bertie. 'So let's walk straight down to the Water of Leith.'

'All right,' said Bertie, breaking into a quick walk. '*Presto*. That means fast in Italian, Daddy.'

31. *Spontaneous Combustion*

Bertie and his father made their way along Cumberland Street in the direction of Stockbridge and the Water of Leith. Cyril, whose encounter with the animal welfare inspector outside the Cumberland Bar had fortunately come to nothing, pulled on his lead with all the eagerness of a dog confident that whatever the purpose of their trip may be – and human purposes are frequently opaque to the canine mind – a challenging range of scents awaited classification. Some of these would be familiar – the human scents that ran like ley-lines along the pavements, or the irritating, provocative scent of cats drifting down from walls and other places of feline safety – while others would require a pause and reflection. Cyril had all the time in the world for the evaluation of scents, but he knew that the same did not apply to humans, who seemed puzzlingly indifferent to the world of the nose. A walk, in the canine view, should be a compromise between these two opposing visions, but usually proceeded at the pace dictated by humans. Boys, Cyril noticed, seemed more receptive to the idea of stopping every few yards to allow dogs to deal with scents, but even Bertie tired of constantly interrupting the walk to permit further olfactory investigation.

'Well, this is fun, isn't it, Bertie?' said Stuart as they reached the top of St Stephen Street.

Bertie nodded. 'I like going for walks, Daddy,' he said. 'Just you and me and ...' He hesitated. He was a loyal boy, and he knew that he should include Ulysses and Irene, but somehow ...

Stuart saved the moment. 'Yes, Bertie,' he said. 'Just you and me. And Cyril, of course – when he's available.'

Bertie reached up and took his father's hand. 'Maybe we could go camping one day, Daddy. You and I could have a big tent and we'd get a small tent for Cyril.'

'Good idea,' said Stuart.

'Could we go camping in Glasgow?' asked Bertie.

Stuart smiled. 'Glasgow? You're rather fond of Glasgow, aren't you, Bertie?'

'Yes,' replied Bertie; Glasgow was freedom to him. 'Remember when we went to Glasgow to get the car? Remember how we went to Mr O'Connor's house?'

Stuart smiled again. 'I remember that well, Bertie. He was quite a man, was Mr O'Connor.'

'I'm sorry that he died,' said Bertie.

'Yes, it's a great pity,' agreed Stuart.

'What did he do for a living, Daddy? Did he work for the Scottish Government, like you?'

Stuart tried to look serious. 'Not quite, Bertie. I think Lard

O'Connor bought and sold things. Or maybe just sold them – I'm not sure if he did much buying.'

'And his friend, Gerry, helped him in the business?'

Stuart said that he thought this was so. Gerry, he imagined, was an enforcer, and would undoubtedly have been able to offer his talents elsewhere.

'Gerry will be missing him,' said Bertie.

'He'll probably be all right,' said Stuart. 'These fellows are quite tough, you know, Bertie. They bounce back. Glasgow's a bit different from Edinburgh, you see. Gerry will be all right.'

Bertie thought about this for a moment, and decided that this was enough about Glasgow and Mr O'Connor. There was something else he wanted to ask his father.

'I was reading something, Daddy,' he said.

Stuart looked at him enquiringly. Bertie's reading habits were extraordinary.

'You like your reading, don't you, Bertie? What was it this time?'

'There was a magazine in the 23 bus,' Bertie said. 'Somebody had left it there.'

'Oh yes?' Stuart sounded cautious.

'There was an article in it that I didn't manage to finish,' Bertie began. 'We reached Holy Corner and we had to get off. And Ulysses had just been sick over Mummy again, and I had to try to wipe it off her jersey. You know that red one? Mummy had given him some squashed beetroot so it didn't matter too much. The sick was all red, you see. It was full of little bits of beetroot.'

'Yes, Bertie, I can imagine. But what was the article you read?'

'It was about spontaneous combustion. It said that people can be walking along and then suddenly – whoosh – they go up in flames. They burn to bits and all that's left is the shoes. There was a photograph.'

'A photograph of somebody spontaneously combusting? I don't think so, Bertie. I don't think they've ever recorded it in a photograph.'

'No, just the shoes,' explained Bertie. 'They had a picture of some shoes with smoke coming out of them.'

Stuart laughed. 'That would be fake, Bertie. Magazines do that sort of thing. There's something called Photoshop. You can do things with photographs.'

'But they said that it really happens. Is that true, Daddy? Can people suddenly burn up altogether – just like that?'

'It's a peculiar thing, Bertie. Some people say that it happens. I read something about it too – quite some time ago. But I think there have been cases where it seems to have happened. And I think that Charles Dickens . . .'

'Did Mr Dickens spontaneously combust, Daddy? Is that how he died?'

'No, Bertie, Charles Dickens wasn't a victim of spontaneous combustion. But he did mention it in one of his books – *Bleak House*, I seem to recall. There's an incident of spontaneous combustion in that novel, I think. It's certainly a very odd thing.'

Bertie looked thoughtful. 'Has it ever happened in Edinburgh?' he asked.

Stuart shook his head. 'I don't think so, Bertie.'

'Maybe it's happened in Glasgow,' suggested Bertie.

'Possibly. Who knows? But I wouldn't worry about it, if I were you.'

But Bertie was still intrigued. 'I wonder if you just feel yourself getting a bit hotter,' he said. 'Then you get hotter and hotter until you start to go on fire.'

'Possibly,' said Stuart. 'But let's not bother ourselves too much with spontaneous combustion, Bertie. As I said, it's unlikely to happen in a place like Edinburgh, and even if it did, we have an excellent fire brigade. I'm sure that they'd know exactly what to do.'

'If you started to spontaneously combust, Daddy,' Bertie asked, 'would you call the ambulance first, or the fire brigade?'

Stuart thought for a moment. 'That's an interesting conundrum, Bertie. Very interesting indeed.'

32. Professor Purdie, Sleepers, Top Hats

The rather surprising conversation about spontaneous combustion saw them the length of St Stephen Street. Now, just before they turned into India Place, Bertie noticed the Floatarium and pointed it out to his father.

'That's the place where Mummy goes to float,' he said. 'See it, Daddy? They have those big flotation chambers and you go inside and it's all dark and you float on the water. Even your pillow floats. They fill the tanks with water from the Dead Sea.'

'Really, Bertie?'

'Yes. Mummy likes it. She takes her friends there sometimes.'

Stuart nodded. 'It must be fun.'

'Remember that therapist? Remember my last psychotherapist, Daddy?'

'Yes, Bertie, I remember him.'

Bertie looked up at his father. 'Not the one I've got now. Not the Australian one. Not him. The one who looked like Ulysses?'

Stuart was silent.

'He went to the Floatarium,' said Bertie.

'I suppose a lot of people go there,' said Stuart evenly. 'It must be very relaxing.'

'He went to the Floatarium with Mummy,' said Bertie casually.

Stuart's pace slowed down. He looked up at the sky.

'I think he liked it,' said Bertie.

They walked on. 'That house over there,' said Stuart, pointing to an ancient stone house standing by itself on a corner, 'that's a very old house called Duncan's Land, Bertie. That's where Professor Purdie lives. He's a friend of Angus Lordie's, I believe. Angus says that Professor Purdie tells some very good stories.'

Bertie looked at the house. 'Did Mr Lordie tell you what they were?' he asked.

'He did, as it happens,' said Stuart.

'Can you tell me one, Daddy?'

Stuart tried to remember; something about the Crown Prince of Japan at Oxford – that was one of them. And then there was the man on the sleeper from London ... 'Oh yes,' he said. 'I remember one, Bertie. There was a businessman in London who got on the sleeper train bound for Glasgow. But just as he left London he had a telephone call from his boss who said there was some trouble at their business in Carlisle. Could he get off the train at Carlisle and then go on to

Glasgow later the next day? So the man went to the sleeper car attendant and asked him whether he could get off early.

'The sleeper car attendant said no, they only stopped for a minute or two to change drivers in Carlisle and it wasn't an official stop. But the man persuaded him to wake him up and put him and his luggage off the train as a special favour. And the sleeper car attendant was a very kind man, and so he said he would.'

'And did he, Daddy?' asked Bertie.

'Well, no,' said Stuart. 'You see, the next morning the man woke up and found that the train was coming into Glasgow. And so he was jolly cross and he went to see the sleeping car attendant and he told him how cross he was. And I'm sorry to say, Bertie, he swore at him very badly. You mustn't swear at people, as you know ...'

'Tofu does,' said Bertie.

'Yes, Tofu ... Anyway, this man was very cross and he swore really badly at the poor attendant. And then the attendant said: "I'm awfie sorry, sir. It's entirely my fault; my mistake. But I can say one thing for you, you're a very good swearer, sir, very good – almost as good a swearer as that man we did put out at Carlisle station ..."'

Stuart looked down at Bertie. 'You see ...' he started to explain.

But Bertie was grinning. 'So they did put a man out at Carlisle station,' he said. 'And that man was jolly cross because he didn't want to be put out.'

'Precisely,' said Stuart.

Bertie smiled. 'I wonder who told Professor Purdie that story.'

'I expect he made it up himself,' said Stuart. 'Angus Lordie says he's very good at these things.'

'Could we go and see him some day?' asked Bertie.

Stuart thought this was possible. 'I think we could, Bertie. We'd get Angus to give us an introduction.'

'A letter of introduction?' asked Bertie.

'Well, we probably wouldn't need anything that formal. I would have thought that maybe just a telephone call from Angus would be enough. He could say that there's this fellow called Bertie who'd like to make your acquaintance ...'

'Who's seven now,' said Bertie proudly.

'Exactly. Who's seven now and who's interested in Scottish history and Robert Burns and things like that. I'm sure that would do the trick.'

Bertie beamed with pleasure at the thought of being introduced to a real professor, and particularly to one who knew a lot of stories and jokes. 'You know that painting in the Scottish National Gallery?' he said to his father. 'I saw it when Mummy took me there. It's called *The Letter of Introduction*.'

'I think so,' said Stuart. 'Is it the one where the boy, or young man, rather, is standing in front of the older man, who's looking at the letter he's given him?'

'That's the one,' said Bertie. 'And the man's dog is sniffing at the boy. He looks very suspicious.' He paused. 'It's by Sir David Wilkie, Daddy. He was a famous artist, you know.'

Stuart laid a hand on Bertie's shoulder and patted him. 'You're a fund of information, Bertie,' he said. 'You really are.'

Bertie looked anxious. 'I'm not showing off, Daddy. I promise you.'

'Of course you aren't, Bertie. I'd never accuse you of showing off. And never be ashamed to know things, Bertie. There are a lot of people these days who think it's smart to know nothing.'

'Tofu,' said Bertie. And added, 'Larch too.'

'Really? Oh well, don't you worry about them, Bertie.'

They were now getting close to the bridge that crossed the Water of Leith at the end of Danube Street. Off to their left, set up against the edge of Lord Moray's Garden, was a large, quite isolated house, deposited as if an afterthought to the elegant Georgian terraces at the top of the cliff behind it. Stuart remembered something that he had heard about that house years ago.

'That house,' he said to Bertie. 'Did you know that a long time ago when it changed hands, the new owners discovered the attic was full of top hats, Bertie?'

'How strange,' said Bertie. 'Why?'

Stuart shook his head. 'I have no idea, Bertie. Nobody has.'

33. By the Water of Leith

There were very few people on the walkway beside the Water of Leith when Bertie and his father reached it. In the distance, a woman was walking her dog on a lead; a young couple were strolling back in the direction of Stockbridge, arms round each other's waists, oblivious of all but their own company. A man clad in an overcoat, in spite of the warmth of the late afternoon, shuffled despondently along, his step faltering from time to time as the burden of his memories, or sorrows perhaps, became too great: sadness has a slow step; cheerfulness, with its clear conscience, has a lighter one.

The river, swollen by heavy rains that had fallen on its catchment slopes in the Pentlands a few days earlier, was in spate, yet its waters, unusually for a river that flowed through a city, were as clear as any Highland stream's – the colour, here and there, of whisky. Below them, but reachable from their footpath, was St Bernard's Well, with its stone-columned temple to Hygieia. Cyril, it seemed, wanted to go in that direction, and tugged them down to the foot of the small building, panting eagerly, as if ready to take the waters himself.

Bertie stared at the statue of the goddess and then looked quizzically at his father.

'Hygieia, Bertie,' said Stuart. 'She was the Greek goddess of hygiene.'

Bertie turned to face the river. 'Could we go and sit down there, Daddy? On the rocks?'

'If we're careful. The river's very full at the moment. All that rain.'

They picked their way gingerly across an expanse of rock until they were just above the level of the water, perched on a smooth and accommodating boulder. Cyril, who was still on the lead, sat next to Bertie, his mouth open to reveal his gold tooth, his pink tongue hanging out. The water, uttering something between a chuckle and a roar as it leaped over rocks impeding its path, was a white torrent here, only a few feet deep perhaps, but voluminous enough to be a set of miniature rapids.

Bertie had to shout to make himself heard. 'The doll, Daddy . . .' he began.

Stuart had been so wrapped up in his conversation with his son that he had almost forgotten that he was carrying the hated present. Now he remembered and felt a sudden pang of guilt that he should have agreed to be party to the throwing of the doll into the Water of Leith. He would have to renege, he thought; he would have to persuade Bertie that no matter how much he disliked the present, it was simply wrong to fling it away. And it was littering too . . .

He extracted the doll from the packet in which he had been carrying it. 'I don't think it's a very good idea to throw poor Jo away like this, Bertie. I think you should think again.'

Bertie had half-risen to his feet, and now leaned forward to take hold of Jo.

'You said I could,' he muttered to Stuart.

Stuart winced. It was a moment of choice. 'You don't like Jo, do you?'

Bertie shook his head. And then, without uttering any warning, he threw the doll out over the river with all his strength.

Jo described a high curve. For a moment she seemed to hang in the air, her little plastic arms wide apart in surprise, and then she fell, head first into the Water of Leith. The river took her, but she did not sink, bobbing about instead on the current, staring at her previous owner with the optimistic fixed grin with which she had left her factory in China. Then she was tugged away, and dipped into the first of a series of rapids that would carry her downstream.

Bertie looked up at his father. His face revealed the sudden wave of regret he felt at the appalling thing he had done.

'I didn't really mean to,' he began, and then trailed off. It had been a terrible thing to do, and he feared that no words of his would excuse him.

He had reckoned without Cyril. The dog had been watching silently, but with interest. Now, seeing Jo hurled into the water, he decided that this was an unexpected, but very welcome invitation for him to fetch her. Angus threw sticks into the water and he retrieved them; this was just a variant of that timeless human-canine game.

Dashing forward, his lead trailing behind him, Cyril lunged into the water. Bertie cried out in alarm and snatched at the lead, but he was too late. Cyril was now fully in the water, scrabbling, half-swimming, through the shallows. Within a few seconds he closed in on Jo, who had been swept into a patch of less turbulent water, and it was there that he closed his jaws around her, his teeth sinking deep into her yielding plastic flesh. Then he turned round and made his way back to the rock on which Bertie and his father were now standing, transfixed by the heroic rescue they had just witnessed.

'Look!' shouted Bertie. 'Cyril's saved Jo!'

Dropping the bedraggled action figure at Bertie's feet, Cyril shook himself vigorously, drops of water spraying liberally over Stuart and the boy.

Bertie picked up the doll, who stared up at him blankly. One of Cyril's teeth had punctured the place where her mouth had been, leaving a small hole, out of which water now dribbled, as if from the mouth of one saved from drowning.

'What are we going to do?' asked Bertie. He suddenly felt protective towards Jo; Cyril had taken such a risk to save her, and it had been so wrong of him to throw her into the river. He could not hurl her back into the water.

Stuart looked at the doll. 'It's up to you, Bertie,' he said. 'Do you want to keep her? You don't have to, you know.'

'It's not her fault,' muttered Bertie. 'She didn't ask to be given to me.'

Stuart frowned. He realised that he would have to take control of the situation. He could not leave his son wrestling with guilt and shame.

'I've had an idea, Bertie,' he said. 'There's a charity shop down in Raeburn Place that takes toys. They'll find a home for Jo.'

Bertie's face brightened. 'Do you think so, Daddy?'

'Yes,' said Stuart. 'I really do, Bertie.'

Suddenly Stuart felt stronger. What was the word Irene always used? he asked himself. She talked about empowerment of women – that was it. Well, thought Stuart, women might be empowered, but so might men, and he felt suddenly empowered. Very empowered.

'220 volts,' he muttered under his breath. 'DC.'

34. Big Lou Makes an Appointment

Big Lou had been waiting rather a long time. She was patient by nature, but after an hour of sitting on an uncomfortable plastic chair in a cramped recess off a corridor, entertained only by a tattered pile of out-of-date magazines and copies of the Edinburgh Social Services Review of the Year, she was beginning to wonder whether three o'clock had really been four o'clock, and whether she had misread her appointment time. But she had the letter with her, tucked away in a pocket, and when she extracted it and read it again, she found that there had been no mistake.

Eventually, though, an official arrived to inform her that she would be seen, and apologies were made. 'We're very sorry to have kept you waiting. We're a bit understaffed at the moment, you see.'

The apology was made with evident sincerity, and Big Lou did not say anything, as she had half-decided to do, about the difficulties that making an appointment entailed for those who ran their own businesses. Her coffee bar, which she ran entirely herself, had been closed for this meeting and she would have lost business. Not much business, it was true – only the sale of three or four cups of coffee, perhaps, as the afternoon was a slack time, but there was the principle of the thing. She paid her business rates as everybody else did, and . . .

'And you've probably had to close your coffee bar to be here,' the official continued. 'We're very sorry.'

'It doesn't matter,' Big Lou said hurriedly. 'I'm under-staffed myself. I know what it's like.'

The official, a woman in her mid-thirties wearing a plain grey trouser suit, smiled at Big Lou as she led her into her office. 'Please call me Marjory,' she said. 'And you're Lou, aren't you?'

Lou nodded. 'Most people call me Big Lou. They always have. You can, if you like. I don't mind it.'

Marjory looked slightly embarrassed. 'Oh well, names ... It's a bit cramped in here,' she said. 'But I chose this room for the view. View over space, I think. Don't you?'

Big Lou looked out of the window. Beyond her was the skyline of the Old Town – a field of spires and chimneys and spikes. Edinburgh was a spiky city, she thought; one so easily forgot that. And there, beyond the rooftops, were the Salisbury Crags and the brooding shape of Arthur's Seat. In the far distance, the Firth of Forth, opening out at that point, was a field of light blue across which a tanker ploughed its furrow.

'A fine view,' said Big Lou.

The official joined her at the window. 'It's better even than the view from the Lord Provost's window,' she said.

They sat down. Marjory opened the file on her desk in front of her. 'Now then,' she said. 'You've had your prelim-inary interviews, I gather. And everything seems to be in order. We're happy to approve you.'

Big Lou's eyes widened. 'Is that it? Approved?'

'You'll need to go to our training sessions,' said Marjory.

'There's a place just come up, as it happens, this weekend. Could you manage that?'

Big Lou said she could. 'I'll close the business on Friday afternoon. I'll be there.'

'Good,' said Marjory. 'It's out at Eskbank. I'll send you the details.'

'And then?' asked Big Lou.

'Then ... well, then we can make a placement. You'll be monitored quite closely to begin with – I'm sure you understand why we have to do that.'

'Of course.'

'But in your case,' went on Marjory, 'your experience working in that nursing home up in Aberdeen is in your favour. We felt we could shorten the training and perhaps have a shorter monitoring period too.'

'I won't let you down,' said Big Lou. 'I would never let you down.'

Marjory looked at Big Lou in silence. It seemed that the younger woman was evaluating her – and she was. 'I can tell that,' she said. She glanced down at the open file. 'Arbroath. The farm ... The nursing home. Frankly, it's the ideal background. I suppose the only thing that perhaps is not ideal, and we have to be open about this, is that you're ...' She hesitated. 'You're by yourself.'

Big Lou did not flinch. 'I see.'

'Because it's sometimes easier for two foster parents,' said Marjory. 'Particularly if there's a boy involved. Boys can be demanding.'

Big Lou said nothing.

'But it's not something we make a fuss about,' Marjory

went on. 'The important thing in looking after children is routine, love, and a proper measure of firmness and consistency. I'm sure that you will be fine with all of those.'

'I'll try,' said Big Lou.

Marjory smiled. 'Good. I have complete confidence in you.' She closed the file and reached for a piece of paper from her tray. 'We have a child in mind,' she said. 'In fact, two – a brother and sister. They're eight and ten. You obviously would need school age children if you're working. And of course you'll have to make arrangements for the period between school and your coming home in the evening.'

'I'll change my opening hours,' said Big Lou. 'I can shut the café at three in the afternoon. Nae bother.'

'Good.'

'Can you tell me something about them?'

The social worker sighed. 'It's not an atypical story, you know. A bad one. Bad adult behaviour and who suffers? The children. The innocent children.'

'I've seen that,' said Big Lou.

'Of course you have. These two youngsters are, I'm afraid, quite badly damaged. They've never had a chance, really. Mother was utterly irresponsible, and how she managed to bring them up as long as she did is anybody's guess. She wanted a good time. Clubbing every night, excessive drinking, and that didn't fit with having two children. Father was nowhere to be seen, of course, which is par for the course. The children were in and out of care, and then Grandmother came into the picture. She was the maternal grandmother and she lived out at Craigmillar – a really good woman. She looked after them pretty well, in the circumstances, but she

144

became ill. One of those quick cancers and there wasn't much they could do for her. She was really worried about the kids and tried to make arrangements – with friends and so on – but it wasn't very satisfactory. Shortly before her death she handed over all her life savings – four thousand pounds – to a friend who promised to use it to help the children after she was gone. And you know what happened?'

Big Lou looked away. She imagined what was coming.

But she was wrong. 'No, the friend didn't make off with the money,' Marjory went on. 'Not at all. She decided to put it into bank shares. This was before the crash.'

'Oh no,' said Big Lou.

'And yet what do we read in the paper?' said Marjory. 'We read about major bonuses for bankers. That's what we read.'

35. The Planning of Happiness

While Marjory made Big Lou a cup of coffee they continued their conversation.

'I've never understood this bonus system,' said Big Lou. 'Don't they pay these people salaries?'

'Of course they do,' said Marjory. 'They pay them handsome salaries.'

'So what are these bonuses?'

'That's a good question,' said Marjory. 'It amounts, in my view, to a skimming off of a substantial part of the profits by the staff.'

'Aye,' said Big Lou. 'That's what it sounds like to me.'

'And the problem is that they're all at it. The shareholders can't control it because the boards are all packed with institutional shareholders. Turkeys don't vote for Christmas, as they say. They're not going to stop a system which they tend to have a stake in themselves.'

'No, they wouldn't,' said Big Lou.

Marjory handed Big Lou her cup of coffee. 'Instant, I'm afraid.'

Big Lou said nothing.

'Of course,' continued Marjory, 'they argue that they have to give these big bonuses in order to attract the talent. They say that they wouldn't get the best people if they couldn't offer bribes of millions. But that's rubbish. People would be lining up for those jobs – lining up; and there are people already working in banks who could do the job every bit as well as the bonus-merchants. There are bags of people who are hungry who would go for that work like a shot. And be able to do it, too. They'd do it for a salary that was a fraction of what these greedy individuals are paying themselves.'

'I can imagine that,' said Big Lou. 'I get some of the more junior staff of one of the banks coming into my café. They're hard-working people, and good at their job. They don't get these bonuses at all.'

'They could do those jobs just fine,' said Marjory. 'They would do them for one fifth, one sixth of the pay – and still be happy with it.'

'The world is in a gae fankle,' mused Big Lou.

'The world isn't,' said Marjory. 'Just bits of it.'

They sipped at their coffee.

'These bairns,' said Big Lou. 'The brother and sister: what happened?'

'The mother couldn't look after them properly,' said Marjory. 'She tried again after the grandmother – her mother – died, but it was no use. We had to take them into care when the school discovered that they hadn't had a proper meal for two days. Mother handed them over quite happily – she couldn't be bothered. So they've been with us. They had a spell of fostering with a very good couple we have off the Easter Road, but that was always going to be short term. The children aren't easy, I'm afraid.'

Big Lou frowned. 'Who can blame the pair wee things?'

'No, one can't blame them at all. You can't ever blame the children, as far as I'm concerned. If a child behaves badly, then it's because of what's been done to him. And if he behaves badly in spite of being treated well, then it's the genes, I'm afraid, and you can't blame a child for his genes either, can you?'

Big Lou supposed not.

'There's no violence, or anything like that, so ...'

'Would a bairn be violent?' interrupted Big Lou.

'Oh yes,' said Marjory. 'We had a six-year-old the other day who threatened to kill somebody. Threatened to throw him downstairs. What can you expect? The child had been dumped in front of the television set for six hours a day and seen images of non-stop violence and aggression. Watch six hours of television, and that's what you'll see.'

'But these bairns ...'

'Their problem is silence,' said Marjory. 'They're very withdrawn. They'll hardly speak, I'm afraid. Mind you, they haven't really been spoken to very much. Their mother certainly didn't speak to them.'

'That's bad,' said Big Lou.

'So they're very withdrawn,' said Marjory. 'They're not autistic, as far as we can make out, because there have been spells of perfectly normal social interaction in the past. We hope that with time they'll come out of their shell.' She paused. 'I hope I haven't put you off.'

Big Lou shook her head. 'It would take more than that to put me off. No, you send me these bairns and we'll see what I can do.'

'Thank you.'

'There was a boy like that at school when I was a wee girl,' said Big Lou. 'He had been bullied a lot. He was a muckle great lad, but he wouldn't stand up for himself. His father had been killed in a road accident. He never said anything. He just looked at you and then looked away.'

'What happened?'

'He joined the Boys' Brigade. There was a good man there and he took him under his wing. He saw him through. He works in Dundee now, that boy. He has a landscape gardening business and has done well enough. He married and has a family – I saw him at the Highland Show last year.'

'It doesn't always work out like that,' said Marjory.

'No, it doesn't.'

'But when it does, it makes everything we do seem so worthwhile.'

Big Lou put down her cup. 'These bairns – what are their names?'

'Luke and Jenny. Luke is ten; Jenny is eight.'

'I like those names,' said Lou.

Marjory handed Lou a photograph from her drawer.

'That's them,' she said. 'That was taken about six months ago.'

Big Lou looked at the picture. The boy was standing; the girl was sitting. They were in what looked like a living room. There was a small fireplace in the background and a shelf of china ornaments. Neither of the children was looking at the photographer. Jenny was looking down at the floor, and Luke was staring at the wall. Neither was smiling.

'They look very unhappy,' said Big Lou. 'What a pity.'

'You're right: they are unhappy,' said Marjory.

'Then we'll change that,' said Lou.

Marjory grinned. 'That's what I like to hear,' she said.

36. Culturally Specific Foods

Elspeth's irritation with Matthew did not last long. She was too fond of him to feel angry for much more than a very short time, and the *casus belli* in this case was hardly a *casus belli* anyway – a tactless remark, and an absurd one at that, was not something that she would allow to rankle. She forgave him, as marriage, or friendship for that matter, ultimately requires of those who wish to remain married or friends.

Their life together, though, was not without its tensions. The birth of a first child is a stressful time for any man, and many men choose that difficult point in their lives to entertain what amounts to a premature mid-life crisis – a short-lived period of rebellion, confusion, or, in some cases, downright bad behaviour. The causes of this are complex: for some men, becoming a father is a psychological Rubicon, the crossing of which brings it home to them that their wings have been clipped – and their metaphors mixed perhaps. Being responsible for a wife or partner is one thing a man who sees himself as a free spirit can still reconcile with the continued enjoyment of personal autonomy, but responsibility for a child is quite another, involving connotations of permanence and seriousness for which he might not be prepared. If a puppy is for life and not just for Christmas, then how much more so is a baby and, *a fortiori*, triplets.

Even if it looked as if Matthew had managed to weather the birth of the three boys, he was still slightly unsettled, and the situation was not made any easier by the arrival of the au pair's au pair – the one engaged to act as assistant to Anna, the original au pair. This young woman, Birgitte, had been recruited in recognition of the sheer volume of work that three young infants created for Elspeth and Anna. She was just nineteen, having left school in Copenhagen a year previously and spent the last eight months working in a hotel in Lemvig. She was attracted by the thought of a job in Scotland, as it would enable her to improve her English, which, thanks to the excellent Danish educational system, was already quite fluent.

Birgitte appeared to be both biddable and cheerful, but her arrival in the household had somehow disturbed the balance of the domestic relationships previously existing in India Street. There is a folk belief that two women cannot share a kitchen. This is probably not true; there may well be cases where women find the sharing of a kitchen difficult, but many modern women, being less thirled to the domestic life than they used to be, no doubt share their kitchen quite amicably with another woman. But when it comes to three women sharing a kitchen with one man – as was now the case in Matthew and Elspeth's flat – then tensions may be expected to develop. With six in the flat – if one included Fergus, Rognvald and Tobermory – there were, it seemed, simply too many people living under one roof.

Some of the kitchen tensions were minor – risible, really. Shortly after her arrival, Birgitte, who, like Anna, was energetic and keen to work, had taken it upon herself to tidy one of the food cupboards. Much of what she did in this exercise was useful: there had been, for example, three packets of hazelnuts in current use – these she reduced to one, by emptying the contents of the second and third bags into the first. Then she wiped the marmalade and jam jars so that they would not be sticky to the touch – again, a very sensible thing to do, even if not a task that the average Scot would think to perform. But then it came to the jar of Marmite, which Matthew used each morning at breakfast.

It is well known that Marmite is not for everyone. While it is much appreciated in Britain – as is its Australian equivalent, Vegemite, in Australia – there are those who find it quite beyond their understanding that anybody should eat dark brown, salty yeast paste and appear to enjoy it. Americans, in particular, have difficulty in understanding the appeal of Marmite, and if they are ever encouraged to sample it tend to wrinkle up their noses, utter expressions of disgust, and immediately try to remove the taste from their mouth by eating something sweeter or blander. Marmite, it seems, is something that one needs to be brought up with in order to appreciate to the full extent; not a surprising thing, as western Europeans and Americans have never quite got the hang of eating sheep's eyeballs, or mopani worms, or any of the other culturally specific delicacies they are on occasion offered when travelling abroad. The idea of the relativity of taste applies in matters of the table as much as it applies in other areas of life; the simple truth is that those who enjoy Marmite enjoy it. As Muriel Spark had Jean Brodie observe: for those who like that sort of thing, that is the sort of thing they like.

On opening the jar of Marmite, Birgitte sniffed at it, unwisely dipped a teaspoon into the jar, and then put the teaspoon straight into her mouth. The recommendation is, spread thinly, and putting a spoonful into one's mouth hardly comes within the scope of that advice. Birgitte gave a cry, and concluded that the contents of the jar – whatever they might be – had definitely gone off or were possibly even poisonous and needed to be thrown away. Which is what she did.

Similar weeding out occurred when she turned her attention to the fridge. A half-eaten haggis, saved for Matthew's dinner that night, also judged to be off, was wrapped in newspaper and put in the bin, the same fate as befell Matthew's supply of Patum Peperium. This was followed by the washing of all the saucepans and kitchen utensils, and their replacing in the wrong place.

'She's just trying to be helpful,' whispered Matthew.

'I know,' said Elspeth. 'But I can't stand this, Matthew. It's my space, you see. My space!'

He looked at her apologetically. It was his fault. He had given her three boys. He had encouraged this new au pair. It was his unsuitable flat they were living in. It was all his fault.

37. *Perjink Bungalows, et cetera*

The awkward state of domestic affairs in Matthew's flat might have continued for some time had it not been for the fact that he and Elspeth one morning happened to find themselves reading the property supplement of the *Scotsman*. Property pages are not just read by those actively searching for a new home – interest in the houses being sold and bought by other people is widespread, and there are many who, although they may never read the business or motoring supplements of newspapers, will nonetheless turn with enthusiasm to advertisements for houses and flats.

There are various forms of motivation behind this. For

some, the reason to scan the property advertisements is to get an idea of what one's own home is worth. This is understandable: for many of us, our principal asset is our house, and to find that it has grown in value provides the reassurance that we are not going to die paupers. Within this group, there are those who, having bought their house for very little, discover that it is now worth so much that they are comfortably millionaires. This may turn their heads, and they may well be reminded that the value of a house is mainly theoretical if one has to live in it. Even if one sold the house for one million pounds, one would have to choose between being a homeless millionaire, or buying a new house, and becoming cash poor again.

Another reason for looking at the property advertisements even if one is not thinking of moving is the sheer voyeuristic pleasure of seeing how other people – both below one and above one on that terrible escalator known as the property ladder – live their lives. In this way, photographs of perjink bungalows in Greenbank will reveal exactly what happens in that particular slice of Edinburgh suburbia – how many bedrooms and bathrooms there are in the lives of those who live there, how large their garages are, and the nature of their outlook – in the sense of both their view and their views. Similarly, the occasional advertisement of large country houses will reveal to those who live in towns just how much room those who live in the country may have. This can be the cause of some distress, as urbanites looking at the leisurely and indulged lifestyle of country gentry may feel a sense that life is not quite as fair as it might be: what gives them the right, after all, to have a gazebo system and a small loch? And if that is not enough to give rise to feelings of frustrated longing, then resort to the property pages of *Country Life* may cause even greater annoyance to those of an envious cast of mind. These pages have full-page pictures of an estate near Inverness (six thousand acres and a salmon river – at least four fish last season); a villa in the Charente Maritime (with hobby vineyard and the most charming chateau); and a bijou mews house in London (Notting Hill tube station just yards away) for a mere four million pounds (rather more in roubles).

Matthew and Elspeth did not fall into any of these categories of reader. They perused the property pages together, taking it in turns to guess what the value of each house might be. Elspeth was extremely good at that, and often got the figure exactly right, while Matthew tended to underestimate the value of the properties she described to him.

'Here's an interesting one, Matthew,' she said that day. 'Moray Place. Two bedrooms. Second floor. A good view of the gardens. What would you guess?'

Matthew suggested a sum, and Elspeth laughed. 'Way out,' she said. 'You might have got it for that ten years ago, but not today. Not Moray Place.'

'What about the nudists?' Matthew asked.

Elspeth looked doubtful. 'They probably make no difference to the people living there. Not all that many people know that Moray Place is the centre of the Scottish nudist movement.'

'Odd, that,' mused Matthew. 'I suppose it's a nice place for nudists to live. The gardens give them a bit of cover, I should imagine. And nudists don't do any harm, after all. They probably make rather pleasant neighbours. They won't have rowdy parties at weekends because they'll all be off at their nudist camps in the dunes in East Lothian, or wherever they like to go.'

Elspeth's attention was distracted by another advertisement. 'What about this?' she said, and then read: 'An attractive house near Nine Mile Burn with an unrivalled view of the Pentland Hills. Well away from the main Biggar Road, this charming old farmhouse (*c.* early eighteenth century) has hosted an array of Scottish notables of the past (David Hume stayed here as a visitor, as did Burns and Robert Louis Stevenson). Seven bedrooms, four public rooms, and considerable attic space. Wine cellar and ice-house in the grounds. The property has ten acres of land attached to it, with stabling for two horses, and a byre in need of some attention. There are several stands of mature trees, and a small walled garden. Within easy reach of Edinburgh.'

She stopped and looked at Matthew, who was gazing up at the ceiling.

'Let me think,' said Matthew. 'I suppose it depends on the state of repair. Some of these old houses . . .'

'Matthew,' Elspeth said quietly. 'Forget about guessing. This house would suit us. Us, Matthew! This could be our new home. Seven bedrooms, and we could put Anna and Birgitte in the byre – once we'd done it up, of course. And the boys could have a wire slide, once they're a bit bigger, from one of the mature trees . . .'

Matthew transferred his gaze from the ceiling to Elspeth. 'Are you serious?'

'Never more so,' she said, passing him the *Scotsman*. 'Look at the picture. Isn't it lovely?'

He looked at the picture of the house. It was a good-sized gentleman-farmer's house, made of stone but with harling that had been painted ochre. He could see the mature trees over to the side of the house, beyond the lawn, which had been neatly cut in stripes. People selling houses know when photographers are coming to take their promotional pictures and they cut the lawn in stripes in time for the photograph. Nobody else has their lawn in stripes – no real people, thought Matthew.

'It looks rather lovely,' he said. 'But it doesn't say what the price is.'

'Doesn't it?' asked Elspeth.

'No,' said Matthew. 'It's rather odd. All it says after the word price is: "Guess".'

38. Birgitte Becomes Irritating

Matthew had his misgivings about moving from India Street, but he was carried along on the wave of enthusiasm that seemed to embrace not only Elspeth but the two Danish au pairs as well. Birgitte, it transpired, was a country girl at heart, and she raised the question of whether she could possibly keep a pony in one of the fields attached to the house. She could teach the boys to ride, she said, and she would do all the work of feeding and grooming.

'All of it,' she said. 'You will not have to lift a thumb.'

'A finger,' muttered Matthew.

'Nor that,' said Birgitte.

He looked at her in astonishment; the boys were still very

small, not even a year old, which made him wonder how long she was thinking of staying with them. You could put a three-year-old on a docile pony, he imagined, but surely it would be dangerous to try it with a child any younger than that. Did she intend to be here for the next two years – or even longer?

'But you'll be going back to Denmark,' he said mildly. 'So I don't know if . . .'

Birgitte waved a hand airily in what she took to be the general direction of Denmark. 'Oh, there's no hurry to do that,' she said. 'Denmark will still be there.'

Anna nodded her agreement. 'Denmark is not as exciting as Scotland,' she said. 'I don't think I shall ever return. I am sure that many more Danish people will be coming over here, once they find out how nice it is.'

This conversation took place after Elspeth had organised a viewing time with the selling agents. Matthew tried to catch her eye, to signal his concern over the assumptions being made by both au pairs, but Elspeth was too enthused to notice.

'We'll all go,' she said. 'Everybody can have a look round.'

'Perfect,' said Birgitte. 'But Anna must stay to look after the boys. I shall have to go so that I can advise on the horse angle.'

'We haven't actually decided about . . .' began Matthew.

'It may be necessary to build new stables,' Birgitte continued. 'But we can decide about that later.'

'I'm not sure . . .' Matthew said.

'Never have just one pony,' advised Birgitte. 'Horses get terribly lonely. They pine for a friend.'

They made the trip in the late morning, Birgitte sitting in

the back of the car offering advice on a range of topics as they drove out of Edinburgh. 'I do hope that the house faces west,' she said. 'Then you get the morning light at the back and the evening light on the front. When I was in Jutland I stayed in a place that was completely the wrong way round. It was very uncomfortable. You knew you were the wrong way round the moment you went in. Mind you, there are some countries that are the wrong way round altogether. France is like that, you know. It faces north and south; it would be far better if it faced east and west, as America does.'

By the time they reached Fairmilehead, Matthew was silently fuming. He had almost said something – something like 'You certainly appear to know quite a lot – for somebody who's just left school' – but stopped himself and kept his silence. He remembered what it was like to be eighteen or nineteen – you are so confident of yourself at that stage and you are so sure that you are right, and yet the world seems not to appreciate your talents. And people in their thirties or forties were just so out of touch, so irrelevant, and yet did not seem to know it. I was every bit as bad as you, he told him-self. It helped.

As they drew level with the Hillend ski-slope, his feelings had softened. It was a clear, bright day and the air blowing in through the open window of the car smelled faintly of gorse and newly cut grass. He looked at Birgitte in the rearview mirror, at the solid, slightly square Scandinavian face framed by its long blonde hair, and smiled. He and Elspeth were secure enough not to be irritated by the pushiness of some-body of the Danish girl's age; they would smile at her ways rather than snarl at them. She was far away from home, too, and she was also their guest – in a sense – which meant that it would have been quite wrong to treat her with anything but gentleness and understanding.

Birgitte was looking out of her window towards the slopes of the Pentlands that rose high beside the road.

'Look at those Munros,' she said, pointing.

Matthew looked in the mirror. 'No, Birgitte, those are not Munros.'

'Yes, they are,' she said. 'I have read all about Munros.'

Matthew saw Elspeth suppressing a grin.

'Munros are mountains over 3,000 feet,' said Matthew patiently. 'Then there are Corbetts, which are between 2,500 and 3,000 feet, and Grahams, which are between 2,000 and 2,500 feet.' He paused, glancing off towards the unambitious slopes of Caerketton Hill. 'That hill, for instance, is only just over 1,500 feet.'

Birgitte stared back at him in the mirror. Their eyes locked.

'I don't think so,' she said. 'It will be much higher than that. I am very sure it's a Munro.'

'I'm telling you, it's not,' insisted Matthew.

'I think you're wrong.'

Matthew looked at the road ahead of him, checked what was behind him, and then pulled into a parking place off the side of the road. Elspeth glanced at him enquiringly and was about to say something, but he signalled for her to keep quiet.

Once the car was stopped, but with the engine still running, he swivelled round in his seat and looked at Birgitte. 'Listen,' he said. 'We don't want to be rude to you, Birgitte, but you're going to have to accept that you are not in

Denmark now – you are in Scotland. If I went to Denmark, I would not – I repeat not – lecture you on the height of your Danish hills – if you have any, that is. Understand?'

Birgitte's eyes widened. 'You say we have no hills in Denmark ...'

Elspeth glanced at Matthew. 'Matthew! Don't be unkind!'

'It's not unkind to say that somebody hasn't got any hills,' snapped Matthew. 'For heaven's sake! There are plenty of people without hills. It's just an observation.'

'How do you know Denmark hasn't got any hills?' asked Elspeth mildly. 'You've never been there, have you? It could be a very hilly country, for all you know.'

Suddenly Birgitte began to sob. 'Yes,' she said. 'You condemn my poor country before you've even visited it. You're very cruel, Matthew.'

39. 'I love it. I want to live here'

The argument about hills in Denmark, as absurd as it was unnecessary, did not persist. Elspeth, who as a teacher had been able to handle Tofu and Olive, not to mention Larch, now used the same techniques to put an end to the unseemly dispute between Matthew and Birgitte.

'Now listen,' she said, 'we're not here to fight with one another about how high any particular hills are, or whether there are any hills at all.'

'That's right,' muttered Birgitte. 'We are not.'

Matthew drew in his breath sharply. 'I didn't start it,' he protested. 'I was merely driving along ...'

'Nobody started it,' Elspeth interrupted. 'Nobody's to blame.'

'That's right,' said Birgitte.

Matthew received a warning glance from Elspeth. 'And so,' she went on, 'I suggest that we just carry on with our journey. The more time we sit here arguing about Munros and things like that, the less time we'll have to look at this house we're buying.'

Matthew frowned. 'We haven't decided yet,' he said. 'We're just looking.'

Elspeth acknowledged that this was so. At the same time, she had a strong feeling about the house, she revealed – an instinct, in fact. 'I really liked the photograph,' she said. 'And I've always liked Nine Mile Burn. It's the light, I think.'

She was right about the light, Matthew thought. He had always liked the light on that side of the Pentlands – a light that came from the south-west, that seemed to grow softer and bluer as one looked down towards the Lammermuirs. And the thought of living out of town appealed to him, especially as this stretch of country was so close to Edinburgh as to be virtually its back yard. He liked the villages hidden in the tiny, crooked glens that one found on these fringes of the Borders. He liked the short horizons in these glens; the occasional views of higher hills in the distance; the secrets of small villages that seemed to have changed so little over the years; the names that spoke of distances and colours and the points of the compass – Nine Mile Burn, Silverburn, West Linton. One might turn a corner here and move from a timeless world of agriculture – from cultivated crops or sheep pasture – to a landscape on which quite other human uses had left their mark: old mines, disused shafts, flattened, ancient bings – mounds dug out by men whose lives had been spent in darkness, danger, and poverty. He imagined how, in a hundred years from now, our own tenancy of this part of Scotland might be similarly written across the land. Would there be broken piles where once had stood our ugly, scarring wind farms – monuments to the temporary, to the thoughtless destruction of natural beauty, to the vainglorious pursuit of quick returns? Would there be great bundles of knitted wire where power cables once had marched across the sky? Would there be ...

'That's it,' said Elspeth. 'Just up ahead.'

Matthew abandoned his reflections on the fate of the Scottish countryside to concentrate on identifying the turning that would lead them off to their new house. The road down which he turned was a paved one, but had not fared well in the severe winter of the previous year; here and there potholes made it necessary for them to slow to walking pace, while at the edges the grass, untamed, encroached on the tar.

A hedge, unkempt and now sprouting skywards, initially obscured the view on either side but this now gave way to a bedraggled sheep fence. And there, at the end of an unpaved branch off the road, was the house they had seen in the newspaper advertisement.

Elspeth gasped. 'I love it,' she whispered. 'I want to live here.'

Matthew took one hand off the wheel and rested it momentarily on her knee. 'Darling,' he whispered, 'if this is where you want to be, then so do I.'

'What was that?' asked Birgitte from the back of the car. 'What did you say? I didn't hear you.'

'I was talking to Elspeth,' said Matthew, through clenched teeth.

'I know that,' said Birgitte. 'But I didn't hear you. What did you say?'

Elspeth now turned in her seat and smiled at Birgitte. She made a gesture of silence, placing an upraised finger to her lips.

The house was approached by a long drive that culminated in a small turning circle before the front door. There was another car there already, an old Bristol in British Racing Green, and Matthew drew up behind this. 'That'll be the owner,' he said.

They got out of the car and approached the door. Matthew looked up at the roof – sound grey slate, he noted – and at the guttering that ran along the front. This looked solid and in good enough condition, he thought. At each end it led into a hopper, a lead tray that served to collect the water before consigning it to a downpipe. These hoppers were decorated with a small ornamental thistle that had been cut out of lead, layered to give relief, and then stuck on.

'Look,' he said, nudging Elspeth. 'Look at the thistles.'

Elspeth glanced up, and smiled at Matthew. 'Don't you love them?' she asked.

He nodded. He did. He loved thistles.

The front door had a thistle too – a large brass thistle made into a knocker. As Matthew leaned forward to examine this, the door was suddenly opened by an impressive-looking man in a kilt. They looked at one another in momentary astonishment. Then Matthew recovered his composure.

'Oh,' he said. 'Is this ... is this your place? We hadn't expected ...'

He did not finish. The Duke of Johannesburg burst out laughing. 'What a pleasant surprise,' he said, gesturing for them to enter. 'I had no idea when the agents phoned that it would be you coming out to view the property. Well, it just goes to show, doesn't it?'

Birgitte looked puzzled. 'Excuse me,' she said. 'What does it go to show?'

The Duke looked enquiringly at Matthew.

'This young lady,' Matthew said, 'is Birgitte. She's an au pair.'

The Duke inclined his head courteously in Birgitte's direction.

'She's Danish,' Matthew went on. 'Birgitte, this is His Grace the Duke of Johannesburg.'

Birgitte's face revealed her surprise. 'A duke?' she said. 'That is very exciting. I have never met a duke before. I've met a count, of course, but ...'

'But they don't count,' interjected the Duke, and laughed.

'Excuse me?' said Birgitte.

'British humour,' said the Duke airily. 'Pay no attention to it. That's what I always tell people who visit this country. Pay no attention to the humour.'

40. Jock Tamson's Bairns

Matthew and Elspeth knew the Duke of Johannesburg, of course. Matthew had first met him some years earlier when he had gone to a party at Single-Malt House, the Duke's seat. Most of us have houses or flats, but dukes have seats, which conjures up an altogether more comfortable set of domestic arrangements. Professors have chairs, which are not necessarily as comfortable as seats, but better, perhaps, than the mere benches on which judges have to spend their working hours. Least fortunate, of course, are people who have posts or slots – arrangements suggestive of impermanence and discomfort. To say of somebody that 'he occupies the post of' is to imply that he has a place, but that he should not become too ensconced as there are others only too ready to take his place, with all the enthusiasm of the would-be stylite, on that post.

At that first meeting, the Duke had explained to Matthew the origin of his title, which appeared in none of the acknowledged works on the ancestry of the various swells who adorn Scottish society. The Duke's real name was Maclean, and he came from a long line of Highlanders, traceable back to an early Irish chieftain who enlarged his suzerainty to embrace a number of Scottish islands and some ill-defended parts of the Scottish mainland. Some genealogies claimed to be able to trace the Maclean ancestry even further back, going as far as Julius Caesar and, in some cases, admittedly more tendentiously, to the ancient Celtic god of the sun. Such claims are dubious, but this does not stop their being made; genealogy is an aspirational, rather than exact, science. But what's the point? Ultimately, as Professor Sykes, the population geneticist, has suggested, all of us have an ancestry traceable back to a handful of ancient ur-mothers, which makes distant cousins of us all.

That fact is humbling, as it underlines the ultimate, simple humanity of all. The Scottish expression 'We're all Jock Tamson's bairns' makes a very similar point, as does Robert Burns's 'A Man's A Man For A' That'. And all of this was accepted by the Duke, who used the title only out of piety to the memory of his grandfather, who had been promised a dukedom in return for a large political donation and had then been cheated of it by a reneging government. This act of perfidy should not go unremembered, the Duke reasoned, and the best way of reminding people of the injustice was to use the title that was never conferred. After all, he said, if someone promises you something and then doesn't deliver it, you have every reason to feel aggrieved.

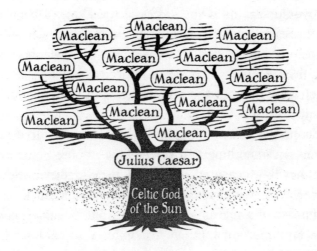

Matthew's second meeting with the Duke had taken place when he, Elspeth, Anna and the triplets had been enjoying a picnic in the Pentlands and the Duke had appeared as if from nowhere. They had engaged in conversation then and the Duke had expressed views on community and the sense of belonging that Matthew had found both perceptive and comforting. He liked this rather unlikely mustachioed figure, he had decided.

'Come in and start taking a look around,' the Duke said. 'I'm never sure whether you should accompany people when you show them a place you're trying to sell, or whether you simply let them wander about themselves. I suppose the danger is that if you don't show them round, they won't know what's what. But if you do, then you might inhibit them. They might wish to express disgust, for example, and may feel disinclined to do so if the owner's standing there.'

'I'm sure we would never express disgust,' said Matthew.

'I wouldn't mind if you did,' said the Duke. 'I believe in direct speaking, no matter how mealy-mouthed our society has become.' He paused. 'Have you noticed how nobody says what they feel today? Have you noticed that?'

Matthew thought for a moment. 'I'm not sure ...' he began.

'People are cowed,' said the Duke. 'They're worried that if they say something that offends the imposed consensus, then they'll be censured, or even punished. They could lose their job, for example. Just for expressing a view. Let's say you disapprove of something – anything – but that thing is held up as an important value by the opinion formers. Can you really express your views these days? Or will you be accused of all sorts of heinous crimes?'

Matthew thought about this. 'I suppose we have lost freedom of speech,' he said. 'But only certain sorts of speech.'

'Such as?' the Duke challenged.

'Speech that diminishes other people. Speech that makes them feel bad about themselves. Speech that disturbs the peace.'

'Such as singing a sectarian football song?' asked the Duke.

'Maybe,' said Matthew. 'What's the point of stirring up animosity between groups?'

The Duke looked bemused. 'I have no time for that sort of thing either,' he said. 'I don't think it's a good thing to make people all hot under the collar by singing rude songs about them. But before we go headlong down the road of forcing everybody to be nice to everybody else, surely we have to ask ourselves: where will it end? Once you restrict freedom of speech in one context, then it's much easier to restrict it in others.'

Elspeth had been following this conversation without joining in. Now she did. 'Sticks and stones will break my bones but words will never hurt me,' she quoted. 'That's what children say, you know, when another child insults them.'

'Exactly,' said the Duke. 'Don't you think that we're making people think of themselves as victims? We're urging them to believe that if anybody says anything hurtful about them they're entitled to run to the police and report it. Aren't we effectively encouraging people to be hyper-sensitive?'

'But what if I said "Dukes are rubbish"?' said Matthew. 'How would you feel?'

The Duke looked at him reproachfully. As he began to respond, Matthew saw that tears were forming in his eyes. 'That's really hurtful,' he said, his voice breaking with emotion. 'We're not rubbish, you know. We really aren't.'

'Look what you've done, Matthew,' hissed Elspeth. 'For the second time in one day. First Birgitte and now the Duke.'

Birgitte was comforting the Duke, putting her arm about his shoulder. 'Dear Johannesburg,' she whispered. 'Please don't cry.'

The Duke winked at Matthew.

41. *The Whole Point of our World*

Pat had spent precisely three hours – to the minute – wondering whether Michael would call. They had exchanged numbers in the Elephant House, Michael writing hers on his wrist with a ballpoint pen she had lent him for the purpose. It gave her a curious thrill – very curious, some might say – to see this breathtakingly good-looking young man put the numbers on his tanned skin; it was such an intimate thing, she reflected, to have one's mobile number inscribed on somebody else. It was as if he had taken her photograph and pressed it to his chest; but then she thought: no, it isn't; he has only written it there because he did not have a piece of paper and he did not want to write in his copy of David Esterly's wood carving book.

He had said that he would call her in a couple of hours to suggest when they might meet again. 'You might like to come and look at this table I'm working on,' he said. 'It has some very detailed inlays. I'm rather proud of them, actually.'

She had accepted immediately. 'I'd love to see your table.' She wanted to add, immediately, 'When?' but did not.

He had eventually finished his coffee and left, as he had to see somebody about a commission, and she had sat by herself for several minutes, savouring the moment.

This is it, she thought. This is definitely it.

But what exactly was it? Love? Had she fallen in love with this boy whom she had just met? Could you fall in love within ... what was it? Twenty minutes? That was the length of time they had spent together over their cup of coffee, and surely it was impossible in so short a time to get any real sense of what another was like. And yet how else could one describe the feeling that had come upon her – that feeling of sudden and intoxicating elation; that feeling of lightness in the stomach, in the head – everywhere, in fact; that feeling of wanting nothing more than to see the other person again, immediately and most urgently?

She closed her eyes, hoping that this might in some way restore her to the way she had felt before she entered the Elephant House. But it did not. When she opened them a few seconds later, she felt exactly as she had felt before. Her world was different now – quite different. An hour or so ago it had been a world in which Michael had not existed in any sense – not even as a possibility, because she had never known that there were woodworkers who made beautiful tables in Candlemaker Row and read books about wood carving and looked like that, and who wrote your number on their wrists in ballpoint ink and smiled in a way that seemed to light up the whole room, and who ... She stopped. As a teenager she had been obliged at school to learn, by heart, several of Shakespeare's sonnets, and had realised, even then, how acutely he had captured the feeling of simple cherishing that lay at the heart of love. Sonnet 18 said everything about that;

it expressed that conviction of the ultimate ineffable value of the one whom you loved. There was nothing more to be said, really, because what it spoke about could only be articulated to an extent; thus far, and no further – thereafter one came up against something mysterious, something immanent that could not be explained. We loved another because we loved him or her. We just did.

And it did not matter who or what it was that we loved. Auden said that when he was a boy he loved a pumping engine and thought it every bit as beautiful as the 'you' whom he later addressed. We loved people because they were beautiful or witty or smiled in a way that made us smile; we loved them because they spoke or walked in a certain way or because they had a dimple in exactly the right place; we loved them because they loved us or, sadly, because they did not love us; we loved them because they had a way of looking at things, or because there was a certain light in their eyes that reminded us of the sunlight you saw caught in a rock pool on a Hebridean island; or because they wore a kilt or black jeans or a Shetland sweater or could recite Burns or play the guitar or knew how to make bread or were kind to us and tolerated us and our ways and our stubborn refusal to stop loving them. There were so many reasons for loving somebody else; so many; and it made no sense to sit about and think about whether it was a good idea or not because love was like a bolt of lightning that came from a great cumulonimbus cloud that was far too great for us to blow it away; and it struck and we just had to accept it and get on with the business of trying to exist while all the time there was this great wave of longing within us like a swell in the sea, one of those great rolling waves that comes in off the Atlantic and hits Ardnamurchan and cannot be fought against, because fighting love like that is hopeless and you should just go under and let it wash over you and hope that when you come out from under the wave you will still be breathing and that you will not have drowned, as people could – they could drown in love, just drown.

Cumulonimbus cloud

She walked out of the Elephant House and made her way slowly down Chambers Street. She was going nowhere in particular, as she had no wish for a destination. She would go down to the Cowgate and walk along its narrow pavements and on to Holyrood and then ... She stopped. What she really wanted was for Michael to phone her, and until such time she would not be distracted by anything that she saw about her. It was as if the whole world were suspended in anticipation of that call; a ridiculous notion, of course, but it was just possible, just, that the world did indeed turn on love, that Professor Higgs's boson was, in fact, love by another name: the guiding force, the centre of gravity, the whole point of our world.

42. 'You all right, hen?'

And he did phone her – three hours after they had said good-bye in the Elephant House, when she was standing on the corner of the narrow lane that led up to the Scottish Poetry Library, having wandered aimlessly about that part of the Old Town, waiting for her telephone to ring. She had spent the best part of an hour in the Canongate Kirkyard, drawn in by the statue at the entrance of Robert Fergusson and remembering that her father had once taken her there, when she was sixteen or seventeen, and shown her the place where the poet was buried. The grave on which Robert Burns, lionised by Edinburgh society at the time but never forgetting who he was or, most important, who his predecessors had been, had paid to have a stone erected to commemorate the young poet whose work, though cut short, had influenced him so much. And her father, who had known Robert Garioch, had quoted to her his poem about the visit that Burns had paid to the Canongate: strong present dool, rugs at my hairt, Garioch had written – strong present sorrow tugs at my heart; and then he had gone on to say: here Robert Burns knelt and kissed the mool – here Robert Burns knelt and kissed the soil.

She had been impatient then, as might any teenager be expected to be when there was talk of poetry and sorrow, but now, recalling the incident, at a time when her senses had been so strangely sharpened, she suddenly felt herself overcome by the emotional tenor of the story. Burns and Fergusson were no longer mere names; they were people, not all that much older than she was; and they had lived right here, in these very buildings that still stood about her – or buildings very like them – and they had presumably felt exactly how she now felt. Burns certainly had, because he wrote about love and you cannot write about love if you've never experienced it; it would be like describing the surface of a completely unknown planet.

She had sat on a bench in the kirkyard. The afternoon sun was on the Calton Hill, touching the monuments with gold. The Canongate Kirk, though, was in shadow, and seemed cold, in spite of the warmth of the summer day. She looked down at the ground and felt for her mobile telephone in her pocket. She took it out and checked that it was on and ready to receive a call; it would be a disaster if she had it switched off or if her battery had run out, because he might try to phone and he would get no reply and might not try again.

It was so unfair, she thought. Boys, she told herself, could phone girls but girls could not phone boys without running the risk of seeming too keen. And if you seemed too keen, then boys were put off, whatever people said about equality and how girls could make the first move if they wanted to. They could not. Ideas of equality were not as powerful as the facts of biology, and a fact of biology was that men wanted women to appear reticent and not be too forward; pushy,

voracious women could make bad mates as they might not stick to their men and do what biology wanted them to do. She was sure that this was true, although when she had mentioned this theory to her father, Dr Macgregor had merely smiled and said, 'Sociobiological nonsense. Nonsense on stilts, to echo the late Jeremy Bentham.'

'So what's your explanation?' she had challenged.

'Social custom,' he had said. 'As simple as that. We do things – or don't do them – according to the precepts that have been inculcated into us by our parents.'

'But they – our parents – must do things for a reason.'

He had thought for a moment before he answered. 'Yes, there may have been a reason – an ur-explanation, so to speak – but those aetiological factors will be pretty obscure and ancient; lost in the mists of time. The point is this, my dear: many of the things we do are done for no discernible reason.'

She had left the kirkyard and wandered back down St Mary's Street, up which she had just walked. A meandering course had taken her to the Poetry Library's lane and there, as she looked across the road to the towering face of the Salisbury Crags beyond, she had heard her mobile ring.

She fumbled with the buttons, and almost lost the call before she answered. And then she said, 'Yes,' because she had momentarily forgotten that she normally said 'Hello'.

'Well, yes sounds positive,' Michael said.

She laughed. 'I mean hello.'

'Well, hello then.'

She felt her knees go weak – just from the effect of the two small words hello then.

She waited. 'I'm glad I got you,' he said. 'I washed my hands and I almost lost one of the numbers on my wrist. It was a close thing. It could have been an eight or a zero. Either. I chose eight.'

'I'm glad you did,' she said.

He cleared his throat. 'You know the Canny Man's?'

'That pub in Morningside?'

'Yes. Do you fancy meeting there tonight? Early-ish.'

She made an effort not to answer too quickly. 'I think that'll be fine. What time?'

'Six? Seven?'

She hesitated. Six might seem too eager, seven less so; sociobiology prevailed. 'Seven?'

'Cool. See you then. Got to go now. Bye.'

She replaced her phone in her pocket. She was shaking. She was crying.

A woman who had been walking past stopped and looked at her with concern. 'You all right, hen?'

Pat nodded.

The woman's concern was still evident. 'Bad news? You're sure you're all right?'

Pat wiped away her tears. 'No, not bad news . . .'

'A feller?' asked the woman. 'Fellers are awfie bad news – always have been. For weemin-fowk, that is. If a lassie greets it often means she's having trouble wi' a feller.'

'Not with this one,' said Pat.

The woman shook her head. 'Oh, darlin', dinnae delude yersel. They're all the same, these fellers. We think we ken a' there is to ken aboot them and then we find oot a wee bittie mair and it's nae pleisant at all. You mark my words, hen. You'll find oot.'

43. Bertie's Fantasy

Bertie's concern that his mother would find out that he had thrown Jo into the Water of Leith, had allowed Cyril to grasp her in his faithful but damaging jaws, and had then given the unwanted doll – or play figure – to a charity shop in Raeburn Place, was in no way alleviated by the knowledge that all of this had taken place under the aegis of his father. Bertie loved and admired Stuart but he was realistic enough to understand that in the adult hierarchy under which he, and all children, lived their small lives, his father was definitely subservient to Irene.

This disappointed him, and sometimes he nursed quite lengthy fantasies – delicious in all their detail – in which his father suddenly ripped off the suit that he wore to work each day, to reveal underneath a green and red outfit of the sort favoured by superheroes. Thus clad, with a few deft acts of realignment Stuart would then fire the psychotherapist, close down, until further notice, Yoga for Tots, inform the saxophone teacher that his services were no longer required, and purchase a large and discouraging dog – a Dobermann Pinscher, perhaps – that would be trained to growl at the slightest sign that the new order was being in any way threatened.

This, he knew, would not happen. Superheroes were as fictional as fairies and just as likely to intervene in human affairs; the reality of the situation was that his father would never dare to challenge in any real way the pervasive, unquestionable power of his mother. That was the order under which he lived his life, and so it would continue until that magical, impossibly distant date: the day of his eighteenth birthday, and his decisive and unambiguous move to Glasgow – and to freedom.

Olive, it seemed, had worked all this out. 'See your father?' she said one day in the school playground. 'See him, Bertie?'

Bertie was silent; wary.

'Well,' said Olive, 'do you want to know what my dad says about him?'

Bertie shook his head. 'No thank you, Olive.'

'You can't run away from the truth forever, Bertie,' interjected Pansy, who, as usual, was standing behind Olive, a faithful lieutenant and Greek chorus rolled into one. 'You have to listen to what Olive says. You can't carry on being in denial.'

'I'm not in denial,' Bertie protested. 'But I don't have to listen to Olive all the time.'

Pansy drew in her breath, shocked at the blatant *lèse-majesté*.

'It's all right, Pansy,' said Olive reassuringly. 'Bertie's just stressed; he doesn't really mean it.' She turned to Bertie. 'My dad says your father's a wimp. That was the word he used, Bertie. I didn't use it. He did. And there's one thing I know about my dad, Bertie. There's one thing I can tell you.'

'Yes, Bertie,' crowed Pansy. 'You jolly well listen to Olive.'

Bertie stared at the ground, but there was no help for him there – or anywhere else.

Olive savoured the moment. 'My dad is always right, Bertie. That's something I've learned.' She paused before continuing. 'My dad also says he's sorry for him, being married to your mummy, Bertie. He says it's jolly bad luck to have a wimp for a father and a cow for a mother. He says that people get taken into care for less. I heard him say all this to my mummy. I heard every word, Bertie.'

'How do you hear everything, Olive?' Bertie mumbled. 'You don't know . . .'

She did not let him finish. 'Because I hide under their bed at night,' said Olive. 'I hear everything, you see.'

'See!' said Pansy triumphantly.

Bertie said nothing.

'Poor Bertie!' said Olive. 'It's bad luck – it really is. You didn't ask to have a wimp for a father. It's not your fault.'

'Then why are you telling me?' muttered Bertie.

'Because I'm on your side, Bertie,' answered Olive. 'Isn't that true, Pansy?'

Pansy hesitated, but only briefly. 'Yes, it's true, Bertie.

Olive has your best interests at heart. She always has had. I promise you, that's the truth.'

'So if I tell you things,' said Olive, 'it's only to be helpful. You do understand that, don't you, Bertie?'

Bertie remembered this conversation as he and his father returned – Jo-less – to Scotland Street that afternoon. But if he feared that Irene would immediately challenge him about the doll, his fears proved unfounded. It was Irene's book group night and she was occupied with putting the finishing touches to a paper she was to read to the members. Her recent observations on the psychopathology of A. A. Milne had been well received, and she had spent some time preparing a deconstruction of Robert Louis Stevenson. This paper, 'Stevenson: the bourgeois transparency of an opaque writer', was, she thought, rather good, and might even be worked up into something publishable. She was pleased.

Nor was there any mention of the doll the following morning, even as Bertie, in an attempt to distract attention away from the absence of Jo, had played ostentatiously with his Junior UN Peacekeeping Kit, winding one of the blue armbands around the upper arm of his young brother, Ulysses, and giving the infant a peacekeeping leaflet to chew upon.

Irene barely noticed. She had received a letter that morning and appeared quite elated by its contents.

'Well, I never!' she exclaimed as she read the contents of the large blue envelope that the postman had dropped through the letterbox.

'Something interesting?' asked Stuart. 'Won the lottery?'

'No,' said Irene. 'But many a true word is spoken in jest. I have indeed won something.'

Bertie looked up from a section of carpet he had designated as a refugee zone. Small UN signs had been placed around this territory and Ulysses was being informed that he was not to crawl into it. 'Is it a big prize, Mummy?' he asked.

'It's a trip to Dubai,' said Irene. 'Well, well!'

Bertie knew where Dubai was. 'There are camels there. And lots of desert.' He paused. 'Are you going to go, Mummy?'

The question was posed with Bertie's usual politeness, but there was a hinterland of longing behind it.

'Of course not,' said Irene. 'Why would anyone wish to go to Dubai, of all places?'

'Don't write it off too quickly,' said Stuart. 'Let's take a closer look at this. Pass me the letter, darling. Let's see what they say.'

44. Irene Makes a Fateful Decision

Stuart smiled as he read Irene's letter. 'This is terrific,' he said. 'What did you have to do?'

Irene clearly did not wish to make much of it. 'Oh, it was just some silly little competition in the *Scotsman*. You had to write a slogan for the Dubai Tourist Board. I admit that I dashed a few words off – just for the fun of it.'

Stuart beamed with pleasure. 'But, darling, that's wonderful! You must have written something really clever.'

Irene shrugged. 'Not really. These slogans are hardly profound, Stuart. They want something they can put on posters or make into a jingle – that sort of thing.'

'Don't be so modest,' pressed Stuart. 'Talent deserves recognition.'

Bertie joined in. 'Yes, Mummy, tell us what you wrote.'

Irene looked out of the window. 'I think it was something like this: Lots of sand – so close at hand.'

Stuart and Bertie were silent. Then Stuart clapped his hands together. 'That's pretty good,' he said. 'No wonder you won. It can be read at so many different levels – well, two at least. It means that there's lots of sand in the desert and then the desert is close to Dubai.'

'Dubai is actually in the desert, I think,' said Bertie.

'Indeed,' said Stuart. 'But it also means that Dubai itself is close to other places. You can get there very easily these days. That's what that means.'

Irene allowed a slightly superior smile to flicker around her lips. 'Perhaps,' she said.

'Well done, Mummy!' exclaimed Bertie. 'You're really clever.'

Irene smiled at him. '*Grazie tante, Bertissimo!*'

Stuart returned to the letter. 'It says that you can take up the offer of a free ticket from Glasgow to Dubai at any point. But ...' He paused as he read ahead. Then he continued, 'Then they go on to say that you may wish to attend the Emirates Literary Festival as their guest. They'll provide a hotel room and full board for five days. Isn't that generous!'

Irene shrugged. 'I have no wish to go to Dubai,' she said.

'But you must, Mummy,' urged Bertie. 'It would be rude to say no to these people once they've asked you.'

'Nonsense, Bertie,' said Irene. 'They're a commercial organisation. You can't be rude to a commercial concern.'

'Actually,' said Stuart, 'I think you can. If commercial concerns can be rude to you, then you can be rude to them. And the Arabs are very sensitive about these things, I understand. They're very good hosts, with such strong ideas of hospitality that you must be careful not to give offence. I think you should go.'

'Yes,' chimed in Bertie. 'Go, Mummy. Go.'

From somewhere down on the floor, where Ulysses was chewing on the UN pamphlet, there came a tiny voice. 'Go!'

'And it is a literary festival, after all,' said Stuart. 'Imagine whom you might be mingling with.' He looked again at the letter. 'It says that many high profile authors will be there and that people will have the chance to ask them questions and mix with them. Think of that!'

Irene did not want to appear impressed, but it was clear that she was. 'Pah!' she said. 'High profile indeed! I'm not impressed by celebrity.' She paused. 'Who are they, by the way?'

Stuart looked at the letter. 'William Dalrymple will be there,' he said. 'Think of that. All those wonderful books about India and Afghanistan. And then there's . . . ' He consulted the letter again. 'Michael Longley, the poet – he'll be there too. And there are lots of others.'

Irene looked thoughtful.

'It starts in two days' time,' said Stuart. 'It's a bit rushed, but . . . '

'I suppose I should make an effort,' said Irene.

'The ticket is business class, of course,' said Stuart.

'I'm not impressed by such things,' said Irene.

'You could always sit in economy on principle,' Stuart

pointed out. 'You could put some poor person from economy in your business class seat.'

Irene ignored the suggestion. 'What about Ulysses?' she asked. 'I could hardly leave Ulysses, could I?'

From under the table, again a small voice could be heard. It was difficult to make out what was being said, but it sounded to Bertie rather like 'Yes, yes!'

'I'll hold the fort,' said Stuart. 'I'm due some leave and I could take a week off. You could probably extend your ticket by a few days if you paid for the hotel part.'

'I'm sure you could do that, Mummy,' said Bertie quickly. 'You could maybe even stay for a couple of weeks.'

'Oh, I couldn't do that, Bertie,' said Irene. 'One week would be quite enough, I suspect.'

She gestured for Stuart to pass her the letter, and she noted down the telephone number of the agency that had organised the competition. 'I assume this is the number I call to accept,' she said.

'I'll fetch the telephone, Mummy,' offered Bertie.

Irene took the telephone and dialled the number. The agency that acted for the Dubai Tourist Board was delighted to hear from her and assured her that a seat could be found on the Emirates flight from Glasgow Airport the following day. Would she mind, they asked, if a photographer were present at the airport to record her departure for *Gulf Life* and one or two other magazines? Irene said she had no objection to this, although the time made available for photographers would be strictly limited.

'We understand,' said the agency manager. 'You will have many calls on your time. Just a quick photo-shoot.'

'You've made the right decision, Mummy,' said Bertie,

after Irene had finished her telephone conversation. 'I'm so proud of you, Mummy.'

Dubai

Irene Pollock
44 Scotland Street
Edinburgh
EH3

'Thank you, Bertie,' said Irene. 'But you will promise to help Daddy look after little Ulysses, won't you?'

'Of course,' said Bertie. 'Cub scout's honour.' And with that he gave the cub scout salute.

'I don't want any of that paramilitary nonsense, Bertie,' said Irene. 'Your own word will be more than enough.'

'Ulysses will be really pleased ...' Bertie began, but did not finish. He had been about to say 'that you're going away', but he realised that this was a bit tactless, and so he said 'that you've won' instead.

45. Irene Embarks for Dubai

Having started off being somewhat unenthusiastic about her trip to Dubai, once she started to make preparations Irene discovered that the prospect of five days away, staying in an expensive hotel – but not paying for it, of course – became increasingly attractive. She packed quickly and then found the time to go up to a bookshop on George Street to purchase a copy of the relevant Lonely Planet guide. With everything else prepared, she left Stuart to attend to Ulysses and to make Bertie's supper while she paged through the guidebook's account of the attractions of Dubai.

'I wonder if I shall swim,' she mused. 'They seem to have some rather nice-looking beaches.'

Bertie expressed concerns about sharks. 'There are sharks out there, Mummy,' he said. 'Please be careful.'

'Don't worry, Bertie, I can cope with sharks,' said Irene.

Bertie looked relieved. He found it hard to imagine his mother coming off second best to anything, even a shark.

'And always remember to bargain when you're shopping in the souk,' said Stuart helpfully. 'The opening price is never what the merchant really expects.'

Irene assured her husband that she would drive a hard bargain. She was interested in getting a new rug for the entrance hall and she imagined that there would be many of these to be had in the souk. 'I shan't have too much time for shopping,' she warned. 'I'm really going for the literary festival.'

'Of course,' said Stuart.

'However, I'm sure I'll find time for a bit of sightseeing. What a pity it is that the prize was only one ticket, rather than four. We could all have gone as a family.'

'A great pity,' said Stuart hurriedly. 'But let's look on the bright side. It's surely better that at least one of us manages to get to Dubai rather than none at all.'

'Daddy's right,' said Bertie. 'Don't you worry about a thing, Mummy. You just go and enjoy yourself.'

Irene smiled at Bertie. 'Dear Bertie,' she said. 'You're so sweet.'

The following morning they loaded Irene's suitcase into the back of the car and drove off along the motorway to Glasgow Airport. It was a bit of a crush in the new car, as this was not as roomy as the Volvo station wagon they used to have. That car, to which Bertie had been particularly attached, had been subjected to the indignity of being mistaken for a car destined to participate in a sculptural installation by a well-known contemporary artist. It had been taken down to London, sliced in two, and then mounted on a board – to win that year's Turner Prize hands down. Bertie had been upset and it had been some time before he had come to accept the substitute Volkswagen Golf that Stuart had acquired in place of the station wagon.

Once at Glasgow Airport, Stuart parked the car while Bertie and Ulysses accompanied their mother to the check-in desk. By the time Stuart came in, Irene had been duly allocated her window seat in the business class cabin and was ready to go through security.

'Now, goodbye, my darlings,' said Irene. 'Be good while I'm away.'

She leaned forward to plant a kiss on Bertie's head. He blushed, as any small boy would do in the circumstances, but did not resist. Irene then took Ulysses from Stuart, who had been holding him, and tried to kiss him on the cheek. Ulysses squirmed in his mother's arms and then, without any warning at all, was sick all over her shoulder.

Stuart tried his best to clean up the side and back of Irene's jacket.

'He always does that with you, Mummy,' said Bertie. 'You shouldn't try to hold him.'

'Nonsense, Bertie,' snapped Irene. 'This is really most irritating. There'll be nobody else in business class with sick all over them – in economy maybe, but ... How can I possibly not hold Ulysses? I'm his mother, after all.' She handed Ulysses back to Stuart. 'And he's your son.'

Bertie frowned. 'Are you sure?' he asked.

'Am I sure about what?' asked Irene.

'Are you sure that Ulysses is Daddy's son?'

Irene looked menacingly in Bertie's direction. 'Now don't talk nonsense, Bertie,' she said. And then, in an obvious attempt to change the subject, 'And look, Bertie, that man in the blue uniform is a pilot! Look at the wings on his jacket.'

Bertie was not to be that easily deflected. 'It's just that he looks so like Dr Fairbairn, Mummy. He really does. Lots of people have noticed it. And people at school said that Dr Fairbairn helped you to make him. Could that be true, Mummy? Or could Dr Fairbairn have made some of him – his ears, for instance – and Daddy made the rest?'

Stuart moved forward to whisper in Bertie's ear. 'Hush, Bertie. I don't think Mummy likes to talk about that sort of thing.'

'Out of the mouths of babes!' joked Irene, uneasily.

Stuart shot her a glance. 'That particular expression may not exactly be appropriate in this context,' he said. 'Usually one would say it when a child makes an unusually perceptive or true observation.'

Irene laughed. She tried to sound casual, but the laugh was forced. 'Such nonsense! Now I think it's time for me to go through security.'

They waved as she went off to join the queue lined up for the search. When she had gone through the metal detector, she turned round and looked back towards them. Stuart raised a hand to wave, and then dropped it. The thought had occurred to him that this might be the last time he saw his wife.

He wanted to follow her. He wanted to call out and tell her that she shouldn't go after all. He wanted to keep her. It would be easy enough to run up to the security barrier and bring her back. She would be cross, of course, but he would beg her to stay. He would say that he had had a premonition – which in a way he had. He saw flames. He heard cries. And then he felt just a terrible heavy sense of dread, like a great weight about him, pressing down on his shoulders.

'Irene . . .' he half-called out.

She did not turn round. She had retrieved her case from the X-ray belt and was moving off towards the departure gates.

He watched her until she disappeared. And then he thought: we leave it too late – we always do – to say the things that we need to say to people.

46. The Dear Green Place

They made their way back to the car park – the small group of Stuart, Bertie and Ulysses, with Bertie pushing his brother in his squeaking, much-in-need-of-oil pushchair. While Stuart paid the parking ticket, Bertie scanned the confusing ranks of vehicles, trying to remember where their own car was parked. Such was his excitement on their arrival at the airport he had not paid attention to where his father was parking, and now, faced with row after row of confusingly similar cars, he was unable to make out their own.

'Right,' said Stuart breezily, as he re-joined his sons. 'Now, off we go to the car.'

He hesitated. Bertie looked at him expectantly. 'Do you remember . . .' he began, but trailed off as he saw his father look anxiously around. Bertie sighed. It was not the first time they had lost their car.

Stuart gave a cry. 'There it is, Bertie! You see that one over there, that red one. That's our car.'

He was right, and they were soon safely strapped in and ready to depart. Bertie opened a window. 'You can get these things that make cars smell better,' he said to his father. 'They're sort of round things that sit on the dashboard. Could we get one, Daddy? It would take away the smell of Ulysses.'

'Maybe, Bertie,' said Stuart. 'But Ulysses doesn't always smell.'

'Most of the time he does,' said Bertie. He paused. 'I'm not being unkind, Daddy. I really like him. But I don't really like the way he smells. He's going to have big problems in life if he carries on smelling like that.'

They drove out onto the motorway that led back into the heart of Glasgow. Bertie watched the unfolding panorama of the city pass them by; this was, in his mind, the promised land, the great beacon of freedom; this was where he would live when he was eighteen and could leave Edinburgh. He looked at the houses. There were Glaswegian boys living there, he assumed – presumably unaware of their great good fortune. There would be no yoga classes in Glasgow, no girls like Olive or Pansy, and certainly no psychotherapy.

'Are they happy in Glasgow?' he asked his father.

Stuart glanced at his son and smiled. 'Are they happy in Glasgow? That's an odd question, Bertie. But I think that by and large they are. They're quite cheerful people, the Glaswegians. They have a very good sense of humour – if you like that sort of thing.'

By now they were in the tunnel under the Clyde, and Stuart explained to Bertie that they were directly underneath one of Scotland's greatest rivers. Bertie marvelled at the thought but was distracted shortly afterwards by a sign pointing to an exit from the motorway. 'Can't we go down there, Daddy?' he asked. 'Can't we go and take a look at a bit of Glasgow?'

Stuart hesitated. He had made no plans beyond returning to Edinburgh, and it seemed to him that a brief diversion off the most direct route would do nobody any harm. It ought to be possible, he thought, to strike off to the left and then work up towards Balfron or Drymen or somewhere like that. Then they could return to Edinburgh by Stirling – a more picturesque route than the dull and rather bleak journey along the spine of the Central Belt.

He made up his mind. 'All right, Bertie,' he said. 'Let's go and take a look at a bit of this dear green place.' He used the name traditionally applied to Glasgow, and Bertie repeated it under his breath. Dear green place; dear green place. The words, powerful and affecting, were like a shibboleth. Dear green place: have you got room for me too? Dear green place.

They slipped off the motorway and into a side street. Stuart had no map with him, and was uncertain as to where exactly they were, but he thought that they were headed in the general direction of the university. Once they were there they could meander off in a generally northerly direction and would eventually get to Bearsden or somewhere like that. They could always stop and ask somebody for directions, if they needed to. And they were in no hurry, after all.

They drove through Kelvinside and into Maryhill. By now he was even less sure where he was, although he was aware of the fact that the urban scenery had changed. After a while he turned off onto a side road and brought the car to a halt in a parking place that had conveniently appeared outside a pizza restaurant. Bertie stared out of the car at the large notice that advertised the pizzas within. 'P I Z Z A,' he read.

Stuart looked down at his son and smiled. 'Would you like one, Bertie? I'm feeling a bit peckish myself.'

Bertie's face broke into a broad smile of delight. Irene did not let him have pizzas, which she described as unhealthy (which they undoubtedly were), vulgar (which was a matter of opinion) and inappropriate (which was unintelligible). Bertie's friend, Ranald Braveheart Macpherson, by contrast, had pizza at home every Friday and sometimes on other days too. 'They're delivered on a motorbike,' Ranald explained to Bertie. 'And you can have all the toppings you like. Salami. Pineapple. Tons of cheese. The works, Bertie. It's a pity you aren't allowed to eat them. I'll try to bring a slice into school for you one day, just to show you what you're missing.'

It seemed to Bertie that there could be no greater pleasure in life than to have your food delivered on a motorbike. That surely was the height, the very pinnacle, of privilege. 'I must get ready for dinner,' you would say. 'The motorbike will be here any moment.'

And then it would arrive, and the man delivering it would get off his motorbike and take your dinner out of the insulated hot-box on the back of the bike and carry it into the house just as those armed guards deliver boxes of money to the bank. He would put it down on your table, and you would open the box and there would be your dinner. Not the healthy fare you were normally enjoined to eat, but a great, vivid pizza, oozing oil, a burst of colour, carrying with it a whiff of everything that was excluded from your life, everything that you could not have but wanted so desperately. And the delivery man would get back on his motorbike and start it noisily; and the roar of its engine would be the sound of freedom, and the smell of the melted cheese would be the odour of happiness.

47. The Association of Scottish Nudists

While Bertie and his father were enjoying their first few hours of freedom – as was Ulysses, although, being so young, he had no idea why exactly he should suddenly feel so liberated – back in Edinburgh a meeting was being convened in the Moray Place headquarters of the Association of Scottish Nudists. This meeting was an extraordinary one, called under a provision of the Association's constitution allowing for at least twenty-five members to call a meeting about any matter 'affecting the vital interests of the Association or of any section of the Scottish nudist community, whether or not the persons affected were members of the Association'. The committee had tried to take a narrow view of this provision, and, sensing that their running of the Association's affairs was being called into question, had attempted to prevent the calling of the meeting. It soon became clear, however, that the determination of those wishing to call the meeting was such that any attempt to thwart them would result in mass resignations. In the light of this, the Chairman very reluctantly agreed that the meeting should be held and notified the four hundred and eighteen members of the Association accordingly.

Voting rights within the Association were far from simple. The constitution, drawn up by an Edinburgh solicitor in 1958, provided for four categories of membership: Edinburgh nudist, resident nudist, non-resident nudist, and emeritus nudist. Edinburgh nudists were defined as 'any nudist living wholly or in part within the City of Edinburgh'. A resident nudist was any nudist having a place of residence in Scotland, while a non-resident nudist was 'a nudist who does not have a residence in Scotland'. An emeritus nudist was one who, 'although no longer a member of the Association, has served the interests of Scottish nudism to such an extent as to merit special recognition'.

Each category of nudist had historically been given different voting rights. Edinburgh nudists had three votes each; resident nudists had two, non-resident one, and emeritus nudists half a vote. This inevitably meant that the affairs of the Association could be entirely controlled by Edinburgh members, effectively destroying the political fortunes of any candidate for office of whom the Edinburgh nudists disapproved. The practical result of this was that no Glasgow nudist was ever elected to the committee, in spite of the Association's claim to speak for all of Scotland – or, rather, for all nudists in Scotland.

But it was not just this fundamentally undemocratic feature of the Association's constitution that rankled with the malcontents; there was a whole raft of issues that they wished to take up with the committee. They had tried to raise these at previous meetings of the Association but had been prevented from doing so by arcane provisions within the constitution that required matters for discussion to be tabled with the committee at a separate meeting to discuss the agenda for future meetings. The trouble was that since that meeting had to be called by the Chairman at his sole discretion, if he did not wish to call it then there was no means of ever getting an item on the agenda. And that is exactly what had happened.

The Association
of
Scottish Nudists

MORAY PLACE

The calling of the meeting had attracted considerable attention. A diarist writing in one of the Sunday papers had referred to 'trouble in the Garden of Eden', and had speculated on the possible ramifications of the dispute. Another journalist talked about entryism and had speculated that a good number of the members calling for the special meeting had joined the Association with a view to winding it up and distributing the assets to the membership. The book value of the Association was, in fact, quite substantial, as it owned its premises in Moray Place along with two other flats in Ainslie Place. If these were disposed of and the proceeds divided amongst the four hundred or so members, each member would be entitled to several thousand pounds – a tempting target for an asset stripper. And if all that one had to do to get this pay-out was to pretend to be a nudist and to pay the five pounds required for membership of the Association, then that was not much of a burden and well worth any concomitant embarrassment.

But it was not asset stripping that motivated the objectors, as became apparent shortly after the meeting had begun. There were at least one hundred and fifty people present – all clad, as was customary at the Association's formal meetings. Behind a table at the head of the room sat the Chairman, an influential Edinburgh accountant, flanked by the four other members of the committee: the Treasurer, the Secretary, the Social Secretary, and the Chairman of the Premises Sub-Committee.

The Chairman looked out over the rows of heads before him. It was difficult to recognise faces, he thought – it was easier to work out who was who when people were unclothed. However ... the troublemakers would be in the front, he thought, having arrived early to get the best seats and to be in a position to make things as awkward as possible for the committee. He scanned the front row; he recognised nobody – a bad sign, as were the one or two hostile stares that were returned to him.

He called the meeting to order and made his introductory remarks. 'I don't think this meeting will need to be very long,' he said. 'Indeed, the committee is of the view that it will probably prove to be unnecessary.'

There were murmurs from the front two rows. The Chairman looked over the top of his glasses.

'That's what you think,' muttered one of the members.

The Chairman hesitated. Had his ears deceived him, or was that a Glasgow accent? He turned to the Secretary, seated beside him, and whispered: 'I think we may be in for a bit of . . . how shall I put it . . . trouble from our dear friends the Weegies.'

'Aye, you definitely are,' came another mutter from the front.

The way that definitely was pronounced, with each syllable being detached from its neighbour and given full value, gave the game away.

'We've had various requests to speak at this meeting,' said the Chairman. 'Mrs Maclehose? Is Mrs Maclehose with us today?'

A woman seated in the second row rose to her feet. 'That's me,' she said.

'Well, madam?'

'The thing I want to know,' she said, 'is this: why have Edinburgh folk got three votes and most of the rest of us –

not just me, there's plenty others in the same position here today – have got only one?'

'Yes,' echoed another voice. 'How come?'

48. Defeated

It was a tricky moment for the Chairman of the Association of Scottish Nudists. But he was not one to give up lightly; as an accountant he had faced hostile meetings before – in winding-up proceedings, for instance, when anxious creditors could become quite forceful in drawing his attention to their claims – and he had never shirked the task of holding his ground. Now, as he surveyed a sea of hostile faces, he realised that his only hope of turning away wrath would be, if not in a soft answer, then at least in a courteous attempt to explain the intricacies of the Association's constitution.

'Look,' he began, 'Mrs ... Mrs er ...'

'Maclehose. That's M-A ...'

'Mrs Maclehose, of course. You see the point is, Mrs Maclehose, this association is a very old one. We were actually founded in 1931, and for many years there was no constitution at all. We shared premises in those days with the Scottish Ladies' Mountaineering Alliance in Albany Place, and we mainly used the Queen Street Gardens for our outdoor meetings. Those were heady days, I believe, and also not without their difficulties.

'We carried on through the war and we had that big period of growth in the membership in the years immediately afterwards. But it was still a small association and, frankly, people didn't think that a constitution was necessary. The world was different in those days. People ran things more informally.

'But then in the mid-fifties it was felt that things had to change and so in 1958 the then chairman thought that it was time to have a constitution drawn up. One of the members then was a partner in one of the big law firms – it wasn't Shepherd & Wedderburn, as I recall. He's long dead, I'm afraid, but he was a very fine lawyer. He drew up our current constitution in the belief that it would give the society a certain amount of stability if it were very clearly run by people who knew one another. And you can see the argument, can't you? If people know one another they know their failings, and that means that you'll never get the wrong sort elected to a committee.

'Now some people seem to think that this is just a bit too cosy, but I really don't think they understand the real reason for having this system of preferred Edinburgh votes. If they did, they'd realise that it's for the best.' He paused. 'And that, I suggest, is where we should leave the matter. I know that some people may feel hard done by – insulted perhaps – by having fewer votes than others, but you really must understand that it's for the good of the Association. Stability is the goal. Stability, stability, stability. If the Association is being well run by Edinburgh people, then surely it's best to leave it that way.'

The Chairman sat back in his seat, looking to either side of him for support from his fellow committee members. They nodded their heads sagely: the case for leaving things as they were had been rather well put, they thought.

A man in the middle of the room stood up. 'Oh no you

don't,' he bellowed out. 'You haven't answered Mrs …
Mrs …'

'Maclehose,' said Mrs Maclehose.

'Yes, her. You haven't answered her, sir.'

The Chairman shook his head. 'I thought it was a perfectly good answer. What more do you expect me to say?'

The man sat down, only to be replaced by a woman sitting a few seats away. 'Excuse me,' she said, 'but you suggested that everything was being very well run by the people elected under the current provisions. Well, some of us would beg to differ.'

This brought a chorus of approval.

'You see,' the woman continued, 'I have heard a whole string of complaints from fellow members. Everybody's saying the same thing.'

The Chairman frowned. 'No complaints have reached us,' he said.

'Because you never listen to them,' snapped back the woman. 'Take the case of that outing to Glencoe last year. Remember? Remember how some of us warned you – warned you again and again – that it was not a good idea to go there in the midge season? And remember what happened? Some of us were so badly bitten as we tried to climb that mountain that we had to run back to the bus. We had to run and get dressed as quickly as we could.'

'I remember that,' shouted somebody from the back. 'I was covered in red blotches for days after that.'

'And then there is the issue of the raincoats,' said somebody else. 'Since when have nudists had to wear raincoats? What's the point of being a nudist if you have to wear a plastic mac all the time? We're the laughing stock of the international move-ment – the laughing stock!'

The Chairman shook his head vigorously. 'That's just part of being a nudist in Scotland,' he said. 'Everybody under-stands that our weather's so difficult that we have to wear these macs. Nobody laughs at us for it. And the same goes for the midges. That's something that Scottish nudists just have to bear.'

There were some expressions of agreement with this, but rather few. The feeling of the meeting was now unambiguous.

'We need a complete change,' said a man with a strong Borders accent. 'Selkirk, Kelso, Jedburgh – all these places need to be represented. There are more and more nudists in the Borders these days. It's our association too.'

The Chairman glanced anxiously at the Secretary, who looked away. 'Do I take it that this meeting has no confidence in the current committee?' he asked.

There came a resounding yes.

'In that case,' said the Chairman, 'I offer you my resigna-tion.'

'Thank you,' said Mrs Maclehose. 'And thank you for all the work you've done for the Association.'

The meeting dissolved. Half an hour later, the Chairman, now the former Chairman, sat with the former Secretary in a small tea-room in the West End. 'It's very sad,' he said. 'It's very sad to see the world change so much.'

The former Secretary toyed with an edge of the gingham tablecloth. 'Edinburgh's changing too,' he said. 'You'd think that there would be at least one place that would be able to . . . able to hold out. But no . . .'

They were sitting at a table near the window. The light that came in was weak, washed out – the light of a late afternoon, late in the day.

49. Big Day for Big Lou

Big Lou rarely felt nervous. 'There is nothing you need to be afraid of,' her mother had repeatedly said to her as a child. 'Nothing at all. Bogles and the like – other bairns may tell you about these things, but they're nothing to worry about. Nothing.' That had been sage advice, and it had made her fearless in most circumstances; but now, waiting for the supervised visit of the brother and sister she was to foster, she felt a raw, gnawing anxiety that, if it was not fear itself, was as close to fear as to make very little difference. And it was not the meeting that worried her – that event she had been looking forward to for some time – it was the fact that the children who were coming to see her would be accompanied by a social worker and this social worker would have the power to take them from her; to find her in some way inadequate as a foster parent. That was what frightened her.

As she waited for the social worker's arrival, she set about some last minute tidying, and rearranged the tea things that had been sitting on her table since she left for work that morning. She had baked a cake and a whole plate of shortbread, and these she now took out of their tins and laid carefully on two of her best china serving plates. But even as she did so, it occurred to her that this was the wrong thing to do. She knew that children liked sugary things – she herself had always had a sweet tooth – but did social workers like sweet things? The thought worried her. People disapproved of others eating unhealthy food, and the social worker could well take the view that it was a bad thing to give children cake and shortbread. So what should she serve them? Carrots? Sandwiches with a slice of lettuce in the middle? Fruit juice? Or was fruit juice too sweet, too acidic?

She looked at her watch. It was too late now; they were due to arrive at four, and it was already three forty-five. She sat down and reflected on the story that Marjory, the social worker, had told her; of how the two children had been effectively abandoned by their feckless, drug-abusing mother and their irresponsible, disappearing father; of how their grandmother had done her best to make a home for them but had died; of how they had withdrawn within themselves and become uncommunicative – poor bairns, she said to herself, of course they would! They would have had none of what she herself had had as a child, of which the first and greatest thing was love, just that – the love of a parent. Well, she would offer them that and she would see what happened; she would get through to them in their turned-in-upon-itself world and lead them out into the open. She would do that.

The bell at her front door rang, and she gave a start. Her heart was beating loud within her; she stood up, and for a moment she felt faint, as one does sometimes when one has been crouching and then stands up too quickly. But the feeling passed, and she made her way through her hall to open the door onto the landing outside.

'Good afternoon, Lou,' said Marjory. 'We're a little bit early, but I thought you wouldn't mind.'

Lou looked at Marjory and then at the child standing half beside, half behind her. She looked down the stair behind her visitor; was the girl still coming up? She transferred her gaze to the boy at Marjory's side. He looked as if he was about nine; not very tall for his age, but not too short. He had a broad, open face and he was smiling at her. He had a tooth missing, and she thought, Of course: they lose their milk teeth – and I had forgotten.

'May we come in?' said Marjory.

'Of course. Of course.' Lou moved aside to let her visitors pass.

'Change of plan,' whispered Marjory. 'I'll tell you all about it after we've settled Finlay here. Can he sit in your living room for a wee moment? You and I ...' She glanced towards the open door of the kitchen. 'This is Finlay, by the way. And Finlay, this is Lou.'

'Big Lou,' said Lou. 'Everybody calls me Big Lou.'

'It's a nice name,' said Finlay. 'I wouldn't mind being called Big Finlay, but I'm no a' that big.'

Marjory patted him on the shoulder. 'You're growing, Finlay. You'll be Big Finlay before you know it.'

Marjory took Finlay into the living room and then joined Big Lou in the kitchen.

'I thought there were two . . . ' began Lou.

Marjory shut the kitchen door behind her. 'No. I did tell you about a very difficult brother and sister we had, but . . . well, I didn't really intend to bring them to you.'

'What happened? Have they gone elsewhere?'

Marjory looked bashful, but a smile played around her lips. 'Those children existed, but they're grown up now. I used their case to . . . Well, have you ever heard of a love test?'

'Where people come up with something that will test their lover's real feelings?'

'Exactly. I know that social workers shouldn't do this sort of thing, but I've found that it works really well. I need to be sure, you see, that your heart is really in this. And you showed me that it was. If you had been lukewarm you would have made some excuse after I told you about the difficulties of those poor children. But you didn't. You did exactly the opposite. You showed me that you're up to the task.'

Big Lou said nothing.

'I hope you're not cross with me,' Marjory went on. 'You don't seem the type to bear a grudge.'

Big Lou shook her head. 'No, I'm not cross.' She paused. 'That wee boy through there . . .'

'Finlay is looking for a foster home. He's had a bit of bad luck too in his young life, but he's a great wee chap. If you think that . . .'

'That I can take him?'

Marjory nodded. 'He's very keen to get somewhere secure. His last foster home was very fond of him, but the woman there retired. She'd had eighteen foster children over the years – she was a real heroine. But she and her husband were moving over to Fife, to a cottage near Crail, and they wouldn't have the room.'

'Of course I'll take him,' said Big Lou. 'Of course I will.'

'Good,' said Marjory.

50. 'They were kind to me.'

Finlay was in an armchair, swinging his legs, when Marjory and Big Lou went back into the sitting room. Big Lou looked in his direction uncertainly – she felt awkward and somewhat unsure, even if her earlier anxiety had been completely assuaged by Marjory's friendliness. She had never had any difficulty in talking to children, but then she had never had to talk to a child for whom she was responsible, or about to become responsible.

She knew that one had to be consistent; she knew that one had to set boundaries; she knew that you had to convey love and affection without smothering the child; but exactly how one did it when one had no experience of parenthood was something of which she realised she was ignorant. Nobody taught you to be a parent – friends with children had often said that to her – you simply had to rely on your instincts and hope that you got it right. In many cases that worked, but in many it did not, and it was so very easy to blight a life by doing the wrong thing or doing the right thing in the wrong way, or by doing nothing when you should be doing something, or something when you should be doing nothing. Big Lou knew all that, and now she was faced with this little boy who was looking at her expectantly and waiting, she thought, for her to say something.

'Cake,' said Big Lou. 'Cake and shortbread. Do you like them, Finlay? Maybe ...'

She stopped herself abruptly, but then, almost immediately, Marjory said: 'Does Finlay like cake? Does Finlay like shortbread? You bet he does, don't you, Finlay?'

Finlay nodded vigorously. 'Lots,' he said. 'I like them lots, Big Lou.'

Lou smiled at the way he used her name. It sounded a bit odd, but she had invited him. 'In that case,' she said, 'let's all have a piece of cake and a cup of tea ... unless, Finlay, you'd like some ...' She hesitated. Irn Bru might be a bridge too far, but he was looking at her quizzically, and she continued: 'Irn Bru.'

The nodding became even more vigorous. Marjory laughed. 'I think you understand boys, Lou. Hollow legs, et cetera et cetera.'

They sat at the table, Finlay in the middle, while Big Lou poured tea for herself and Marjory and Irn Bru for Finlay. She cut slices of the cake, which was a sponge with a thick layer of strawberry jam in the middle, and placed them on plates. Finlay watched her every move, his eyes wide with anticipation.

'You should start, Finlay,' said Big Lou. 'You should start so that I'll be able to give you a second slice.'

The boy reached out and took the cake in his fingers. Lou noticed that his fingernails were dirty; but that was what a boy's fingernails were meant to be. And she remembered how, when she was a girl back in Arbroath, a boy from a neighbouring farm, a boy called Alastair who had a thick thatch of jet black hair and whose nose always seemed to be running, had taken a splinter out of her father's collie's paw, and she had watched and noticed that the fingers that performed the deft operation had nails under which thick dirt was encrusted. She saw it still; a boy's nails, and a picture of them lodged somewhere in her brain, a memory ready to be invoked now, decades later, in such a different place.

Finlay talked. He told her about his last foster home and what they had given him for breakfast each day. He told them how they had taken him with them to their caravan, which they kept in a park outside Callander, and how they had stayed there for weeks at a time in the summer and how he had swum in the river that flowed out of the nearby loch. 'They were kind to me,' he said.

Marjory and Big Lou exchanged glances. 'Yes,' said Marjory. 'They were kind to you, Finlay. There are lots of kind people, you know. Sometimes we don't meet them right at the beginning of our lives, but then we do later on.'

The boy was scraping up the crumbs of cake on his plate. Big Lou reached for her knife, cut another slice of cake, and passed it to him. Then she poured Marjory another cup of tea and they talked about the zoo. Finlay had never been there and Big Lou said she would take him. The boy turned to Marjory and said, 'She says she'll take me.'

'Then I imagine she will,' said Marjory.

Big Lou looked at her watch. She did not want them to go.

'I'd better be on my way,' said Marjory.

'I can give Finlay a bag to put some cake in. He'll be able to take it away with him.'

Marjory frowned. 'But he's staying.'

Big Lou looked momentarily confused, but recovered quickly. 'Oh, of course.'

'His things are in that bag I had with me,' went on Marjory. 'I left it in the hall.'

Marjory said goodbye to Finlay and left. Big Lou returned to the boy and sat down opposite him at the table. She smiled at him, and he returned her smile with a broad grin.

'Enough cake?' she asked.

He nodded. 'Thanks.'

They sat in silence for a moment. Then Big Lou said, 'We could go and take a look at the Water of Leith, if you like. Then we could get some chips from the chippie on the way back.'

Finlay said he would like that, and they did as Big Lou promised. When they returned to the flat later, Finlay took a bath, changed into pyjamas, and was installed in the spare bedroom. As she turned out his light, he said, 'I'm a bit scared of the dark, you know, Big Lou. Still.'

She did not ask him why, nor did she ask what the still meant.

'Then I'll stay with you,' she said. 'You don't have to worry, Finlay.'

She brought a chair into the room and placed it alongside the top of his bed. Then she held his hand as he drifted off to sleep. It was so small in her own hand, and it felt warm and dry. She pressed his hand gently, and his fingers returned the pressure, but only just, as he was almost asleep by then. She remembered, but not very well, what it was like to fall asleep holding the hand of another; how precious such an experience, how fortunate those to whom it was vouchsafed by the gods of Friendship, or of Love. She thought she had forgotten that, but now she remembered.

51. 'We are dust before the wind.'

On the day that Finlay moved in with Big Lou, Antonia Collie, author of an as yet unpublished book on the lives of the early Scottish saints and survivor of a nasty attack of

Stendhal Syndrome that had come over her in the Uffizi Gallery, moved in with Domenica and Angus. Antonia's move was on a more short-term basis, of course; while Finlay hoped to stay forever, Antonia knew that she was merely a guest for the next three weeks. This had not discouraged her, though, from bringing with her one of the sisters from the convent to which she had become attached as a resident lay member – the Convent of the Holy Flowers, tucked away in a small village not far from the hill town of Montalcino, in Tuscany. It was this nun, Sister Maria-Fiore dei Fiori di Montagna, who, suitcase in hand, now stood beside Antonia on Domenica's landing in Scotland Street.

Antonia paused before ringing the doorbell. 'This is all so familiar to me,' she said to her companion. 'I used to live here, you know. That was my door.' She pointed to the door on the right, now disused since Domenica and Angus had acquired her old flat and knocked the two flats into one.

Sister Maria-Fiore dei Fiori di Montagna smiled benignly. 'The doors we have used in this life are very important,' she said. 'They are the way we got into places.'

Antonia nodded absent-mindedly. Sister Maria-Fiore dei Fiori di Montagna had a tendency to make philosophical remarks, and she had become accustomed to them, whether issued in the nun's native Italian or, as now, in her passable, though sometimes halting, English. There had been one such remark when they had arrived at Edinburgh Airport. There, as they walked through the door into the arrivals hall, she had said, 'Airports are the places where we land – where we come to earth.' In Antonia's view, this observation, although incontrovertibly true, was not one that was pressing to be made.

But she was tolerant of the sisters and their occasional failings; they had been egregiously kind to her in her time of need, and she now rewarded them with fierce loyalty.

Antonia had noticed something. Leaning forward, she peered at the side of her old doorway. 'There used to be a brass plate there,' she said. 'It had my name on. It was not very big and it just said Collie.' She paused, and turned to look at her friend. 'Now it's gone. They've removed it.'

Sister Maria-Fiore dei Fiori di Montagna frowned. 'You must be very sad,' she said. 'When our names are removed, they are removed. There is no going back.'

'You'd think that they might have left it,' said Antonia. 'It would not have cost them anything to leave it – as a sort of … as a sort of reminder of the fact that I lived here. Now it's as if there's no trace of me.'

'We are dust before the wind,' said Sister Maria-Fiore dei Fiori di Montagna. 'That is what we are.'

Antonia shook her head sadly. 'It would have been a gesture,' she said. 'A gesture to my past.'

She reached forward and pressed the bell on the other door. As she did so, she noticed the shining new brass plate screwed firmly in the middle of that door. *Macdonald-Lordie*, it said. She smiled bitterly.

Angus answered the bell. 'Well, well,' he said. 'Antonia! Here you are!'

He stepped forward and embraced her, kissing her on each cheek. There was real warmth in his welcome in spite of everything; he had decided that Antonia and her friend were his guests, whatever the background of self-invitation, and it was incumbent on him to behave as a good host. This was not surprising, of course; Angus was a man with good manners, who never expressed himself in any extreme way – except, of course, when it came to the Turner Prize, which was another matter altogether. And in that respect, he felt he was entirely justified in becoming animated; how anybody could be taken in by that ridiculous, pretentious, absurd display of utterly banal posturing was beyond him; how anybody could fail to see the complete lack of artistry of any sort in collecting quotidian objects and piling them up, one upon another, and then calling it art, was equally beyond him. But that was not on his mind as he now turned to Sister Maria-Fiore dei Fiori di Montagna and offered her his hand to shake.

'This is Sister Maria-Fiore dei Fiori di Montagna,' said Antonia. 'It's her first time in Scotland.'

'The first of many visits,' said Angus warmly, although it occurred to him that this was perhaps slightly unwise. If one said that sort of thing to Antonia, it could certainly be interpreted as an invitation that was really meant, as opposed to being a remark made purely out of politeness.

'I'm looking forward to seeing *Scozia*,' said the nun. 'And you are so kind to receive us.'

'The pleasure is entirely mine,' said Angus. And realised, as he spoke, that this was probably more true than one might imagine: the pleasure was entirely his in the sense that Domenica had not appeared to take any pleasure at all in the prospect of this visit. Still, Angus thought, this Sister Maria-Fiore of the something-or-other seems nice enough, and perhaps Domenica will be able to regard the whole visit as some sort of anthropological field trip in which the subjects of research visit you rather than you visit them. One never knew.

Angus helped them with the suitcases, which were left in the hall while Domenica, who had appeared from her study, greeted Antonia and was introduced to Sister Maria-Fiore dei Fiori di Montagna.

'You're looking so well,' said Domenica, as politely as she could.

'Not surprising,' said Antonia briskly. 'In view of my life. We have a very simple existence in the convent, you know. We rise early – four o'clock in the summer. We eat simple fare.'

'And nothing to drink?' asked Angus, slightly wistfully.

Antonia allowed herself to smile. 'We have the occasional glass of wine. One of the sisters is a very good wine maker, and we have our own vineyard. We are very close to Montalcino, of course.'

Angus rolled his eyes. 'Brunello territory!'

'We just produce a simple Rosso di Montalcino,' said Antonia. 'Nothing grand.'

'Wine is wine,' said Sister Maria-Fiore dei Fiori di Montagna.

This remark was delivered with a great air of authority, and Angus looked at her with interest. 'Of course,' he said. 'You're absolutely right.'

Domenica looked at the suitcases. 'We must get those through to your rooms,' she said. 'Please follow me.'

52. A Case of Blue Spode Again

Domenica knew that it would be tricky, and now, as she led Antonia and her friend through the door they had made to

215

allow them access to what had been Antonia's next-door flat, she found that her misgivings had been well placed.

'So,' said Antonia, as they approached the new doorway. 'So, this is where you punched your way through.'

Domenica bit her tongue. 'We didn't exactly punch,' she said. 'It's not as if we hired a tank and drove it through the wall.'

'I use the word punch in a loose sense,' retorted Antonia. 'Any violence done to an old building is a sort of punch, I find.'

Domenica gasped. 'Violence?'

Antonia smiled sweetly. 'Not personal violence, of course. But battering these lovely old buildings is an act of violence – in a sense.'

Domenica was not going to let her get away with that. 'Nobody battered any lovely old building,' she said, trying to sound as firm as she could. 'The whole process was actually rather gentle. There was a man with a hammer – admittedly quite a large one – but he wielded it with real consideration for the rest of the structure. He didn't want anything to fall down.'

Antonia shrugged. 'Oh well, be that as it may, this is where you effected entry.'

Domenica struggled to remain polite. 'Effected entry? My goodness, Antonia, you make us sound like burglars. Burglars effect entry, as you put it.'

Angus, who was standing behind the women, caught his breath. This was dangerous territory, as he remembered very well how he had effected entry into Antonia's flat one day when she was out. He had done so with the full connivance of Domenica in order to retrieve the blue Spode cup that she was sure Antonia had stolen from her kitchen. The cup had been retrieved, with Angus narrowly evading detection, and they had thought themselves justified, only to discover, much later, that their own blue Spode cup had all the time been lurking in Domenica's kitchen. Mentioning effecting entry like this was surely to risk the resurrection of an event that was best forgotten. And he was right. His heart sank as Antonia spoke.

'Effecting entry?' she said. 'Yes, you're absolutely right, Domenica. Burglars do effect entry. It's funny that you should say that because I've often thought that I myself must have been the victim of effected entry.'

Domenica said nothing; she glanced at Angus, who had now turned pale.

'You see,' said Antonia, turning to Sister Maria-Fiore dei Fiori di Montagna, 'although Edinburgh is not a place with a very high crime rate, there are some offences that are more common in a place like this, given the widespread ownership of *objets de vertu*.' She paused. 'There are many people, for instance, who have collections of china. Or at least have some cherished china, even if they don't have a very large collection. I think, for instance, of those who own blue Spode.'

'What is this blue Spode?' enquired Sister Maria-Fiore dei Fiori di Montagna.

Angus opened his mouth to answer, but Antonia preceded him.

'Blue Spode is a very beautiful sort of English china,' she said. 'Like many things English, it is understated. English china can often be very quiet, very unassuming, but very beautiful nonetheless.'

'And Scotch china?' asked Sister Maria-Fiore dei Fiori di Montagna. 'What is that like?'

Antonia raised a finger. 'Not Scotch, dear Sister Maria-Fiore dei Fiori di Montagna. *Da noi, diciamo Scottish*. We say Scottish not Scotch.'

Angus saw his opportunity. 'Excuse me, Antonia, but I'd be tempted to argue that point.'

Antonia turned to him and fixed him with a discouraging stare. 'Well,' she said. 'You may argue all you wish, Angus, but what I've told dear Sister Maria-Fiore dei Fiori di Montagna is absolutely correct. It's Scottish, not Scotch. We may as well help her to be correct and to avoid solecism. We wouldn't want her to be jeered at in the streets of Edinburgh for saying Scotch rather than Scottish, would we?' She then answered her own question. 'We would not, I think.'

Angus raised a finger in an admonitory way. 'Show me,' he challenged, 'you just show me where it says you can't use a word that was completely acceptable for heaven knows how many years. Burns used it. He used the word Scotchman. It was perfectly acceptable until people suddenly decided that they wanted to be refined. That's when they started saying Scottish or using the word Scots as an adjective.'

'Usage changes,' said Antonia. 'You don't expect me to start calling my book *The Lives of the Scotch Saints*, do you?'

'I'd see nothing wrong in that. You have Scotch egg and Scotch mist. And what about Scotch whisky? If you can use the adjective with these, then why can't you use it elsewhere? I've got no time, Antonia, for this fussy, refined insistence on Scottish.'

Antonia shook her head. 'I suggest we leave the topic,' she said. 'I would not want Sister Maria-Fiore dei Fiori di Montagna to conclude that we stand about arguing about the correct use of adjectives.'

Sister Maria-Fiore dei Fiori di Montagna made a conciliatory gesture. 'These are very interesting questions,' she said. 'The Lord has undoubtedly put them before us in order to test us. There can be no doubt of that.'

'I suggest we get everybody established in their rooms,' said Domenica, relieved that the awkward moment involving the blue Spode cup seemed to have passed. But her relief was premature; their way led through Antonia's old kitchen, and it was here that Antonia stopped and turned to Sister Maria-Fiore dei Fiori di Montagna. 'This used to be my kitchen,' she explained. 'I spent so many happy hours sitting at my table – which used to be over there, but appears to have been moved. I used to sit there drinking tea …' she paused, 'from my favourite blue Spode cup. That's where I sat – right over there – with my cup – the blue Spode one – on the table before me.'

Domenica looked out of the window. 'Memories!' she exclaimed. 'Isn't it wonderful to have memories of precious moments like that? However, one doesn't want to become too nostalgic. One has to look forward rather than back, I find.'

'Of course,' said Antonia. 'Of course I agree with you on that. I am very forward-looking myself, but that doesn't mean that one cannot privately regret those things that are lost ... those things that are taken from you in this life.'

She waited while her words took effect. Then she continued. 'However, so much for that. Water under the bridge.'

Domenica glowered.

53. Unexpected Turbulence

The great plane lumbered into the air above Glasgow, the folds of Renfrewshire, the twisting ribbon of the Clyde, the distant Campsie hills – all visible to Irene Pollock from her comfortable business class window seat. Irene looked down on the scene below her until a cliff of white cloud embraced them and the world of greens and browns became one of murky white. Then, quite suddenly, as in a *paysage moralisé*, where effort or forbearance is repaid in better surroundings, they broke free of the cotton wool and levelled off in a world of brilliant clarity. In this higher world, the sunlight glinted off the aircraft wing, filled the vault of the sky, made the clouds a field of gold. Irene felt the warmth upon her face and closed her eyes. She was off to Dubai, of all places! She, who had never been out of Europe, with the exception of a short trip to

New York in her student days, was bound for the Gulf of Arabia, no less; a place of burning landscapes, of shimmering mirages, of glittering, artificial cities. And all this because she had created a simple slogan for the Dubai Tourist Authority …

She ran over the words in her mind: So much sand – so close at hand. Yes, perhaps it was rather clever, and certainly it was streets ahead of the slogans that had won second and third places. These had been awarded respectively to an entrant who had coined On the gulf you'll find there's golf! and to the inventor of Dubai, de best buy!

Irene thought that both of these were really rather weak. In her view they showed the deleterious effect of modern tourism, in which what should otherwise be an exotic and culturally distinctive destination was re-interpreted in terms of contemporary western consumerist preoccupations. What sort of person went to play golf in the United Arab Emirates? Presumably such people were ignorant of and indifferent to the rich and ancient cultures of the Gulf. Presumably they were unaware of the price paid in ecological terms to make the desert bloom sufficiently to provide grass for a golf course. And after they had played their golf, these people would go shopping for things they did not really need. How shallow, she thought; how appalling.

She looked about her in the cabin and tried to work out whether her fellow passengers were people of this stripe. She decided they were, and she felt her nose wrinkle involuntarily. But she would not let herself become depressed by the silliness of humanity. She, at least, was above all that and could afford to be generous to these lesser people with their more limited horizons.

As the plane settled into its flight path and the captain switched off the seat belt sign, the cabin staff moved quietly along the rows of seats, offering passengers drinks and small bowls of heated nuts. Irene ordered a gin and tonic. Five days of freedom, she thought; five days of not having to worry about getting Bertie to school or dealing with Ulysses, who was, when all was said and done, a rather demanding baby. What a contrast, she thought. To be sitting at thirty thousand feet or whatever it was, drinking a gin and tonic, was a form of freedom to which she could easily become accustomed.

The gin and tonic was followed by lunch, which was served, in the business class section, on china plates deftly laid on starched linen. Irene chose smoked salmon roulade followed by lamb cutlets, mashed potatoes, and peas. With this she drank a glass of New Zealand Sauvignon Blanc and a glass of Médoc. Then it was time for petit-fours and coffee . . . which was poured at exactly the moment that an unexpected pocket of turbulence threw the plane bucking and shuddering about the sky.

Irene, along with a number of other passengers, gave an involuntary gasp. In her case, though, the gasp was the louder and the more justified by virtue of the fact that an entire pot of airline coffee, down to the last drop – fortunately rather lukewarm at the time – was spilled over her.

The plane corrected itself, and the sound of crashing china faded from the galley.

'Oh my goodness,' exclaimed the attendant out of whose hands the coffee pot had jumped. 'I'm so, so sorry.'

Irene stared at the extensive brown stains that now covered her outfit from head to toe. 'I'm soaked,' she said. 'Soaked.'

The attendant began to dab a damp cloth at Irene's coffee-sodden clothing. 'Oh no,' she said. 'This is just awful. Poor you!'

Irene struggled to continue. 'I can't ... ' she began. 'How can I ... '

The attendant reassured her. 'I've got a spare uniform in my bag. You could change into that. It would make me feel much better.'

'A uniform?'

'Yes,' said the attendant. 'You're more or less my size, I think. And our uniform is rather smart – this nice long skirt and so on. You'll be perfectly comfortable.'

Irene looked down at the light-coloured trouser suit she had been wearing. The wet cloth was sticking to her uncomfortably. 'Well,' she said. 'I suppose it would enable me to get out of this.'

'Exactly,' said the attendant. 'Come with me and we'll get you all changed.'

Irene rose to her feet, attracting several sympathetic looks as she did so. Then, accompanying the attendant, she made her way forward to the galley area. Another attendant appeared and solicitously helped her to take off her jacket, revealing below a blouse covered in dark brown coffee stains that had spread out, like continents on a map.

She went into the washroom and took off the rest of her ruined clothes, taking from the attendant the items of uniform she passed through to her. After a few minutes, with her old clothes in a sodden heap on the floor, she glanced at herself in the mirror. She looked to all intents and purposes like an Emirates cabin attendant.

'There you are,' said the attendant. 'That's much better. I felt so bad when you were covered in coffee.'

Irene admitted that she felt much more comfortable and was even able to crack a joke. 'I hope you're not going to ask me to serve drinks,' she said.

The attendant laughed. 'Good,' she said. 'And thank heavens it happened to such a nice person as you. Others could have been very nasty about this, you know.'

54. Misunderstandings at Altitude

Now clad in a borrowed Emirates cabin attendant's uniform, her own coffee-soaked clothes neatly bundled into a plastic bag and stored in the luggage bin above her head, Irene sat back to enjoy the rest of the flight. She had brought several books with her, but she was not in the mood for reading anything serious, and so spent her time looking through the selection of magazines that the airline made available for perusal by its business class passengers. She also dozed a bit, lulled into somnolence by the steady drone of the jet engines and the comfortable temperature of the cabin. Waking up, she decided to get up and replace the magazine she had been reading with something else. She rose to her feet, adjusted the long brown skirt that was part of the uniform of the female cabin attendants, and made her way to the back of the cabin, where the magazine rack was located.

It was while she was choosing a new magazine that Irene was tapped on the shoulder. Turning round, she was confronted with a rather harassed-looking woman who had made her way up from the economy class section.

'Excuse me,' said the woman. 'Could you come and give me a hand?'

For a moment Irene wondered why this woman should have approached her, and then she remembered what she was wearing. 'I'm sorry,' she said. 'I'm not—'

She had been intending to explain that, although she was wearing a crew uniform, she was a passenger, but the woman cut her short. 'Look,' she said. 'I really need you to help me. I pressed the button some time ago and nobody came.'

'But I'm—'

Again the woman stopped her. 'I'm not interested in excuses,' she said. 'It's your job to help people.'

Irene sighed. 'Very well,' she said. 'What's the problem?'

'Come with me,' said the woman, leading Irene back into the economy class cabin. Irene looked about her; this part of the aeroplane was less luxuriously appointed than her own cabin, and there seemed to be rather more people. How did they all fit in, she wondered? How many were there in a row? She started to count, but was distracted by the woman's tugging at her sleeve. 'We're over there. That's my husband, and those are the kids.'

A few rows away, a mild-looking man in a beige cardigan and tobacco-coloured trousers was holding a baby – no more than a few months old – on his lap. Next to him was a child who looked as if he were three or four, and then another child, of six or seven, who was herself holding another baby.

'They're twins,' said the woman. 'The little ones, that is.'

'Ah, yes.'

'They both need changing,' said the woman. 'But Ed's got to look after the four-year-old because he panics on planes

225

and you can't leave him. In fact, if either of us leaves for more than a moment or two, he goes bananas, and we can't have that.'

Irene frowned. 'Do you want me to babysit?' she asked. 'If you need to go to the bathroom, I could, I suppose.'

'No,' said the woman. 'Could you go and change the babies – one at a time? Take Willie first and then little Gordon.'

Irene caught her breath. 'Me?' she said. 'Change your children?'

The woman looked surprised at the note of indignation that had crept into Irene's voice. 'Yes. Why not? It's your job to look after people, isn't it? Well, we need to be looked after.'

Irene smiled. 'I really need to explain something,' she said. 'I may be wearing—'

She was not allowed to finish. The woman had stepped forward, lifted up one of the babies, and was now pushing it into Irene's unwilling arms. 'There,' she said. 'That one's Willie.'

Finding herself holding the infant, Irene could hardly drop him. She looked at him; he had a small, wizened face that was flushed and angry. He stared back at her. He did not smell fresh.

'Here's his nappy,' said the woman. 'Put the old one in this bag and then please dispose of it.'

'Excuse me,' protested Irene. 'I have no intention of changing this wretched child.'

The woman stared at her in astonishment. 'Wretched child? Did you call my baby a wretched child?'

226

A middle-aged woman sitting nearby confirmed that this was so. 'Yes,' she said. 'I heard her. I heard her say exactly that. Shocking, if you ask me.'

Irene spun round at this intervention. 'Mind your own business, you stupid old—'

'Did you hear that?' shouted the object of Irene's insult. 'Did you hear what she said?'

A number of other passengers sitting nearby nodded their heads. 'Send for the captain,' said one.

Irene tried to give the baby back to his mother, but failed to do so, as the mother had now folded her arms defiantly, holding her ground. The baby himself glared at Irene with growing animosity, his little face puckering in outrage. Then he was copiously sick, mostly over the front of Irene's uniform.

'Look what you've done,' complained the mother. 'Here, give him back to me. You're useless, you know, just useless.'

Irene thrust the baby into the mother's arms and then turned on her heels and stormed back to her seat. There she tried to wipe the mess off the front of her tunic – succeeding to an extent, but not completely. She felt her face glowing with anger. How dare that woman assume that she should change her wretched baby – and it was wretched, a most ugly and unattractive infant altogether. She closed her eyes. This trip was proving to be something of a disaster. First, Ulysses had been sick over her at the airport; then she had had coffee spilled all over her; and now this ghastly economy class baby had been sick over her too. It was very unfair. This was her one opportunity to travel somewhere in comfort and style, and she had been humiliated and insulted.

She took a deep breath. She would control herself. She would not allow these ridiculous setbacks to spoil the essential fact that she was about to rub shoulders with the literati – the real, international literati, at the Emirates Literary Festival. Ultimately that was what counted; that was what made it possible to bear all sorts of humiliations. She felt much better with this thought. It put things in perspective, which is how things should always be viewed, no matter what temporary irritations may occur.

55. At the Grand International

They landed at Dubai in darkness, taxiing up to the cathedral of light and glass that was the terminal building. The cabin attendant who had lent Irene the uniform came to discuss its return, suggesting that it could be left at her hotel to be picked up by the airline the following day. Irene agreed to this and gave the name and address of her hotel, the Grand International. She felt a certain thrill in revealing the identity of the hotel; to say 'I'm staying at the Grand International' had a ring to it which was rather different from saying that one was staying at a bed and breakfast.

She was pleased that the business class passengers were allowed out first; this enabled her to avoid being confronted with her detractors from the economy class cabin, some of whom she had noticed in the distance, glaring at her resentfully. Once inside the terminal, she followed the signs to immigration, through which she passed surprisingly quickly. It occurred to her that this was because of the uniform – and that explained, too, she decided, the smiles and nods of greeting she got from aircrew who walked past her.

One woman in an Emirates outfit even stopped and asked her whether she was going off duty and which run she had been on. Irene thought that explaining might be too complicated and could also possibly arouse suspicion, and so she simply said, 'Glasgow. And it was very busy.'

'Yes,' said the other attendant, who sounded Australian. 'I've just come in from Melbourne. I can't wait to crash.'

Irene smiled. 'That's an odd thing for an airline person to say.'

The attendant looked at her. 'Excuse me?'

'You said you couldn't wait to crash.'

'That's right. I'm keeping my eyelids open with matchsticks.'

Irene nodded. 'It doesn't matter.' And she thought: how literal can you get! Really!

They went their separate ways as Irene found the carousel on which her suitcase was due to emerge. After forty minutes, when all the other passengers had collected their cases, Irene found herself standing at a now-static luggage belt without her luggage.

She reported the matter at the appropriate desk. Computers were consulted and an explanation given. 'That case never left Glasgow, I'm afraid. Sorry.'

Irene bit her lip. She had no clothes now – just the Emirates uniform.

'When will it arrive then?'

The clerk looked again at the screen. He glanced at her, as if assessing her likely reaction, and then returned to read the screen. 'I'm afraid it's in Helsinki.'

Irene gave a cry. 'Helsinki!'

The clerk looked apologetic. 'In fact, it's left Helsinki. Something's just come up to say that it's left Helsinki.'

'Well, that's something,' said Irene. 'When does it get here?'

The clerk bit his lip. 'Well, that's a bit of a problem. They seem to have put it on a flight for Buenos Aires. I can't understand why, but that's where it seems to be heading. Via Amsterdam, that is.'

Irene was silent.

'I know it's really awkward,' said the clerk. 'It's not the airline's fault. It's the baggage handlers. You know what they're like.'

'Do I?' said Irene, through clenched teeth.

'Yes. I sometimes think that they do this sort of thing to prevent themselves from getting bored.'

'I see.'

The clerk reached for a form. 'I'll put in a tracer. Where are you staying?'

'The Grand International,' hissed Irene.

'A nice place,' said the clerk. 'They look after your luggage there.' And then he added, somewhat apologetically, 'If you have any, that is.'

The lost luggage report filed, Irene followed the taxi sign and was soon ensconced in an air-conditioned car heading for the Grand International. She was struggling to maintain such equanimity as she had left. She was determined to enjoy herself, and this meant that she would not let these setbacks depress her. No, she told herself. I am above all that. Here I am in Dubai by myself. No husband. No children. No grey skies. No rain.

She looked out of the window. High modern buildings reached into the sky – needles of light. Traffic sped past – important-looking cars with shaded windows; refrigerated trucks; a sleek prowling police car with blue lights and a nagging siren.

'You go to a very good hotel,' said the driver suddenly. 'The Grand International is very good.'

Irene smiled. 'Yes, certainly. Very nice.'

The driver watched her in his rear-view mirror. 'First time in Dubai?' he asked.

'Yes,' said Irene. 'My first time in Dubai.'

'You are very welcome,' said the driver.

'Thank you.'

He looked at her in the mirror again. 'And your husband? You have left him at your place?'

'Yes. He's in Scotland.'

The driver nodded. 'Scotland. That is good. He let you come by yourself?'

Irene pursed her lips. 'My husband does not control me,' she said. 'I can do what I like.'

The driver shook his head. 'Very bad,' he said. 'Tell me: why are you wearing an Emirates uniform if it's your first time in Dubai? Does your husband know about that?'

Irene met his eyes in the mirror and gave him a discouraging look. 'Mind your own business,' she said.

The driver shrugged. 'Sorry. It's just that the police ask us to report anything suspicious. I think you are maybe a bit suspicious.'

'I most certainly am not,' said Irene sharply. 'Now just drive to the Grand International, if you don't mind.'

They were not far from the hotel, and the driver soon swung the car onto a slip-road that led to the front of a towering glass hotel.

'The Grand International,' he announced.

Irene paid him off and entered the hotel lobby. At least they were expecting her at reception, and were sympathetic about the lost suitcase. 'Suitcases always turn up in the end,' they said. 'Very few disappear altogether.'

She was shown to her room, a spacious bedroom on the thirty-second floor. She eyed the marble bathroom longingly while the porter explained the controls of the large television set and the automatic coffee maker. She was tired from the journey and wanted only to sink into a luxurious bath and then throw herself down on the king-size bed with its inviting crisp sheets and pillows. She was still feeling positive.

Everything – absolutely everything – had gone wrong, but at least that meant that nothing further could happen to mar her trip. Surely that was the way it worked. If things started badly, then the odds were that they would get better. She remembered her husband. He was a statistician. Surely he would agree with that.

56. Pat Thinks, and Is Almost Run Over

The euphoria that Pat felt after the telephone call from Michael had not worn off. She had made her way back to the flat dreamily, hardly noticing where she was going and almost being run over as a result at the edge of the Meadows, the expanse of grass and trees that divided the

Old Town, where she studied, from South Edinburgh, where she lived. She had been standing at the Dick Vet corner, looking up at the monstrously ugly building that the university had placed next to the comfortable old Veterinary College – a mistake from a period when such mistakes were made with impunity. Now, of course, it was an embarrassment – a reminder of architectural arrogance and aesthetic shortcomings. Her studies in fine art had had the desired effect, and Pat, who had walked past that building as a schoolgirl and thought nothing of it, now experienced real discomfort at its modernist brutality. Such buildings, she thought, were acts of aggression, which is surely what Michael would think of it. He obviously understood beauty, because he was an artist who made beautiful things, and she would soon see the wonderful table he'd been working on ...

She closed her eyes, and tried to imagine what the table would look like. It would look like ... She stopped, and realised that she knew nothing about tables – nothing at all. What if he asked her to comment on it, to say how she felt it fitted in with other tables, how it related to French tables, for instance; what could she say? She wanted to impress him, to make him think that she knew about the things that he appreciated, and all she knew about tables was that they generally had four legs, except where they had one, or sometimes three. Were there any two-legged tables ...

'Watch out!'

The car that had almost run her over had skidded to a halt. The driver, winding down his window, looked at Pat with disbelief.

'I'm so sorry,' he called out. 'But you were about to cross the road with your eyes closed!'

Pat put a hand to her mouth, her heart thumping with shock. 'I'm sorry too,' she stuttered. 'I was thinking. I'm really sorry.'

The driver shook his head. 'I almost hit you,' he said. 'It was that close.'

'I was thinking,' said Pat. 'I know it sounds really stupid, but I was thinking.'

The driver smiled with relief. 'Well, as long as you're all right. That's the important thing.'

Pat returned his smile. 'And you? Are you all right? That's important too.'

'I'm fine,' said the driver. 'It was you I was worried about.'

'And I was worried about you,' said Pat. 'Are you quite sure you're all right?'

'No, don't worry about me,' said the driver. 'And it would appear that both of us are fine. That's ultimately what matters, wouldn't you say?'

'Yes,' said Pat. 'I'd agree with that, I think.'

The driver waved. 'Well, so long,' he called out. 'Sweet dreams – but not while you're crossing the road!'

Pat watched him drive off and thought: that's the nice thing about Edinburgh. These little encounters – traffic altercations – were so civilised, so courteous. She would tell her father about that; he was always interested in examples of civic decency. He would like this story, although he would be worried, no doubt, at the thought that she had almost been run over.

Dr Macgregor, in fact, was particularly interested in the way people behaved in their cars. Although one never saw it in Edinburgh, in other places driving behaviour was astonishingly aggressive. People who would normally never dream of shouting at others, or intimidating them, seemed to think that they could do this with impunity once they got behind the wheel of a car. On foot, amongst fellow pedestrians, one would never scowl or swear at somebody who made some minor navigational error – perhaps took a step to the side, thus putting himself in one's course and requiring a correction of direction on one's part – but if this happened on the road, it was a different matter. There would be soundings of horns and aggressive gestures and the like, as if the error were an act of extreme and unforgivable hostility or in effect a declaration of war. Why did people behave like that? Were there deep wells of antagonism within them that yearned for release, and found their expression in the driving of a vehicle? Perhaps it was something to do with personal space, he had suggested. The strong sense of being enclosed that came with being in a car seemed to remove social and psychological restraints. It was as if within the car one were invisible, and this invisibility conferred some sort of power, some invincibility.

Pat continued her journey, soon forgetting about her narrow escape and thinking, instead, of her future. Earlier that day she had felt that she had little to look forward to. Graduation, which was imminent, would be the end of the life she had been accustomed to leading for so long. That, in itself, was not something she should worry about, she felt, but the problem was that she had had no sense of what lay beyond. But then there had been that encounter in the Elephant House, and now everything seemed, quite suddenly, to be completely changed. What did Yeats say? Changed, changed utterly ... a terrible beauty is born.

She had learned that poem at school without really liking it or understanding it. Now it spoke to her. It did not matter that Yeats was talking about the higher purpose of political commitment; it was surely the same. Passion was passion, whatever its direction; it gripped the soul in much the same way. Now she had a purpose. Michael. He was her destiny, and she was going to meet him in a couple of hours at the Canny Man's in Morningside Road. She shook her head at the mystery of it. Everything was now subservient to her feelings for him. Everything. How absurd! How ridiculous that another person can come into one's life like that and make everything else seem unimportant and immaterial. Where did this come from? Not from the mind, surely, because the mind took it as its business to reason with you – wherever that you was located. Were we mad to behave like that? Or simply human?

57. *At the Canny Man's*

Pat returned to her flat and, being in a mood to do something, but not knowing what it should be, washed her hair. Afterwards, as she sat on the floor of her bedroom using her hairdryer with its cord that was too short to allow her to stand or sit on a chair, she came to a realisation that was as shocking as it was surprising: This is the first time I have ever been in love.

Those newly in love, of course, are the easiest victims of self-delusion. This time, they tell themselves, it is quite different from the last time. Of course, they are often wrong; love, as the folk-wisdom has it, has the ability to blind us to the obvious – and the obvious, for many, is that love, even if it is not exactly a recurrent infection, visits us more than once. And yet even if this is true, a new love may indeed be stronger, more absorbing, than an old one, just as a new cold may be more severe than the cold we had six months ago. This was probably the case now with Pat. It was not the first time altogether that she had fallen for somebody; but it was the first time that her fall had been so intense, so complete, and so utterly intoxicating.

At last she was ready, and went out of the flat, fumbling

with her key with nervous, uncooperative fingers. Love-struck fingers, she thought to herself, and smiled. Everything now seemed precious: the simple act of locking the door behind her became significant because she did not want anything to happen that would threaten this sudden heightened preciousness of life. None of us – or very few of us, perhaps – wants to die, and this desire to survive becomes all the stronger when we are suddenly given something that we have longed for, never thought we would get, and now, unexpectedly, possess. We want to prolong the moment, to secure it. We know in our bones that what we have in this life we have on loan only, and the term of the loan will always be finite. We know that suddenly the referee's whistle will be blown and that will be the end. But now, at least for the moment, we have it, and want it to last for as long as possible.

It was a fifteen-minute walk to the Canny Man's and she had left it too late to arrive in time. This did not worry her, though: she did not want to be early as this could give the impression that she was keen to see Michael. Which she was, of course, but she did not want him to know – or at least not to know just yet. A few days earlier she had picked up a magazine in a friend's flat and opened it at the problem page, the page to which we all so guiltily gravitate. One of the letters was from a young woman who was seeking advice about a romance that she feared she had killed in its infancy through her being too quick to return a young man's call. 'He seemed surprised that I had called him only an hour after our first meeting,' she said. 'I could hear the change in his tone, as he cooled off. Was I wrong to call him so soon?' And the agony aunt, with all the patience and understanding of one who has seen all human folly, had gently replied that one should never appear too eager. 'It's something to do with men's psychology,' she wrote. 'They are programmed to pursue. That's what they feel they have to do. And if we make the pursuit too easy, or, worse still, do the pursuing ourselves, then they'll lose interest and we'll have only ourselves to blame.' Pat had taken all this to heart; one ignored the advice of agony aunts at one's peril – and if one did, of course, one would only have oneself to blame.

Pat's arrival in the Canny Man's was well timed, as Michael was already there when she came through the side entrance. He saw her immediately, and slipped off his bar stool to greet her. He reached out, took her hand, but only held it briefly before dropping it. It was just right, she felt, for a first date on the evening of the day on which they had met. A kiss would have been too much – too affected; this brief touching was far better.

She felt her knees weaken, and for a moment it seemed to her that there was a danger that they would not support her.

'You haven't been waiting too long, I hope.'

He shook his head. 'Five minutes. Maybe ten.'

She felt her breathing becoming shallower. What if I faint? What would the agony aunt have to say about that? Whatever you do, don't faint on your first date – just don't! And if you do, you'll have only yourself to blame . . .

He ordered her a drink. Handing it to her, he said: 'I'm glad you came. I thought you might not.'

She was surprised. 'Why? Why wouldn't I come?'

He shrugged. 'People sometimes have better things to do than meet me,' he said. 'I would have understood.'

The remark seemed unduly self-deprecatory, but she did

not think so much about this aspect of it as of the attractive lilt in his voice.

'Surely not,' she said. 'People will want to see you ...'

He raised an eyebrow, and then smiled. She was not sure whether he was serious. 'You think so ...'

She was about to reply, but she had become aware of somebody entering the bar behind her. She half-turned round, and glanced towards the door. A moment later she turned back to face Michael, but then she realised what she had seen, and swung back again.

'Somebody you know?' asked Michael.

Pat said nothing. Her eyes had met the eyes of the man who had just walked through the door, and for a few moments the gaze of each of them was locked on the other.

Dr Macgregor was accompanied by a woman. He stopped when he saw his daughter, and turned round to say something to the woman but she did not seem to hear him. She gave him her coat and then looked up, directly into Pat's startled gaze. Somebody else was coming in the door and Dr Macgregor had no alternative but to take a step forward. Now he could hardly leave, and it was too late anyway.

'Daddy?'

He looked down at his shoes, like a schoolboy caught in the wrong place, doing something forbidden.

58. *A Mercenary Conversation*

'Well!' said Dr Macgregor.

He paused, and then, struggling to regain his composure,

added: 'Isn't the Canny Man's popular these days?' There was a further pause, and then, as if to fill the silence, he said, somewhat lamely: 'It always has been, I suppose.'

He glanced anxiously at the woman beside him, who was now staring at Pat with undisguised curiosity. 'This is my daughter, Pat. And ...' He looked at Michael.

'Michael,' said Pat. 'Michael, this is my father.' She hesitated. 'And ...'

'Anichka,' said Dr Macgregor.

Michael reached across to shake hands with both of them. As he did so, Pat took the opportunity to look at Anichka. She noticed the low-cut red top. She noticed the curious brooch in the form of a diamanté sailing ship, the rigging of tiny filaments of silver. She noticed the hair, dyed blonde, but with its dark roots. She saw the handbag, which was of patent leather, with a flashy gold clasp.

Anichka was looking at her with interest. 'So you're Pat,' she said. 'The apple of your father's eye.' She spoke heavily accented English, and she seemed proud of her use of the metaphor, glancing at Dr Macgregor for approval.

Pat felt herself blushing. 'Oh, I don't know ...'

'Yes, you are,' insisted Anichka.

Dr Macgregor's embarrassment seemed to deepen. 'Of course she is. But ... well, I suppose you've got a drink already Pat, and ... well, I suppose ...'

Anichka announced that she would like a gin and tonic. 'With two lemons,' she added. 'You know how I like it.'

'Two slices,' muttered Dr Macgregor. And then he tried to make a joke of it. 'Not two whole lemons! Goodness no!'

'Not whole lemons,' said Anichka gravely.

Michael glanced at Pat.

'I like your name,' said Pat. 'Anichka's unusual, isn't it? It's very nice.' It isn't, she thought. I hate it.

'Not in the Czech Republic,' said Anichka. 'Many people are called Anichka in the Czech Republic. Many women, that is – not men.'

'The Czech Republic?' said Pat. 'So . . .'

'That is where I am from,' said Anichka. 'But now I live in Scotland.' She looked challengingly at Pat as she made this statement, as if her words were the declaration of some irredentist territorial claim.

Pat said nothing. This was the woman who had bought her father those socks.

Anichka turned to Michael, looking at him with frank appraisement. 'You're Pat's boyfriend? Yes?'

Pat stared down at the ground. She had seen sexual interest in Anichka's eyes as she looked at Michael. It was unambiguous. The look. The look! You couldn't mistake it.

Michael smiled. 'We've just met. Only today, actually.'

Anichka stuck her tongue slightly out of her mouth; a tiny, red bud, wet, glistening. It was a gesture that Pat found hard to read. 'Ah. Love at first sight! Very nice. People say that this does not happen, but it does. I think it does.'

Pat did not dare look at Michael.

'Maybe it does,' said Michael. 'For some people. Not for everyone. But for some, yes, maybe.'

Dr Macgregor returned with a glass in each hand. Anichka took her gin and tonic and raised it to her lips. Pat noticed the tongue reappear.

'I suppose we should sit down,' said Dr Macgregor. 'Unless we stand, of course. We could stand.' He looked about him hopelessly, with the air of one who was trapped.

Pat was thinking about love at first sight. If that existed – which of course she was sure was the case – then presumably so did the converse: dislike at first sight. And she felt no doubt about that as she took another look at Anichka. Suddenly she felt sad. She loved her father, and now this woman, this ghastly woman with her obscene red tongue and her patent leather handbag and her ... now this woman was going to take her father away from her and there would be no more dinners in the Grange, no more listening to his going on about Rob Roy, about how to grow tomatoes under cover, and about the *British Journal of Psychiatry* and ... and all the things that fathers go on about and that daughters listen to patiently and think how boring while all the time they love everything their father says and all his beigeness and bad fashion sense and ...

Dr Macgregor was attempting to engage Michael in conversation. 'You're a student, are you? The same course as Pat?'

'No,' said Michael. 'I make furniture.'

Dr Macgregor was interested. 'What sort of thing?'

'Tables. Chairs. Sometimes more complicated pieces. I did a desk a few months ago. I'm working on a rather special table right at the moment. It's fairly—'

'A table?' interjected Anichka. 'How much does it cost, this table?'

Michael frowned. 'Well, there's quite a bit of work in it. Something like that—'

Anichka cut him short. 'How much? In pounds.'

Pat shot her a glance, but it went unnoticed.

Michael's tone was even. 'It's difficult to say. I haven't decided yet. You have to bear in mind that if you charged per hour it could be too expensive for the client. So you often don't work it out that way.'

'No?' said Anichka. 'So what do you do? How much?'

'I really can't say,' said Michael. 'I just don't know yet.'

Anichka was not deterred. 'But how much was the last table you made? How much did you charge for that?'

Pat noticed with concern that Michael had reddened. 'It's difficult,' she said. 'Some people don't like to talk about what they charge. Artists don't like that.'

Michael looked at her with gratitude. 'No, I suppose people like to think of the thing itself, and of what it means. That's not the same as what it cost.'

'But what did it cost?' asked Anichka. 'The last table you sold – how much was that?'

Michael sighed. 'Nine hundred pounds,' he muttered. 'There was quite a lot of work in it.'

Anichka looked thoughtful. 'Nine hundred?'

'Yes.'

Anichka took another sip of her drink. Pat found herself studying the other woman's lips. There was a small piece of lemon on them; small, but noticeable. Then the tongue came out and licked it off.

'And your workshop?' said Anichka.

Michael answered patiently. 'It's near Greyfriars. You know where that is?'

Anichka nodded. 'I know.' She paused. 'How much did it cost?'

Michael stared at her blankly. 'I rent it. I don't own it.'

'But if you had to buy it,' said Anichka, 'how much would you have to pay?'

Michael shrugged. 'I don't know. I have no idea.'

Anichka moved her head slightly to one side. It was not a nod, more a slight shift of vantage point. 'Can I come and see it?' she asked.

59. Thoughts at the Wallace Monument

Bertie, having said goodbye to his mother at the airport, had enjoyed his visit to the Glaswegian pizzeria.

'That was the best thing I've ever done,' he said to his father as they left the restaurant and made their way back to the car.

Stuart, who was carrying Ulysses in his arms, looked down

at his son. 'Ever?' he asked. Could pizza be that important to a small boy?

Bertie nodded. 'I think so,' he said. 'Although there was also that time we went fishing in the Pentlands. Do you remember that, Daddy? And I almost caught a fish and we went to that farmhouse and there was that boy there called Andy. And he gave me a Swiss Army penknife.'

'Yes,' said Stuart. 'I remember.'

'Which Mummy then took away from me,' continued Bertie. 'Straightaway when I got home. Remember that?'

Stuart nodded. 'I think that Mummy felt that it was a bit dangerous,' he said.

'Not if you use them carefully,' said Bertie. 'I wouldn't be like Tofu. Or Larch. He cut his finger off with his penknife. They took him to hospital, you know, and the finger as well. They put it in a packet, Larch said. Then they sewed it back on. But he says that he thinks they might have sewed on some-body else's finger by mistake because that finger keeps wanting to play the piano, and Larch has never had piano lessons.'

'A bit unlikely, Bertie,' said Stuart.

They reached the car. Bertie helped Stuart to strap Ulysses into his child's seat and they began the journey back to Edinburgh, taking a circuitous route that brought them within sight of Stirling Castle and the Wallace Monument. Stuart pointed the monument out to Bertie, who nodded sagely. He had read about William Wallace.

'Mr Wallace was jolly brave, Daddy,' he said. 'He saved Scotland, you know. You do know that, don't you, Daddy?'

Stuart smiled to himself. 'I know that, Bertie. He believed very strongly in freedom, you see.'

Bertie thought for a moment. He looked out of the car window at the Wallace Monument in the distance, towering and unlikely on its hill. 'Should everybody be allowed to be free, Daddy?'

Stuart did not reply immediately. But then he said, 'I think so, Bertie. People feel very strongly about their freedom.'

'They don't like being told what to do?'

'You could put it that way, Bertie. I suppose that William Wallace didn't like the idea of the English telling him what to do.' As he replied, Stuart wondered what William Wallace would have made of Brussels. It was all very well getting irritated with England telling Scotland what to do, but what if the orders came from Brussels? William Wallace would not have liked that very much, he suspected.

For his part, Bertie was considering what Stuart had said about William Wallace. A large truck passed them, speeding, its slipstream causing their car to swerve slightly. 'But everyone's got the right to be free? Everybody? Including boys?'

Stuart hesitated. 'Well, I suppose you would have to say that – within reason. Boys and girls can't run their own lives entirely. They can do that when they're grown up . . .'

'When they're eighteen?' interjected Bertie.

'Yes, certainly when they're eighteen. But these days . . .'

'Yes?' said Bertie, eagerly.

'These days, people are allowed to decide for themselves a bit earlier. Things have changed, you see.'

Bertie was listening to this very carefully. 'So people who aren't eighteen yet can decide what they'd like to do? Is that what you're saying, Daddy?'

'Yes, I suppose it is.'

'And if there was something that I really wanted to do, then I could decide to do it?'

Stuart was cautious. 'It depends, Bertie. It depends what it is.'

Bertie had been waiting for his moment. It occurred to him that he would probably never have a better opportunity, now that his mother was in Dubai and they were still within sight – even if distantly – of the Wallace Monument and its message of freedom.

'You know that tomorrow is my cub scout night?' he said.

'I believe I do, Bertie,' said Stuart. 'Do you still want to go?'

'Yes,' said Bertie, hurriedly. 'And we have to take the letters from our parents about going on the camp. Will you sign mine for me, Daddy? It's going to be next weekend.'

Stuart glanced at his son. 'Did you speak to Mummy about it?'

Bertie hesitated. He did not like lying, and never did. 'Yes,' he said, his voice small and tentative.

'And did she say no?' asked Stuart.

Bertie hesitated again. Irene had not said no; she had said 'Out of the question'. That was not 'no'. It was a whole different set of words, thought Bertie.

'She didn't say no,' he said. It was true – absolutely true. The word 'no' simply had not been used.

'Well,' said Stuart. 'I suppose that'll be all right.'

Bertie felt a sudden welling of joy within him. He had set his heart on going to the cub scout camp but had imagined, quite correctly, that his mother would never allow him to go. Now the whole wonderful prospect seemed to be within his grasp.

The camp was going to be on Ardnamurchan, in Argyll. They would be staying in the grounds of a real castle, Glenborrodale Castle, and there would be sailing lessons and kayaking too. They would sleep in tents, and eat food cooked over an open fire. It was a vision of complete heaven for a seven-year-old boy.

He counted the days. It was now a Sunday and departure for Ardnamurchan was scheduled to be the following Friday. His mother had gone to Dubai for five days – or so she had said – and that meant that she would be back on Friday – the very day that he was to leave. That was if you did not count today as one of her five days. If you did, then she would be back on Thursday, which would be in time to stop him going. Unless ... An idea occurred to Bertie. It was a rather good idea, he thought, and he imagined that it would work, even if Irene were to return on Thursday. All it involved was putting a pillow under his bedclothes and hoping that she would think it was him. Bertie had read about that old trick and was surprised that it had worked. He would never be taken in by something so patently false, but mothers, he believed, were different.

60. 'There's a bit of Aberdeen in everybody.'

Irene managed to sleep very well that first night in Dubai even though her vivid dreams, with the geographical dislocation so common to the dream-world, seemed to be set firmly in Edinburgh, and in particular in Drummond Place Gardens. These gardens, which were at the top of Scotland

Street, were a favourite haunt of Bertie's, and indeed Bertie was present, although not prominently, in the dream she had shortly before she woke up in her room in the Grand International Hotel.

In Irene's dream, she found herself walking in the gardens, following a path through vegetation that was considerably thicker than the well-regulated shrubs that made up the flora of the real gardens. She was puzzled by this, and also by the noise that seemed to be coming from the far end of the gardens, from behind a towering yew hedge that had been allowed to grow almost to the point of obscuring the rival trees.

Approaching this hedge, Irene found that there was a small opening cut into it, and this she was able to negotiate by dropping down to her hands and knees. As she made her way through the gap, she became aware of a cluster of people on the other side. There was her husband, Stuart, and there were Bertie and Ulysses, and there, rather surprisingly, were several members of her book group. When Irene emerged from the hedge, everybody turned, stared at her, and began to laugh, apparently at her clothing. Ulysses, who in the dream had grown into a boy of thirteen or fourteen, and was wearing a kilt and jacket, was laughing too, and Irene felt a particular pang that he, above all others, should find something amusing about her outfit.

She approached her son. 'You're not to laugh,' she said. 'I'm your mother. I love you. I love you very much. I always have.'

Ulysses looked at her. She saw that his eyes were of a strange grey colour and that on his upper lip he had an incipient moustache. 'I'm not laughing,' he said. 'I'm crying.'

'Why are you crying? What is there to cry about?'

The boy looked at her accusingly. 'What about my father?' he said quietly. 'Why did he go to Aberdeen?'

Irene looked about her. Stuart had been there, but now he seemed to have vanished. Instead, a small spotted dog had appeared, and was looking up at her with reproachful eyes. It was wearing a collar, and she bent forward to look at this. A tin plate on the collar announced the dog's name: Cyril Lordie. But it was not Cyril; Cyril had no spots. She reached out and rubbed the dog's coat. The spots seemed to be made of an inky substance that rubbed off on her hands.

Then the dog spoke and Irene was surprised to hear that he spoke with a Glasgow accent. 'My real name is Truth,' he announced. 'And I am not your dog.'

She stood up. Ulysses had disappeared, and so had Bertie. Now Dr Fairbairn emerged from the hedge and stood in front of her.

'Remember me,' he said.

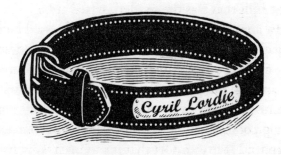

'Why did you go to Aberdeen?' Irene asked.

'Aberdeen came to me,' he replied. 'There's a bit of Aberdeen in everybody, you know, even you, Irene.'

Dr Fairbairn began to fade away.

'Did you say remember me or remember me??' asked Irene. 'There are two question marks, you know. It makes a difference.'

Dr Fairbairn smiled. 'There are so many question marks,' he said. 'Even in Aberdeen.'

She awoke. Dr Fairbairn. Aberdeen. That strange spotted dog whose name was Truth. And now, much more real than the world of that strange phantasmagoria, her room in the Grand International came into focus: the large television set with the glowing red spot at its base, the vulgar picture of an Arab dhow, the half-open wardrobe with its ghostly white bathrobes on their sandalwood hangers, the obedient coffee maker with its neat little kitchen of plastic-packed coffee and sugars – all the accoutrements of a modern hotel that could be anywhere. Only the Arab dhow gave a sense of place, but even that was redolent of an Arabia that was being pushed out onto the periphery by the creeping forest of high concrete ant-hills that was the modern city.

After a long and lingering bath, Irene dressed herself in the only clothes she had – the now rather crumpled uniform of the Emirates cabin attendant. The hotel had promised that they would bring her suitcase up to her room first thing in the morning – if it were to be delivered – and there was still no sign of it. That did not surprise her, of course, as she had been told at the airport that it was on its way to South America, via Amsterdam. Even if it were to be located and apprehended as quickly as possible, surely it would still take a day or two to negotiate its way to Dubai. And that meant that she would simply have to buy a new set of clothes to see her through until she was reunited with her own clothing. She would claim that from somebody, she thought – perhaps from the travel insurance she had bought for the trip. She seemed to remember that it had said something about lost luggage, which, she imagined, might be interpreted to cover not only luggage that was lost forever, but that which was lost for a few days.

Irene remembered that she had noticed a shop in the hotel lobby – or boutique, as it announced itself. She had noticed, too, that there had been some items of clothing in its window display – scarves and the like – and it was possible, she imagined, that they would have more clothing within. After all, people must often find themselves in her predicament and need to make temporary arrangements.

Dressed in the Emirates uniform, Irene took the lift down to the lobby, thirty-two floors below. The boutique was open, and she saw in the back, to her relief, a small rack of clothing that looked like dresses.

A saleswoman came up to greet her, but spoke in Arabic.

'Actually ...' said Irene.

The woman smiled. 'Of course, sorry. What can I do for you?'

Irene explained about the uniform and the suitcase and the woman smiled sympathetically. 'You poor thing,' she said. 'But of course we can help you. We only have fashions for Arab ladies, but I'm sure we'll find something suitable, even if our stock's a bit low.'

Irene followed her to the rack, and thought: from one identity to another.

The saleswoman turned and smiled. 'Black's in this year,

you know. You do know that, don't you?' She paused, before adding, 'I do hope that you're conservative. But, you know, I have a strong sense that you are.'

61. A Change of Clothing

Had there been a better selection of women's wear in the hotel boutique, Irene would undoubtedly have declined the entirely encompassing traditional desert outfit that the helpful assistant selected from the rack. She would not have chosen to have her face entirely obscured, with the exception of a small slit to allow her to look out, nor would she have chosen something that covered her hands and ankles. But she was not in a position to choose: the cabin attendant's outfit was now much in need of dry-cleaning and was becoming increasingly uncomfortable. This new outfit, by contrast, was voluminous to the point that it could easily have accommodated two, rather than one woman. Indeed, as Irene looked at herself in the mirror, the assistant observed that this particular dress was designed for the use of up to three ladies, simultaneously. 'I sold one to three sisters the other day,' she remarked. 'They went out of the shop wearing it and you would never have noticed that there were three people inside.'

'Remarkable,' said Irene. She had not heard of this before, but had read somewhere about Scottish two-man kilts, designed to be wrapped round two men at the same time, thereby saving money. These kilts were uncommon, but had gone down well in Aberdeen, she understood.

With some relief, Irene abandoned the cabin attendant's outfit, which the assistant promised she would have dry-cleaned and then returned to the airline. Then, clad in the traditional outfit and concealed from view, Irene stepped out into the hotel lobby and made her way towards the hotel dining room, where breakfast was being served.

The buffet table was set out with appealing things: peeled oranges, figs, yoghurt, honey, an array of cheeses and so on. Irene filled a plate, thinking of her normal breakfast at home – a bowl of reduced-sugar muesli and two slices of thinly cut toast; and of the boys' breakfasts too: Bertie's of bread, malt spread, and carrots, and Ulysses' of liquefied prunes and beetroot. Those were good healthy breakfasts, even if somewhat less varied than the breakfast she now took for herself, and they would stand both children in good stead as they grew up. Of course there were complaints, and requests for entirely unsuitable things – like sausages – but she had always resisted those, and they would thank her one of these days. There had been no sign of that, just yet, but it would come; Irene was sure of it.

She sat down at her table and reached for a spoon to tackle the large helping of honey-and-date yoghurt that she had ladled onto her plate. But then, as she lifted the spoon, it dawned on her that the traditional desert dress covered her mouth, and that there was no apparent opening for food. She put down the spoon and considered her predicament. How on earth did traditionally minded women cope with eating? Perhaps they ate before they put on the outfit, and therefore did not need access to their mouth once they were fully dressed. Perhaps there was some other trick of which she was culturally ignorant that made the whole process possible. As it was, all that she could think of was to pull the headdress part of the dress downwards, so that the slit for the eyes was now in front of her mouth. That worked as far as access was concerned, but the problem then was that she could not see anything. She felt for her spoon, and eventually located it, but then she had to find the bowl of yoghurt, and that took quite some time.

Eventually, after a good half-hour of laborious eating, Irene finished her breakfast and prepared to leave her table. As she was marshalling the folds of cloth that surrounded her, she saw, through her eye-slit, that a lively group of people were taking their seats nearby. One of them, in her direct line of vision, was a woman carrying a copy of the Literary Festival programme.

Intrigued, Irene moved her head slowly in order to be able to peer at the rest of the party. She stopped. Yes! It was him. It was that famous writer on Indian history. She looked about the others, deciding that there were one or two faces she thought she recognised but was not sure about. She felt a distinct thrill of excitement. She could join their table – and their conversation; it was perfectly acceptable for those attending literary festivals to talk to the participants.

She rose to her feet, gathering up the yards of black material that flowed about her. Her opening gambit, she thought, would be to congratulate the writer on his new book – which she had not exactly read yet, but of which she was otherwise fully informed. Then she could ask if she could sit down.

As she neared the table, looking out of her eye-slit in

much the same way as a tank commander peers through his vehicle's tiny letterbox-like sights, Irene saw the literary faces all turn to look up at her.

'Sorry to disturb you,' she said. 'I wanted to say . . . '

Unfortunately, because of the nature of the cloth about her mouth, Irene could not be heard. There was a sound, of course – a sort of muffled groaning – but no recognisable words, in any language.

The woman she had seen holding the programme now stood up and addressed Irene – in Arabic. What she said was: 'Please do not disturb our distinguished foreign guests.' But Irene, of course, could not understand this.

'But,' she protested. 'I wanted to . . . '

Being in no position to object, Irene was led quickly from the dining room. Now she was in the lobby; although she could not see anything at all clearly, she could tell from the glow through the cloth that she was standing under one of the large chandeliers she had noticed earlier on.

Then a voice said something in English. 'I think this lady was going to be collected by somebody.' And then, after a pause, the voice continued. 'Yes, here they are.'

Irene decided that the time had come to remove her head-dress and make it known who she was. She reached up within the folds of material, but could not find any way of escaping the embrace of her new outfit. Now she was being shepherded in the direction of the door. She tried to protest, but nobody heard her. There was heat – the sudden furnace heat of the open air – and then she was half-pushed into the air-conditioned interior of some sort of vehicle. An engine started; there was movement.

257

62. *Auras, Chakras, Halos*

Angus was pleased with the way that Domenica had handled the arrival of Antonia and her friend, Sister Maria-Fiore dei Fiori di Montagna. Of course there had been every provocation on Antonia's part, in spite of the evidence that there had been earlier on of a change of heart. When she first went to live with the community of nuns near Montalcino her tone had changed from the confrontational to the conciliatory; now it seemed that her tongue had sharpened again. Domenica, however, had shown great patience, and had simply remained silent when faced with some cutting remark, some finely honed put-down. These would have infuriated a lesser woman, but not Domenica.

'I shall rise right above her,' she confided to Angus. 'Every time Antonia makes one of her barbed remarks, I shall simply sit on the moral high ground, which is situated a short way behind her left shoulder. From there I shall look down on her with amused tolerance.'

Angus closed his eyes and tried to imagine the moral high ground. It would look, he thought, rather like some of the higher ground in a Renaissance painting – an idealised, Italianate landscape of cypress trees and distant blue hills. Of course, the moral high ground would be somewhat crowded by now, given the number of people who sought to occupy it. He smiled at the thought. And smiled again when he thought of what a good name it would be for a house. Retired philosophers, for instance, could name their villas that, and certain, but not all, politicians might do the same. It might also be a good name for the headquarters of certain political parties: Moral High Ground House. He stopped himself. That was an unworthy thought, and he would not dwell on it.

At least Antonia required no entertainment, as she had spoken of her intention of spending most of her time engaged in research for her book on the early Scottish saints.

'I shall be in the National Library for most of the time,' she announced at breakfast. 'There is much to be done.'

Domenica eyed her from the other end of the table. 'I'm sure there is,' she said. She was not sure, in fact, as she doubted whether there could be many, if any, new sources for information on the lives of such people. Many of them, as far as she could make out, did not even exist, although she was prepared to accept the historicity of the likes of Ninian and Kentigern.

'They were often rather ordinary, were they not?' said Angus. 'If you were the local priest you were more or less certain to be called a saint, weren't you?'

Antonia nodded. 'Yes, that's true. And your wife was called a saint too. And your children were saints.'

'How nice,' said Angus. 'A whole family of saints.'

Sister Maria-Fiore dei Fiori di Montagna had been following this conversation with some interest. 'Saintliness is a very special quality,' she observed, as she spread marmalade on her toast. 'It is the quality that one finds in saints.'

Angus thought about this for a moment. 'True,' he said.

Domenica said nothing.

'One of the ways in which we can recognise the existence

259

of saintliness,' went on Sister Maria-Fiore dei Fiori di Montagna, 'is the halo that appears above a saint's head. That is a very powerful sign.'

'Indeed,' said Antonia. 'The halo, also called a nimbus or aureole, has a very clear meaning.'

'But surely that's only a convention,' said Domenica. 'It's an iconographical convention. Artists put in halos when painting the saints. This had nothing to do with reality.'

Antonia shook her head. 'Wrong,' she said, simply. 'I've seen it myself.'

'You've seen a halo?' asked Domenica incredulously.

'Yes,' said Antonia. 'Shortly after my unfortunate illness—'

'Your Stendhal Syndrome?' interjected Angus.

'Yes, shortly after I had been unfortunate enough to go down with that in the Uffizi Gallery, I was placed in the care of the wonderful sisters. And I can tell you this: I am convinced that some of the women who looked after me were candidates for saintliness themselves.'

At first this remark was greeted with complete silence. Then Domenica said, 'You mean you saw ...'

'I saw what some people might describe as an aura,' said Antonia. 'That's the term that's used these days by New Age people. We all have an aura. Some people mix them up with chakras. That's the Indian term for centres of energy. Auras are an altogether wider field of energy.'

'Interesting,' said Domenica.

Antonia nodded slowly. 'Indeed. It's a question of sensitivity,' she said. 'We all have the power to detect the moral nature of those with whom we come into contact. It is really just a question of whether one is sufficiently receptive.'

'Do I have an aura?' asked Angus suddenly.

Antonia looked at him over the table. 'You do,' she said. 'You are vaguely benevolent. It is not a very powerful aura, I'm afraid, but that is nothing to be ashamed of.'

'We all shine in different ways,' said Sister Maria-Fiore dei Fiori di Montagna. 'But there is light in every one of us, even the least of men.' She gave Angus a sympathetic look as she spoke, making him wonder whether this was because he was the least of men.

'Of course,' continued Antonia, 'auras and halos are slightly different things. Everyone may have an aura, but only those who follow the ways of the Church can have a halo.'

Sister Maria-Fiore dei Fiori di Montagna nodded in confirmation. 'Yes,' she said. 'That is true. It may seem a bit hard on some, but a line has to be drawn.'

Antonia now delivered her bombshell. 'I do not wish to embarrass anybody,' she said, 'but as I said, the sisters who, in their goodness, looked after me were of a very saintly disposition – and none more so than dear Sister Maria-Fiore dei Fiori di Montagna.'

The nun made a gesture of modesty. 'Please, Antonia, I am flawed, like everybody else.'

'And I would go further,' said Antonia. 'I have noticed – and I really don't think I'm mistaken – a certain glow about her head. Look, can you see it?'

Domenica peered from the other end of the table. 'I might need to fetch my glasses . . .'

Angus held up a hand. 'No flippancy, please,' he said. 'You know, Antonia, I think you may be right.'

63. Materialism, Belief, et cetera

While Antonia made her way off to George IV Bridge to pursue her research in the National Library, Angus helped Domenica with the washing-up of the breakfast plates, Sister Maria-Fiore dei Fiori di Montagna having returned to her room to complete her morning devotions.

'I do hope that the need to complete devotions will not totally preclude all help in the kitchen,' said Domenica. 'What with research and devotions, you and I might have to do all the work, Angus.'

Angus smiled. 'I'm sure that she'll pull her weight, even if Antonia won't. Nuns are very hard-working in my experience.'

'In your experience?' asked Domenica.

'Well, so I've heard,' said Angus. 'They get up terribly early in the morning and scrub the floors and the like. By eight o'clock they've been up for hours, and done a great deal of work.'

'I suppose so,' said Domenica. 'Perhaps Sister Maria-Fiore dei Fiori di Montagna will scrub our kitchen floor for us some day. I can't recall when I last scrubbed it – in fact, I'm not sure if I've ever done such a thing. Mopped it, perhaps, but not scrubbed.'

'We certainly don't scrub things enough,' said Angus. 'I remember my father telling me that it was important to scrub one's back once a week. We had a long-handled brush in the bathroom and you scrubbed your back with that while sitting in the bath. But now ...'

'I suspect virtually nobody scrubs their back any more,'

said Domenica. 'There may be some, I suppose, who keep up the old ways, but most people, no, they don't scrub their backs.'

'Perhaps we should make some sort of New Year resolution next year. We might both resolve to scrub our backs.' He paused. 'Does one's back get particularly dirty? One's neck does, I suppose. If you look at your collar when you take off your shirt, you can see that the neck is somewhat inclined to dirt. But I'm not so sure about the back.'

Domenica handed him a tea towel. 'Let's not talk too much about people's backs; it's somewhat too intimate a subject for morning conversation. Would you care to dry the dishes?'

Angus set to work. 'I must say that I rather take to Antonia's friend,' he mused. 'She has a rather appealing way of making very obvious remarks sound full of significance. I rather like that.'

Domenica nodded. 'I rather like her, too,' she said. 'But when Antonia implied that she had a halo ... well, I thought that was a bit much. I've never had a guest with a halo. Never.'

Angus laughed. 'I've always taken the view that Antonia is a bit odd,' he said. 'I'm not surprised that she's gone off to live in a convent. I always thought it was on the cards that she'd do something extreme. Commit murder, or rob a bank, or marry somebody from Glasgow. Something like that. Only joking.'

Domenica chuckled. '*Très drôle*. Well, it's all harmless enough. Mind you, I have difficulty in imagining her scrubbing floors ... or carrying out devotions, for that matter.'

Angus looked thoughtful. 'Do you think she believes?'

'Believes what?'

Angus shrugged. 'In God?'

'As a general rule,' said Domenica, 'those who live in convents believe in God. I suspect that in Antonia's case, she's persuaded herself to believe in him. People do that. They make themselves believe in something that they otherwise would not believe in. There's comfort in that.'

'Is there?'

While Angus had been drying the plates, Domenica had been preparing them another cup of coffee. Now she handed a cup to Angus.

'Yes, there is comfort,' she said. 'Because what's the alternative? A belief that life is without meaning, without purpose? If we consider our position – our real position – what are we? A life form on this tiny rock hurtling about in space – perhaps even a hologram, if some theories are to be believed.' She paused to take a sip of coffee. 'But, however small and insignificant we are in a cosmic context, one thing that we do understand is that we have consciousness and that we are capable of certain emotions. We like some things and dislike others. We feel happy or unhappy. We experience pain and pleasure. These are facts.'

'So?'

'So, given that we really have no idea about why we are here – and it's true that we have no idea about that, no matter how much we like to think we do – then our options are . . . are what? To shrug and accept that we mean nothing, or to create some sort of system of beliefs, some myth that will sustain us. Which of these do you think makes life less terrifying? A belief in nothingness and irrelevance, or a state of denial of the emptiness?'

Angus did not take long to answer. 'The latter,' he said. 'If it's empty, that is. But . . . '

Domenica looked at him expectantly. 'But?'

'But believing in something that you know is inherently likely to be false is surely a form of self-delusion. And isn't it counter-intuitive to believe in something that you suspect doesn't exist? I could tell myself that Santa Claus exists, or fairies, and I may be happier for thinking that, but I'm abusing my capacity for reason and that means I'll be less of a rational man.'

Domenica sighed. 'I know. But, on the other hand, look at results. The rational person will believe only those things he can see – and prove. He tends, therefore, to be a materialist. But where does materialism lead us?' She pointed out of the window, in the direction of Princes Street. 'Go up there,' she said. 'Stand on Princes Street for a few minutes. Look at the people walking along the street. Look at their faces. Look into their faces. All those people going shopping. Buying things that they probably don't really need.'

'They're satisfying reasonable material appetites,' said Angus.

'Yes, I suppose we all need shoes and pullovers and . . . and whatever people buy on Princes Street. But look at the emptiness. Look at the aimlessness of people's expressions. How many people will you see on Princes Street who look really alive?'

'Oh come on, Domenica!' said Angus.

'No,' she said. 'I'm serious. The materialist view is like weedkiller. It kills all possibility of the spiritual.'

'So you're saying that the people you see on Princes Street have nothing in their lives?'

Domenica did not answer immediately. One could not condemn an entire cross-section of the population of Scotland too quickly. One needed to think about it.

But then she had a thought. If God existed, his other name, she felt, might be Good. And good existed because we felt it, as surely as we felt the sun on our faces. We knew it was there.

64. The Unexpected

'I think,' said Angus Lordie to Sister Maria-Fiore dei Fiori di Montagna, 'that we should start off the day with a cup of coffee in a typical Edinburgh coffee bar . . .'

He paused, and asked himself: was Big Lou's coffee bar in any sense typical? A coffee bar run by a widely read but down-to-earth autodidact from Arbroath? A coffee bar that used to be a bookshop, down the stairs of which the late Christopher Murray Grieve – Hugh MacDiarmid, the poet – had once tripped, and avoided serious injury, unlike the Glasgow informal businessman, the late Lard O'Connor (Aloysius Xavier O'Connor) R.I.P., who had left this world while trying to negotiate his bulk down those very steps? A coffee bar frequented by the occasional Jacobite and art dealer and the only dog in Scotland with a gold tooth? Was any of that typical?

'Perhaps not entirely typical,' Angus added.

'What exists is typical,' said Sister Maria-Fiore dei Fiori di Montagna. 'There is nothing that is not created for a purpose. Everything has its point.' She looked at Angus, as if to ensure that he had understood. 'And so a flower that may have no apparent reason for existence is there because it beautifies that little bit of space.'

Angus stared at her. 'I see ...'

Sister Maria-Fiore dei Fiori di Montagna smiled benignly. 'May I tell you a little story, dear Mr Lordie?'

'Of course,' said Angus. 'But would you like to tell me as we walk to the coffee bar? It's a fine morning, and it'll be very pleasant walking along and listening to you.'

Sister Maria-Fiore dei Fiori di Montagna said that she thought this was a good idea. 'I do love to walk,' she said.

Angus waited for her to say something else, as this statement seemed rather short for her. Surely there was some greater purpose in walking – some connection between walking and understanding, for instance; but no, she had nothing to add.

Cyril, who had been sitting at Angus's feet, recognised the word walk, even when uttered with an Italian accent, and immediately shot off in search of his lead. This he brought back and dropped before his master.

'Your dog is very charming,' said Sister Maria-Fiore dei Fiori di Montagna. 'St Francis himself would have loved him. I am quite sure of that.'

'Possibly,' said Angus. 'He can be a bit malodorous at times, but I suppose that was nothing to St Francis. I assume that he loved smelly animals too.'

'Undoubtedly,' said Sister Maria-Fiore dei Fiori di Montagna. 'All types and conditions of animal flocked to St Francis. There is that lovely picture in Florence of him preaching to the birds. Perhaps you know it? And all the birds are lined up before him, entranced by the saint's words.'

They set off, Cyril straining eagerly at the leash.

'Your story?' said Angus.

'Ah yes,' replied Sister Maria-Fiore dei Fiori di Montagna. 'My story is about a monastery in Tuscany – a very beautiful place, tucked away in the Sienese hills.'

'A very fine setting for a story,' Angus ventured.

'Indeed,' said Sister Maria-Fiore dei Fiori di Montagna, giving Angus a cautionary glance; she clearly did not want interruptions. 'Now, in this monastery there was a young novice – not much more than a boy, really – a young man of nineteen; but very spiritual, of course.'

Angus thought of the few Scottish nineteen-year-olds he knew – more interested in spirits (such as vodka, for example) than in spirituality; but he did not say anything.

'And this young man used to go for a walk every day. He left the monastery and walked along a path that went up a hillside. It was very beautiful, with groves of olive trees on both sides and a small stream – almost invisible in the dry summer months. At the foot of the hill was a farmyard in which were kept two white oxen of quite exceptional loveliness. They were used to pull an ancient wooden cart kept by the farmer – a cart that might have been there for hundreds of years, pulled by the oxen's ancestors.'

Angus could picture the scene. He had seen white oxen in the Tuscan countryside before, and he could picture them now, with their drooping ears and their black noses, and their sweet oxen's breath.

'Now, one of the other monks,' continued Sister Maria-Fiore dei Fiori di Montagna, 'became suspicious of this young man's regular walks. It occurred to him that he might be meeting one of the village girls, which, of course, was something that the Order discouraged. So he went to the Father Superior and voiced his doubts to him. The Father Superior listened gravely and then said, "We should not think the worst of our brethren, but at the same time, we should not close our eyes to the obvious. Follow that young man – discreetly – and then report back to me."'

They had now reached Great King Street. 'So,' said Sister Maria-Fiore dei Fiori di Montagna, 'the senior monk followed the young man, taking care not to be spotted. His route took him up the path almost to the top of the hill, and then he went off on a much smaller path that ran along a ridge. The senior monk was now certain that the young man was meeting a girl, as he had stopped to pick a number of wild flowers and had made these into a posy.

'Keeping well back, the senior monk followed the young man round a corner, and then, quite suddenly, all was revealed. The young monk had stopped and was placing the flowers in a small vase that had been placed on a ledge in the rock. And on this shelf was a small picture of a Madonna and child.'

Sister Maria-Fiore dei Fiori di Montagna turned and smiled at Angus. 'You see?' she said.

Angus nodded wisely. 'The suspicious mind!' he said. 'I am sure that he felt bad about harbouring such suspicions.'

'He did indeed,' said Sister Maria-Fiore dei Fiori di Montagna. 'As did the Father Superior.'

'I bet he did,' said Angus.

'Mind you,' said Sister Maria-Fiore dei Fiori di Montagna, 'because the senior monk sneaked away guilty and ashamed, he did not see what the young man did next.'

'What was that?' asked Angus.

'He went round the corner, where he met a local girl from the village. They had been meeting every day.'

Angus stopped. 'Oh,' he said. 'I wasn't expecting that.'

Sister Maria-Fiore dei Fiori di Montagna smiled. 'I'm sure you weren't. The unexpected, you see, dear Mr Lordie, is what we do not expect, except when, as is sometimes the case, we expect it.'

65. *La Vie Bédouine*

Stuart received the telephone call at the office. It came at an awkward time, in the middle of a meeting with his immediate superior. The two statisticians had been discussing how to present the results of a major survey that had revealed that the Government's claims of improvement in many areas of Scottish life were, to say the least, optimistic.

'It breaks my heart to see these figures,' said Stuart's boss, Andrew. 'Those poor government ministers – working away to put a positive gloss on things, and then all this ... ' He searched for a word to express his distaste. 'All this ... all this evidence.'

Stuart shrugged. 'I suppose that's the risk,' he said. 'You

ask a question and you get an answer you don't like. Then what do you do?'

'You try to see what scraps of comfort are in the answer,' said Andrew. 'Or at least, that's what I've always done.'

Stuart looked at the papers before him. 'Well, let's try that. Let's look at obesity rates.' He read out some figures.

'Those sound as if they're inflated,' said Andrew.

Stuart shook his head. 'No, it's the people who are inflated.'

Andrew was not one to give up. 'Are you sure those aren't pounds you're talking about? It sounds ... well, it makes a difference, you know.'

'No, the figures are in kilos.'

'So the country's getting bigger,' said Andrew. 'Perhaps we could regard that as something positive. People are always going on about growth.'

'In the economy,' said Stuart. 'Not in the national girth. And ...'

'And what?'

'The country itself is actually getting smaller.' He turned to another page in the document before him. 'Look, this column here is all about land area. It seems that because of erosion caused by the sea, Scotland is actually being washed away.'

Andrew shook his head. 'Are you sure? Where's it going?'

'I haven't got a clue,' said Stuart. 'I suppose if bits of land are washed away on the east coast, they must end up on the shores of continental Europe or ...' He hesitated.

Andrew pressed him. 'Yes?'

'Or if the sea currents run north to south, they end up being added to England.'

Andrew's eyes flashed a warning. 'Don't say that,' he muttered. 'Some ministers will not like that.'

Stuart had an idea. 'Of course, it might be possible for them to say that England is actually taking Scottish territory. How about that?'

Andrew made a note. 'Possible. We can run it past them.'

Stuart looked thoughtful. 'What was that research we had to dig out last month? That stuff about air quality?'

Andrew looked puzzled for a moment, but then remembered. 'Oh yes, there was that MSP who wanted to find out whether Scotland got more carbon dioxide from England than England got from Scotland. He wanted to find out whether England was using more than its fair share of air.'

Stuart smiled. 'And we found out they were,' he said. 'That went down well.'

'But there was a bit of a problem, wasn't there? Didn't the

scientists say that the only way in which that could be addressed would be for the English to breathe a bit less? Quite a bit less, in fact.'

'A sort of West Lothian question,' mused Stuart.

It was at this delicate point that Stuart's mobile phone rang.

'Mr Pollock?' enquired a woman's voice.

Stuart rose to his feet to take the call by the window, leaving Andrew at the desk. 'Yes?'

'I'm sorry to disturb you,' said the woman. 'I'm actually calling from the Foreign Office in London. Are you in a position to take this call?'

Stuart's heart lurched. He was back at Glasgow Airport. He saw Irene walking towards the entrance of the security bay. He saw the ceiling, which, curiously, he remembered. There were air-conditioning ducts.

'I'm very sorry to inform you,' said the woman, 'that your wife has been involved in an incident in the UAE. She's still alive, I hasten to tell you – it's not bad news in that sense.'

He breathed again. More carbon dioxide, he said to himself; and then he thought: how strange that the mind can be irreverent, juvenile, at a time like this.

'Is she all right ...'

'We think so,' said the woman. 'It's a rather strange affair. We've had a call from our *chargé d'affaires* there who says that for some reason your wife was attired in such a way that she was mistaken for one of the new wives of a Bedouin leader. She was bundled off into the desert, apparently.'

Stuart was at a loss.

'Are you still there, Mr Pollock?'

'Yes,' he answered weakly. 'I'm still here.'

'Well, when the hotel noticed that she hadn't slept in her bed they made enquiries and pieced the whole thing together. Apparently she purchased a traditional desert outfit and, for some reason, wore that in the hotel lobby. That led to her being mistaken for the other lady – the wife – and carted off by this Bedouin chap's men. We've used our contacts to try to get a picture of what happened then. The Dubai police have been tremendously helpful – as usual – but the problem is that communications in the desert are a bit difficult. We've found out where she is, though.' There was a pause. 'Mr Pollock? Are you still there?'

'Yes, I'm still here.'

'She's in a desert encampment – in the wives' quarters, we're told. Apparently she's in good health, so there's no worry on that score.'

Stuart breathed a sigh of relief. 'When's she coming back?' he asked.

'Well, that's a bit of a problem, I'm afraid. They're touchy, these Bedouin. Noble sons of the desert, and all that – but they're tough negotiators. This chap says that she's his wife now and so it's going to take quite a bit of time for the authorities out there to lean on him. It could be weeks – months, I'm afraid.'

'Oh.' That was all Stuart could say.

'Here's your Foreign Office Distressed Person reference number,' said the woman.

She gave him a number and Stuart wrote it down. As a

statistician, he could not help noticing that it contained an inordinate number of sevens and threes.

66. A Paternalistic Issue

Stuart decided that he would not tell Bertie about what had happened to Irene. In general, he did not like to keep the truth from his son, and had always answered his questions as truthfully as he could. Very occasionally, though, there were situations in which a paternalistic concealment of reality was justifiable – and if a father could not legitimately be paternalistic, then, he wondered, who could?

Bertie was an intelligent child, though, and would need some explanation of why his mother, who was due to arrive home from Dubai any day now, might not be returning for some time – weeks or months, according to the Foreign Office.

That afternoon when Stuart, using his entitlement to flexi-hours working, collected Bertie from the Steiner School, he raised the subject of Irene's delayed return in as casual and non-alarmist a tone as he could.

'The desert has its attractions, you know, Bertie.'

Stuart made this remark as the 23 bus began its dignified way along George IV Bridge. They were sitting on the top deck, in Bertie's favourite position, one that afforded them a good view of the road ahead.

Bertie nodded. 'If you like sand, the desert must be very nice.'

'Ah,' said Stuart, 'but there's more to the desert than sand, Bertie. Much more.'

Again Bertie nodded. 'T. E. Lawrence thought that,' he said.

Stuart's eyebrows shot up. 'T. E. Lawrence? Where on earth did you hear about him, Bertie?'

Bertie shrugged. 'I read something – I forget where. T. E. Lawrence was also called Lawrence of Arabia, Daddy. He was very brave. Everybody was very brave in those days.'

Stuart smiled. 'Do you think so? I wonder whether there weren't lots of people just like ... ' He was about to say 'me', but he stopped himself. He did not want his son to think him a coward; every boy likes to think of his father as being brave, and able to take on anything. Is that what I am? Stuart asked himself. Have I ever stood up to ... my wife?

He finished his sentence. 'Just like the rest of us, Bertie.'

'Maybe,' said Bertie. 'But I think they might have been a bit braver because they were allowed to be.'

Stuart was puzzled by this. 'Because they were allowed to be, Bertie? What do you mean by that?'

Bertie took a few moments to answer. 'Their mothers ... '

Stuart watched his son. He wanted to hug him, to comfort him, to reassure him.

'They were allowed to have penknives,' Bertie said quietly. 'I bet Lawrence of Arabia had a Swiss Army knife, Daddy. I bet he did.'

Stuart touched his son on the shoulder. 'The desert, Bertie. Mummy is going to spend a bit more time in the desert. Maybe a few weeks – maybe even a few months. She's not quite sure.'

'That's all right,' said Bertie. 'We can cope. We can buy some pizzas. Maybe twenty or thirty, and put them in the freezer. Ulysses will eat them too.'

'All right, Bertie,' said Stuart. 'We'll buy some pizzas. Mind you, you won't be needing them for a little while. You're going off to cub scout camp in Ardnamurchan. I've spoken to Akela and it's all fixed up. You're going later this afternoon.'

Bertie spent the rest of the journey in a state of unconcealed joy. When they got off the bus on Dundas Street, he ran all the way along Cumberland Street, having promised his father to wait for him at the Dundonald Street end. And once Stuart had caught up with him, he then ran the remaining distance to their front door and was waiting for Stuart when he arrived.

Bertie's packing was accomplished quickly, and for the remaining two hours before it was time to go off to the hall at Holy Corner from which they would be leaving, he sat on a chair by the door, watching the slow movement of the clock's hands. At last it was time to go, and Stuart, bringing Ulysses in his pushchair, led Bertie off to the bus stop.

When they reached the hall, there was already a small crowd of parents and children contributing to a rising buzz of conversation. Bertie quickly found his friend Ranald Braveheart Macpherson, who was sporting a heavy rucksack that was distinctly too large for him. Ranald, who had notoriously spindly legs – the object of many critical remarks by Olive and Pansy – was clearly very proud of this rucksack, even though it threatened to topple him at any moment.

'I've got a whole lot of new gear,' said Ranald to Bertie.

'I've got a folding shovel, a groundsheet, a GPS, and a set of matching aluminium mess-tins. I'll let you look at my stuff if you like, Bertie, although I may not be able to let you use it much.'

'Thanks, Ranald,' said Bertie, looking about him to see who else had arrived.

Tofu was there, listening glumly to his father, who was lecturing him severely, and there were Olive and Pansy too. Olive, seeing Bertie, came over to speak to him and his father.

'You mustn't worry about Bertie, Mr Pollock,' she said to Stuart. 'I'll keep an eye on him.'

'I don't need ...' began Bertie, only to be cut short by Olive.

'He can put his tent right next to the tent that Pansy and I are going to share,' she continued. 'That way, we'll be able to reassure him if he gets nervous, which he probably will do.'

'That's kind, Olive,' said Stuart. 'I'm sure that Bertie will be able to look after himself.'

'I'm not so sure, Mr Pollock,' she said. 'But we shall see. Have you signed the form yet?'

Stuart frowned. 'Is there a form to sign?'

'Oh yes,' said Olive. 'It's a form that says you won't blame the cub scout movement if Bertie gets killed on this trip. It's a good idea to sign it, Mr Pollock – just in case anything goes wrong.'

Stuart smiled. 'That's a bit alarmist, Olive, don't you think? This will be a very safe trip, I should think.'

'Well, you never know,' said Olive. 'Boys can do some stupid things.'

Stuart winked at Bertie. 'I'm sure Olive's only joking, Bertie.'

'No, I'm not,' said Olive. Now she turned to Bertie. 'And Bertie, I'm really sorry to hear about what happened to your mummy.'

Bertie looked puzzled. 'She went to Dubai,' he said. 'She's in the desert.'

Olive smiled knowingly. 'My father showed me the *Evening News*, Bertie. It says that she's been seized by some desert sheik and is being held prisoner in a harem. That's what it says, Bertie. I could have cut out the article for you. I'm sorry I didn't.'

Bertie looked up at his father.

Stuart groaned. 'Don't worry about it, Bertie,' he said. 'The papers often get it wrong. They love to sensationalise.'

67. *Ardnamurchan*

That evening, in the soft light of summer, William Hunter's beige and brown private coach conveyed twenty-seven members of Bertie's cub scout pack across the high wastes of Rannoch Moor and down towards Glencoe. To their left, Buachaille Etive Mhor, the great shepherd at the mouth of Glen Etive, towered watchfully; to their right, beyond the Kings House Hotel, the slopes of mountains that were now, at their peak, topped by a wraith of wispy cloud.

'Now, boys and girls,' announced Rosemary Gold, Akela of the pack, 'we are about to enter Glencoe, which is a very important historical place.' She paused, wondering how to explain to the children one of the most notorious dinner parties in Scottish history. 'It witnessed a very sad event, I'm sorry to say.'

'I know all about that,' volunteered Tofu. 'The Campbells fell upon the Macdonalds and cut their throats. Just after they'd had their tea together. There was blood all over the place.'

Olive turned and stared at Tofu in disgust. 'You'd better watch out, Tofu. The Campbells will get you one day.'

There were titters of laughter.

'That's not very helpful, Olive,' said Akela. 'We must put such things behind us.'

'Then why are we having a referendum?' asked Ranald Braveheart Macpherson.

'The referendum has nothing to do with Glencoe,' said Akela. 'Nothing at all, as far as I can see.'

The discussion moved on to less fraught terrain. Akela pointed out the sweeping fields of boulders, remnants of the passage of glaciers, and drew attention to the gullies carved into the mountainsides by the action of water. Then, as the road levelled out and they left Glencoe village behind them, they saw their first sea loch, Loch Leven, spanned, in the distance, by the Ballachulish bridge.

An hour or so later, having negotiated the crossing of Loch Linnhe on the Corran ferry, the coach drew up at the field near Glenborrodale upon which they were to pitch their tents. Several helpers had come with the children, and they supervised the erection of rows of small green tents, each pitched carefully on a waterproof rectangular ground-sheet.

Bertie found himself sharing a tent with Ranald Braveheart Macpherson, while Tofu and Larch shared next door. Beyond that, pitched as far away from Tofu and Larch as they could manage, was the tent occupied by Olive and Pansy – a tent that was very soon enhanced by the addition of several cushions that Pansy had brought with her, along with a scented candle, and a box of McVitie's finest Edinburgh shortbread.

The tents erected, an evening meal was served around a large cooking fire made by the adults – sausages, baked beans and large squares of fried bread.

Bertie sat on the ground with Ranald Braveheart Macpherson, his paper plate of food before him, his heart filled with pleasure at the prospect of the two days of camping ahead. Ranald had already checked their GPS position, marked it on the map, and taken a compass bearing on the tower of Glenborrodale Castle, tucked away in the trees behind them.

'This is very good fun, Ranald,' said Bertie.

Ranald nodded, but Bertie could tell that he was anxious about something. 'Do you think it gets really dark here?' he asked.

Bertie shrugged. 'Same as Edinburgh, or maybe not quite so dark,' he said. 'My dad told me that in places this far north it's often quite light even at midnight.'

Ranald looked relieved. 'Because we haven't got any lights in our tent, Bertie.'

'No,' said Bertie. 'But we won't need them, Ranald. We'll be quite safe.'

Ranald Braveheart Macpherson looked unconvinced. 'What about Campbells?' he whispered. 'What if there are some Campbells round here?' He looked in the direction of a clump of bushes at the edge of the field – perfectly adequate cover for Campbells.

Bertie sought to reassure him. 'They won't bother us,' he said. 'Campbells stay in at night – most of the time.'

After supper, there was a quick game of rounders before it was time for everybody to go to bed. Bertie and Ranald Braveheart Macpherson slipped into their sleeping bags and lay down on the groundsheet that formed the floor of their tent. Bertie said goodnight to Ranald and lay quite still, his eyes closed, waiting for sleep to come. But he soon became aware of a chattering sound from Ranald's side of the tent.

'Is that noise your teeth?' he asked in the semi-darkness.

'I think so,' said Ranald, his voice small and nervous. 'They're making a funny sound.'

'Are you frightened?' asked Bertie.

There was a short silence before Ranald replied. 'A little bit,' he said. 'The Campbells ...'

'You shouldn't be frightened of Campbells,' said Bertie. 'You really shouldn't, Ranald.'

'I know,' stuttered Ranald. 'But my teeth seem to be frightened. Do your teeth get frightened sometimes, Bertie?'

Bertie said that he was not sure. Then he said, 'Roll over to this side of the tent, Ranald. You'll be safe over here.'

Gratefully, Ranald rolled in his sleeping bag so that he was lying just a few inches away from Bertie. Bertie reached out and placed a protective arm over his friend's shoulder. Slowly, the sound of chattering teeth became fainter, and then stopped altogether.

'Better now?' asked Bertie.

'Yes,' whispered Ranald. 'I'm sorry that I'm not all that brave, Bertie. I'm really sorry.'

'You don't have to say you're sorry,' said Bertie. 'Everyone gets frightened now and then. You don't have to be ashamed, Ranald.'

Bertie closed his eyes. Underneath his arm, he felt the slow up and down movement of Ranald's chest as he breathed in and out. He would leave his arm where it was until Ranald was safely asleep, and then he would move it. It gave him a warm feeling to be protecting his friend from whatever it was that frightened him – whether it was Campbells, or the dark, or things that had no name. And it was not surprising, perhaps, that he should feel it – this little boy who felt things so deeply; for we all feel that about our friends; we all feel that about those around whom we might put an arm. We all feel that about the darkness into which we go with others and about the very understandable fears that can be so easily dispelled, put to flight, by a simple gesture of the human arm, at once so easy and yet so hard to make.

68. Fear and Loathing in Las Vegas; Joy and Delight in Morningside

Dr Macgregor and Anichka did not stay long in the Canny Man's. Even so, the ten minutes or so that they spent in the bar seemed an eternity to Pat. The conversation was awkward, and her father steadfastly avoided her eye. Anichka, who spoke in a high-pitched rather nasal voice, prevented anybody else from saying very much, and Pat found herself cringing whenever the Czech woman spoke. At length, finishing the last of his drink with evident relief, Dr Macgregor looked at his watch and declared that their dinner reservation required them to leave.

'It is a very expensive restaurant,' said Anichka. 'Maybe eighty pounds a head. Ninety sometimes.'

Pat glanced at her father, who again looked away. 'No, it's not cheap,' he muttered. 'But it's very good.'

Pat looked at Anichka. 'Well,' she said, 'it's always nice to be taken out to dinner, isn't it? And not to have to pay.'

Anichka's eyes narrowed. Pat had not intended to insult her, but somehow the remark had slipped out.

Michael touched Pat's arm gently. 'I think we should go too.'

Pat was not sure where they were meant to be going, but nodded her assent. 'Yes, it's late.'

'Bedtime?' said Anichka, looking at Michael.

Pat caught her breath. How dare she?

Michael blushed. He tried to make light of the remark. 'I never go to bed before midnight,' he said.

Pat looked again at her father. How could he tolerate this crude . . . this vulgar woman? Yes, she decided, vulgar was the word. People did not use it very much any more because it sounded elitist, or even snobbish. But there were people who were just . . . well, just vulgar, pure and simple. There was no other word for it.

For a moment Dr Macgregor seemed unwilling to catch his daughter's eye, but then he looked up, and their gaze met. He knows, thought Pat; he knows what she's like. But then if he knew, why did he continue to spend time in her company? Or was it simply physical? She did not like to think of that; what child imagines his parents to have an interest in such matters? But he was human, of course, like the rest of us.

They let Dr Macgregor and Anichka leave first. There were awkward farewells; then, as the door banged shut, Pat turned to Michael. 'My father . . .'

He shook his head. He was smiling. 'You don't have to say anything.'

She was relieved. He understood; of course he would – he was so nice himself that he was bound to understand. 'He's such a kind man, and I wish you hadn't met him with that . . .'

He reached out and placed a finger gently across her lips, in a gesture that was one of both silence and comfort.

'You needn't explain,' he said. 'Sometimes one's parents get things wrong. My father had a very strong West Highland accent. When I was young I remember being embarrassed by the way he spoke. We lived in Stirling, you see, and nobody spoke like that there. The other boys used to say things like "Your dad's a real teuchter". I hated it.'

'I like a Highland accent.'

'So do I. Now. But not when I was twelve, or whatever it was. At that age you want your parents to talk exactly the same as everybody else.'

She looked up at the display behind the bar: bottles of whisky with obscure names; malts with labels she had never seen before. She imagined what he had been like when he was twelve.

'Thinking of something?' he asked.

She laughed. 'Yes.'

'What?'

She hesitated before answering. She felt that she could tell him; there was something about him that encouraged confidence. Curiously, since she had just met him, she felt the sort of trust that one normally feels with an old friend.

'I was thinking about you, actually.'

'Me? Well, that's nice to know.'

'I was wondering what you were like when you were twelve.'

He smiled at her. 'I can show you a photograph, if you like. I had a brace on my teeth.'

'Did you?'

'Yes. I was embarrassed about that too. In fact, come to think of it, I was embarrassed about just about everything.'

'And now?'

He shook his head. 'Nothing to be embarrassed about.' He paused. 'And you?'

'At that age? I was embarrassed too. I remember being embarrassed by the furniture in our house. Other girls had houses with modern furniture – ours was ancient and the chairs had threads hanging down from them where the cat had sharpened its claws. I was embarrassed by the cat.'

'Yes,' he said. 'It's awful for everybody at that age. I sometimes think how great it would be if you could take a pill at the age of fourteen, say, and then wake up when you were seventeen. The worst teenage years would be over and you would have been spared all the indignities that went with them. Bad skin. The embarrassment we've been talking about. Awkwardness. Anxiety that people aren't going to like you because you're not cool enough. Everything.'

'Fourteen to seventeen?'

'I was thinking of boys,' he said. 'Those are the really bad years for boys. Then, suddenly you're through it all. Eighteen is actually quite exciting.'

'And it gets better, doesn't it?'

He nodded. 'Yes.'

He had been looking at her when he replied, and she felt a momentary thrill that perhaps he meant that it got better because one met people, and in particular because he had met her.

Now he was smiling again. 'Oh well,' he said. 'We should go.'

'Yes,' she said, without knowing where they were meant to be going. He had said nothing about dinner: was he going to take her to a restaurant?

He rose to his feet holding out a hand towards her. 'My place is just round the corner. Maxwell Street. I wondered if you ...'

She busied herself with her coat.

'... if you wanted to have dinner there. I can cook, you know.'

'Yes, I'd love that.'

He went out first, and she followed him. Outside, the evening sun bathed the buildings behind them in warm light, bringing out, through the grey of the stone's discoloration, the original colour of honey. A woman walked past them carrying her bags of purchases from the supermarket further up

Morningside Road. A young girl on the other side of the road, walking beside her mother, holding her hand, suddenly skipped, as if for sudden, unexpected joy. Pat thought: and so could I.

69. Pythagoras's Trousers

His flat was on the top floor of a tenement block. The stair was typical of buildings of that sort, with that slight smell of dust and something else that it was always rather difficult to pinpoint – did stone have a smell? Chalk did, if you put it under your nose – a chalky smell. Sometimes, of course, a common stair trapped cooking smells, and you could tell what was on your neighbour's menu as you walked past their door: curry, perhaps, or something fried; the sweet smell of steak under the grill. Sometimes you would hear them, too: the sound of laughter, or voices raised in anger; the sound of children shouting or crying – the background noise of communal life.

He fiddled with the key in the lock, which was stiff, and then pushed open the door. 'My place,' he said. 'It's a mess. Sorry about that.'

It was not a large flat, and as she stood in the hallway Pat realised that it consisted of only two rooms and a bathroom. Through an open door off the hallway she could see into a living room beyond; it was light, a benefit of being on the top floor. 'It's not a mess at all,' she said. 'It seems very nice.' She peered through the door. 'May I?'

'Of course. Go right in.'

The living room turned out to be a bed-sitting room; there was a bed at the other end of the room, under the window. It was one of those beds done up as a sofa, a brightly coloured spread across it and a couple of cushions in place of a pillow.

She looked about her. 'Do you live by yourself?'

He nodded. 'Yes. Mostly.'

She wondered what he meant by that. 'You sometimes have a flatmate?'

Michael had crossed the room to a table on which there was a CD player and speakers. He had a disc in his hand and it caught the light, casting a dancing spot of colour onto the ceiling. He answered her without turning round. 'Sometimes.'

The disc inserted, he pressed a button. There was a sudden burst of music – too loud, and he quickly turned it down. The music was bright and compelling.

'You've heard them before?' he asked.

She shook her head. 'Who is it? It's very . . . '

'Infectious?' he offered.

'Yes. It makes you want to dance – almost.'

'It's the Penguin Café Orchestra,' he said. 'There's nobody like them, really. It's wonderful. The man who started it, Simon Jeffes, was a fantastic musician. He composed this stuff and there's nothing like it.'

She listened carefully. A hurdy-gurdy was being played alongside light percussion; she thought she heard a piano accordion too.

'This is called "Pythagoras's Trousers",' Michael said. 'He went in for great titles. There's another one, a bit later on, called "Music for Helicopters". And there's "Music for a Found Harmonium". Simon Jeffes was in Japan once and he went out and found an abandoned harmonium in the street. Imagine that. Imagine finding a harmonium . . . ' He paused. 'Are you hungry?'

She was not sure if she was. She had not eaten for hours, but she had not been thinking of food. 'Yes. Not ravenous, I suppose, but hungry enough for dinner.'

'Good,' he said. 'And do you like scallops?'

She did.

'That's good too,' he said. 'Because I've got some and I thought I'd cook them for us. With rice. Wild rice.'

'That sounds really nice.'

'It is,' he said. 'You know something about cooking scallops?

You mustn't wash them, because they absorb water and it ruins them.'

Pat said she did not know that. 'I know nothing about scallops,' she said.

He smiled. 'Well, you know something now. I could tell you a whole lot more, if you wanted to know.'

'Such as?'

He put on an expression of mock seriousness. 'Such as that people who cultivate them are called scallop ranchers. How about that?'

'I love it. And?'

'And there's a big difference between hand-dived scallops and the scallops that are sucked up by trawlers. The hand-dived ones aren't damaged – the ones they vacuum up from the seabed are battered about. Then, of course, some of them put them in fresh water so that they increase their bulk by about twenty-five per cent. A quarter of the weight you pay for is just water.'

He pointed towards the door. 'I need to go through there to get things going. Give me a few minutes. I'll get you a glass of wine.'

He left her. In the background the Penguin Café Orchestra played optimistically. She picked up the sleeve of the CD and studied the picture. A penguin stood before an open door, looking out. Why had they chosen that name? And did Pythagoras wear trousers? If he did, then the sum of the legs would be equal to . . .

She moved away from the table. On the opposite side of the room there was a small fireplace and mantelpiece. The fire had long since been blocked in, as happened, and replaced with a flat, white-painted board. Once there would have been a range there, she thought, and it would have been the focal point of the room, the family's hearth.

She looked at the objects on the mantelpiece. A ruler, a tape measure, a book into the pages of which slips of paper had been inserted as bookmarks. She looked at the title of the book: *An Anthology of Nature Poems*. He read poetry. It was unexpected. He read poetry and he knew all about scallops and how to cook them. There was a card tucked under the book, and she picked it up. It was a birthday card. She opened it. She was not thinking.

She read the inscription. *To my darling lovely Michael*. She dropped it, from shock. She picked it up with fumbling, nervous fingers. Underneath was written: *From your fiancée, who loves you so, so much*.

He came into the room. She held the card loosely.

'You're engaged . . .'

He frowned, and then moved forward, taking the card from her hand.

'Was,' he said.

She could not think what to say.

He spoke quietly. 'She died. A year ago. A bit more, actually. Fifteen months.'

'I'm really sorry.'

'I miss her so much.'

'Of course, you must.'

He went over to the table and silenced the Penguin Café Orchestra.

'I've been hoping to meet somebody else,' he said. 'I was hoping . . .' He trailed off, and then, with a playful movement of his right hand, he pointed at her. 'You?'

70. On Loch Sunart

Bertie awoke before Ranald Braveheart Macpherson. For a few moments he was uncertain where he was, but then, seeing the sloping canvas roof of the tent above his head, he remembered. And with that came the realisation that he had spent his first night in a tent, in a field, in the middle of Argyll, and had survived. The knowledge was exhilarating, and he found himself smiling in delight at the thought that he had another two nights of this ahead of him before they went back to Edinburgh; it was good fortune of an utterly over-whelming nature.

He slipped out of his sleeping bag and dressed in his uniform as quietly as he could so as not to disturb Ranald. Then he unzipped the doors of the tent and went out into the field. The sky was clear and the sun was on the hills and the waters of Loch Sunart. Bertie stood still for a while, taking in the beauty of his surroundings. It was a landscape full of possibility for adventures – on either side of the sea loch were mountains, tree-lined at the lower levels and bare further up. There were few signs of human habitation – a house here and there, nestling into a hillside or clinging to the shore on the edge of the loch; a small road cutting into the forest.

Bertie was distracted by a shout. Turning round, he saw Tofu emerging from the trees at the edge of the field.

'Bertie!' shouted Tofu.

Bertie waved to Tofu as he walked over to meet him.

'I've found a boat,' said Tofu. 'Come and see it.'

Bertie followed the other boy down a path that led down

to a rocky shore below. A small sailing dinghy bobbed on the surface of the water, tethered to a mooring ring in the rock.

'Do you want to come with me?' asked Tofu.

Bertie frowned. 'In the boat?'

'Yes,' said Tofu. 'Breakfast won't be ready for ages. All the grown-ups are still asleep. They're really lazy when you give them half a chance.'

Bertie looked doubtful. 'I don't think we're allowed ...' he began.

Tofu cut him short. 'We won't go far. And we're not going to do any harm. I'm a really experienced sailor, Bertie.'

Bertie still looked doubtful. 'I didn't know that you sailed, Tofu. Where have you been?'

'We went to France on a ferry,' said Tofu. 'And came back.'

There was a noise behind them – the sound of stones slipping down the path. Bertie turned round and saw Ranald Braveheart Macpherson.

'What are you doing?' asked Ranald.

'We're going to have a sail,' said Tofu, scrambling down to the boat. 'You coming, Ranald?'

'Is Bertie going?' asked Ranald.

'Yes,' said Tofu. 'Unless you're too scared. You don't have to come if you're scared. You can go and play with Olive and Pansy.' He laughed at the slur.

Ranald looked anxiously at Bertie. 'We're not scared, are we, Bertie?'

Bertie shook his head. 'But we mustn't go far, Tofu,' he said. 'It's not our boat.'

'Don't worry,' said Tofu. 'Come on. Get on board.'

They climbed aboard gingerly, and Ranald cast off the line securing them to the ring. As he did so, a small gust of wind sprang up and the boat began to drift away from the shore.

'Where are the oars?' asked Bertie.

Tofu looked round. 'Oars? This is a sailing boat, Bertie – you'd think you'd know that sailing boats don't have oars.'

'Then how do we move?' asked Ranald.

Tofu extracted a sail from a bag under the midships seat. 'We put up this sail,' he said. 'Come on, give me a hand.'

It took some time to raise the sail, but eventually it was in position and had filled with wind. 'There,' said Tofu with satisfaction. 'We're sailing. I told you we didn't need oars.'

The dinghy, with the nimbleness of its breed, was now moving swiftly over the water. Within a few minutes they were out in the sea loch, having slid out past a few tiny islets that marked the entrance to Glenborrodale's bay.

'We're really moving now,' said Tofu. 'You see?'

Bertie looked back at the shore. 'I think we should go in soon,' he said. 'We don't want to go too far.'

Tofu shook his head. 'We'll turn round in a few minutes,' he said. 'Once we reach that headland over there we can turn and come back.'

Ranald Braveheart Macpherson, who had so far been silent, now spoke. 'How are we going to get back?' he asked. 'You can't sail against the wind, you know, and it's behind us now. If we turn round it will just carry on pushing us this way.'

Tofu made a dismissive gesture. 'What do you know, Ranald? Nothing. You know nothing. So shut your face.'

Bertie came to Ranald's defence. 'I think Ranald may be right, Tofu. You don't know everything, you know.'

'My dad's got a boat on the Clyde,' said Ranald. 'I think he stole it from someone, because we never see it. But he told me about how you can't sail against the wind. He knows about these things.'

Tofu was now showing the first signs of anxiety. 'It's easy,' he said. 'You see this thing here? That's called the tiller. You turn it like this.'

The boat heeled over dangerously as Tofu swung the tiller to starboard. Quickly he returned it to its original position. The wind had come up now, swirling off the face of Ben Hiant, and was propelling them even faster.

'We're going to die,' said Ranald Braveheart Macpherson. 'We're going to be swept out to sea and drowned.'

'Rubbish,' said Tofu. 'The wind's going to change direction and push us back. We'll be back at camp for breakfast, like I said.'

Bertie shook his head. 'I don't think so, Tofu. I think we are really going to be swept out to sea. Our only hope is that we see a fishing boat or something and they save us . . .'

'Otherwise we're dead,' said Ranald.

Tofu was silent now, having realised the full seriousness of their position. 'I don't want to die,' he said.

'Then you shouldn't have taken this boat,' said Ranald. 'If you hadn't we would have survived. Now we're finished.'

'You shouldn't give up too quickly, Ranald,' said Bertie gently.

Ranald looked miserable. 'My dad told me a story once about how three sailors were shipwrecked in a lifeboat and they were there for ages and ages. They became hungrier and hungrier and eventually they ate the cabin boy.'

Tofu looked at him. 'That's you, Ranald. We'll eat you.' He paused. 'I'm not joking, you know.'

71. *Lord of the Flies*

The wind that had blown the small sailing dinghy past the towering green shore of Ben Hiant now swept the hapless boat, and its three unhappy young sailors, out through the northern reaches of the Sound of Mull. Now Ardnamurchan Point revealed itself, a great bulwark against the Atlantic, with its lighthouse white and glorious in the morning sun; scant pleasure though did this sight give the three boys, nor were they moved by the view they now had of the distant shapes of Muck, Rùm, and Eigg.

Ranald Braveheart Macpherson sat up at the bow, looking out for any sign of a boat to which they might signal for help, but there was nothing. So far they had seen only one other vessel, a small yellow fishing boat that had been steaming off in the direction of Tobermory but had been too far away from them to notice or answer any waving or shouting on their part.

'We're going to be carried right out,' he said to Bertie. 'All the way to Canada.'

Bertie tried to comfort him. 'Don't worry, Ranald. We'll get to the Outer Hebrides first. Maybe Barra, or South Uist, or somewhere like that.'

Tofu, who had begun the trip with his usual bombast, was severely diminished now. 'I can't swim,' he said miserably. 'What if a wave breaks over us and the boat gets full of water? What then, Bertie?'

'I don't think that will happen, Tofu,' said Bertie.

'If we're too heavy, we could throw Ranald over the side,' Tofu mused. 'That might help. Do you think we should do that, Bertie?'

'Definitely not,' exclaimed Bertie. 'We're all in this together.'

'Yes,' said Ranald. 'That's what the Government says, Tofu. We're all in this together.'

'I think we should just sit still,' said Bertie. 'I'm sure that somebody will see us sooner or later.'

Now that they were out in the open sea, with the coast of Mull receding behind them, the boat was being tossed about a bit on an ocean swell. The wind, though, had picked up, and what way they might have lost from the force of the oncoming swell was more than compensated for by their increased sail power. Bertie had now taken over the tiller from Ranald, and was sitting at the stern, making sure that they avoided broaching. He was thinking of all the things that he had not done in his life and would now never have the chance to do. He would have liked to have lived at least for a little while in Glasgow; he would have liked to have owned a Swiss Army penknife; he would have liked, per- haps, to have written a book. He was not quite sure what book he would have written, but perhaps it would be a book that helped other boys who were in the same position as he was. Perhaps he would have written *Bertie's Guide to Life and*

Mothers. It would have been such a useful book, that one, and now he would never be able to do it.

Suddenly Ranald gave a cry. 'Look, Bertie! There's land ahead.'

Bertie abandoned his reverie and stared in the direction in which Ranald was pointing. Sure enough, there on the horizon was a cluster of small, low shapes, and to the south of them a larger land mass – a substantial island.

'There you are,' said Bertie. 'We're going to be washed up on some islands. We're going to be safe after all.'

'I told you,' said Tofu.

Now helped by the current, the little boat sailed swiftly through a channel between a larger island, flat and uninhabited, and a small cluster of rocky islets. Some of these were topped with vegetation, with an overcoat of grass, and one, to which the current was propelling them, had a curved beach of inviting white sand. It was here that they made landfall, the nose of the dinghy obligingly gliding into the embrace of the sand.

'There,' said Tofu. 'We've arrived. I'll take over now.'

Ranald Braveheart Macpherson cast an anxious glance at Bertie.

They stepped out onto the shore. Behind them, in the small bay formed by the curve of the island, seal heads popped out of the water, watching them with that curiosity that seals have for intruders. On the island itself, above the line of the sand, a carpet of wild flowers, in full summer bloom, made a private garden for nesting sea-birds.

Bertie, followed by Ranald Braveheart Macpherson, made his way up to a vantage point above the beach, clambering over the rocks. Tofu remained below with the boat, busying himself with securing it to an outcrop of rock.

'Where do you think we are, Bertie?' asked Ranald.

Bertie thought for a moment. He was intimately acquainted with his parents' bookshelves, which he happily browsed at such times that he was not attending the various classes organised by his mother. He had pored over *A Gazetteer of Scotland* and remembered the maps: Colonsay, Mull, Tiree, Coll . . .

'I think we must be on the Cairns of Coll, Ranald,' he said. 'That big island over there must be Coll itself.'

Ranald peered across the sound towards the other shore. 'Coll has people, doesn't it, Bertie?'

Bertie nodded. 'Yes, there are people, Ranald.'

Ranald still looked worried. 'Campbells, Bertie?'

Bertie shook his head. 'I don't think so, Ranald.'

There was a shout from Tofu. 'Boat coming!'

Bertie and Ranald had been looking out towards the open sea; when they turned, they saw a trawler-sized boat making its way through the channel separating the Cairns from the shore of Coll. They shouted and waved, as did Tofu, and several figures on the boat waved back to them.

Tofu ran forward to meet the inflatable tender that the now anchored boat dispatched to the beach. As he did so, Bertie and Ranald made their way down the slope, slipping and sliding over the humps of grass in their haste and elation.

'Did you lads get all the way out here in that wee thing?' asked the man as he beached his tender.

'We were blown here,' explained Bertie.

'Tofu took the boat,' began Ranald Braveheart Macpherson, only to be silenced by a glare from Tofu.

The man now asked them their names, and gave his own: Captain Campbell. 'Well, you'll be coming back with me,' he said. 'Come on; we can tow the dinghy back. Mull, is it?'

'Ardnamurchan,' said Bertie.

They began the journey back. They had been on the island for such a short time, thought Bertie, and there had been no time for Tofu to ... He paused. He had seen a book once that seemed to talk about something rather like this. There had been some boys and they had found themselves on a desert island, and there had been a boy with glasses and a boy who was kind and a boy called Jack who was rather like Tofu ... and things had gone badly wrong. He glanced at Tofu, and then at Ranald Braveheart Macpherson, who seemed strangely silent. Then he looked back towards the mainland, and what it represented.

72. Tea for Three

'It's been a long time,' said Domenica as she welcomed her friend Dilly Emslie into her drawing room. 'We should see our friends more frequently, but do we?' She answered her own question as soon as she had posed it. 'We do not.'

Dilly smiled. 'I know what it's like, but at least I have the chance of catching up with Angus too. That's a bonus.'

Angus was in the kitchen, making tea for the three of them. He had also baked scones and was setting these out now on the three-tiered cake stand that Domenica used – with proper irony, of course: it's quintessentially Edinburgh, she had said when she had first shown it to him. Now he brought the tray through and set it down on the table.

There was a lot to catch up on. Dilly enquired after Angus's health. 'And how is your somnambulism, Angus?' she asked.

'Completely cured,' he said. 'Relegated to my medical history – or shall I say my psychiatric history? I saw Dr Macgregor about it – he's a well-known shrink – and after one or two sessions the whole thing went away. He told me that the solution to so many psychological problems is to talk about them. If you talk freely about a problem, then you take away its power to distress you.'

'That's a great relief,' said Dilly. 'Perhaps we should talk a little bit more about our tram system. Perhaps that would take away its power to distress us.'

Domenica laughed. 'So droll,' she said. 'So very droll. But what if one has no problems? Should one talk about the problems one doesn't have, or perhaps about the problems that others have?'

'Maybe a bit of both,' said Angus.

'It's always so very satisfying to talk about the problems that beset one's friends,' said Domenica. 'In a proper spirit of sympathy, of course.'

'If they have any,' said Dilly. 'And now, with Angus's somnambulism dealt with, you won't have any yourselves.'

'Oh, we do,' said Domenica. 'We have Antonia ...'

Dilly sighed. 'Of course. I was forgetting.'

'And there's Sister Maria-Fiore dei Fiori di Montagna,' continued Domenica. 'She's an Italian nun who's staying with us at the moment. She's full of observations. It's like living with an anthology of aphorisms.'

'How trying,' said Dilly. 'I don't know if I could bear too many aphorisms in the home. May I make a suggestion?'

'Anything,' said Domenica.

'Why don't you introduce her to somebody and get her launched in Edinburgh society, even if she isn't here for long? I believe they're crying out for a new enthusiasm as they're fed up with hearing the same old thing time and time again. When did you last hear a good aphorism at an Edinburgh dinner party?'

Domenica looked thoughtful. 'That's possible,' she mused. 'But I'm not too exercised about it. The visit has had its moments, of course.'

Angus said nothing, but he felt his neck getting warm as he remembered the reference that Antonia had made to the blue Spode cup. That had been one of the visit's saliences, so far, and it really was confrontational on Antonia's part to drag that up when it could so easily have been consigned to history. There was no doubt that he did not emerge very well from that story, even if he had acted in the belief that he had been entitled to reclaim his – or Domenica's – own property. Was he destined now to feel this great burden of Spode-related guilt more or less forever?

Dilly replaced her cup on the table. 'You have such lovely Spode,' she said.

Domenica glanced at Angus, but then very quickly looked away.

'It is nice, yes. Of course, we also have a very nice set of Mason's that came from . . . '

She did not finish. Dilly had picked up her empty cup to examine it. 'Where does one get blue Spode these days?' she asked. 'I've heard it can be difficult.'

'There's that shop behind the Museum,' said Angus quickly.

'I'm not sure if they have Spode,' said Dilly. She paused, holding the cup up to get a better view of it. For a few moments it seemed to Angus that she had perhaps discovered something in the particular cup that she was about to remark on – the owner's initials, for instance, somehow inserted into the glaze. He felt the hot patch behind his neck get larger.

'It used to be very popular,' Dilly remarked. 'Fewer people have it now, of course.'

One fewer, thought Angus.

Domenica came to his rescue. 'Yes,' she said firmly. 'Antonia can be trying. But then, I suppose most of us have what I call our quota of lame-duck friends.'

'Absolutely,' enthused Angus, with relief. 'And I suppose we have to put up with them.'

'I suppose that's true,' said Dilly.

Domenica expanded on the theme. 'There must be very few people who, when contemplating their friends, can't list at least some whom they view with a certain ... how shall I put it? A certain sinking of the heart?'

Angus thought of his friends. There had been one or two at art college who had always tagged along and who ... He thought of charity, and our obligation to be charitable, and then suddenly he thought of the late Ramsey Dunbarton, whose portrait he had painted and whom he had found so very tedious but who had looked upon him as a friend and had sought out his company at the Scottish Arts Club. Poor Ramsey, with his interminable tales about playing the role of the Duke of Plaza-Toro in the Church Hill Theatre's production of *The Gondoliers*; and his account of playing bridge at Blair Atholl; and his story of how the senior partner in his legal firm had invited him as a young man to have a glass of sherry and made a joke about the Water of Leith; and his story of how he had seen the *Gardyloo* in the Firth of Forth, and so on, and so on ... until he had died, and suddenly Angus had realised that he could have been nicer to him and given him more of his time; which, he reflected, was a thought that all of us might think about those whom we know, but that in general we did not, because life got in the way, which it always did, until suddenly . . .

73. The Innocent Games of the Innocent

Bertie returned unscathed from the cub scout expedition to Ardnamurchan. The ill-fated trip to the Cairns of Coll that he made with Tofu and Ranald Braveheart Macpherson had not had the serious consequences it might have had. For some reason their absence from breakfast had gone unnoticed – such was the general excitement – and by the time they were eventually missed they had been landed by their rescuer and were making their way up the brae to the camp ground.

The boys agreed that nothing would be said about their experience. 'There's no point making adults worried,' said Tofu. 'You know how anxious they get over nothing.'

Both Bertie and Ranald Braveheart Macpherson remained silent over this. Ranald opened his mouth to speak, but was warned off by Tofu, who leaned towards him in a way that was unambiguously threatening.

'Agreed, Ranald?' growled Tofu.

Ranald nodded. He did not express the wish he privately felt, and had whispered to Bertie, that Tofu had taken the boat by himself and had been blown over to the Outer Hebrides, possibly never to return. But such sentiments had no effect on his, or on Bertie's, enjoyment of the next few days, and when the time came to return to Edinburgh they were in a state of complete bliss.

When the bus arrived back in Edinburgh, Stuart and Ulysses were waiting to meet Bertie. On seeing his brother, Ulysses let out a shriek of delight and waved his tiny arms about hysterically.

'You see,' said Stuart. 'He's been missing you, Bertie.'

'I think he needs changing,' said Bertie, wrinkling his nose.

'All in good time,' said Stuart.

'And is Mummy still . . . ' Bertie's voice trailed off.

'She's still in the desert, Bertie,' said Stuart. 'They say it might be as long as three months.'

Bertie absorbed this information stoically. The true period, which Stuart did not communicate to Bertie out of sensitivity to his feelings, was six months – or so the Foreign Office had recently revealed. They had been in touch with the Bedouin sheik who was holding Irene and he had disclosed that he was in no hurry to release her. Apparently Irene had organised a book club for the wives in the harem, and this had proved immensely popular. The sheik, who was used to grumbling wives, was pleased with the relative peace that prevailed in the harem and had no inclination to bring it to an end.

As they made their way back to Scotland Street, Stuart mentioned a conversation that he had had with Angus on the stair.

'I was talking to Mr Lordie, Bertie,' he said. 'He had been taking Cyril for a walk. I think Cyril is missing you – he looked around my feet just to check that you weren't somewhere there.'

'He's a very good dog,' said Bertie.

Stuart nodded. He wondered whether it was hard to be a good dog – whether they had to make a moral effort – or whether it came naturally. Was human goodness natural? He looked at his son; he was naturally good, he thought, but no doubt the world, alas, would chip away at that as he got older. The doctrine of original sin, Stuart had always thought, was an utter nonsense – a miserable notion, full of fear and negativity about human nature; if anything we arrived in this world, he thought, endowed with original goodness rather than burdened with evil.

'Mr Lordie made a very interesting suggestion,' said Stuart. 'I thought I'd run it past you, Bertie.'

Bertie looked at his father expectantly.

'He had heard that your birthday party had never really got off the ground,' said Stuart. 'What with Mummy being very busy and then having to go off to Dubai at short notice. So he wondered whether you would like to have it at the same time that he and Domenica have a little party they've been planning. You could ask your guests and they could ask theirs. Mr Lordie would open up the Drummond Place Gardens for you and your friends to play whatever it was you wanted to play.'

'Chase the Dentist?' asked Bertie excitedly. 'Could we play that, Daddy?'

'Of course,' said Stuart.

'And Greeks and Turks?' asked Bertie. 'Could we play that one as well? We'll need some mud for that.'

'How do you play it?' asked Stuart.

'Well,' said Bertie, 'you have two sides, see? And one side are the Greeks and the other side are the Turks. And they shout at each other. The Greeks shout "Horrid Turk!" and then the Turks shout "Horrid Greek!" And then they throw mud and hit each other – not hard, just pretending – until somebody shouts "European Union!" and they stop. Then somebody shouts: "European Union Over!" and it all starts over again.'

'What fun,' said Stuart. 'I'm sure we can arrange that.'

'And could we play Campbells and Macdonalds too?' asked Bertie.

'Yes,' said Stuart. 'If there's time.'

'I think it'll be really good fun,' said Bertie. 'When will it be?'

'On Saturday,' answered Stuart. 'It will be a sort of lunch for the adults and you and your pals can have a separate lunch—'

'Of sausages?' interjected Bertie.

'Yes. Sausages,' said Stuart.

The question of the guest list was then discussed. 'Do I have to have Olive?' asked Bertie.

Stuart shrugged. 'Not if you don't want her to be there, Bertie. It's up to you.'

Bertie frowned. He was a kind boy, and he did not want to hurt Olive's feelings. Perhaps she could come, after all, but would find it difficult to order him around if she were outnumbered by boys.

'She can come if she wants to,' he said at last. 'And she can bring Pansy too. But no other girls will be allowed.'

'Fair enough,' said Stuart. He paused. 'What about your friend Tofu?'

Bertie hesitated. 'He can come,' he said. 'And so can Ranald. But not Larch or Eck.'

Again Stuart readily agreed. 'There's another boy you might like to ask,' he said. 'Big Lou – you know that woman with the coffee shop, round the corner – she's looking after a boy of about your age. He's called Finlay, I'm told. I hear he's very nice. It would be good to have him along, don't you think?'

'Yes,' said Bertie. 'He can come.'

74. *Architecture, Love, Desert*

The lunch party took place on a Saturday, with guests, both juvenile and adult, arriving at shortly before one. The guest list was an eclectic one – Domenica's parties had always involved people of every talent, and very rarely of none. She believed, though, that everybody present should know, or know of, at least half the other guests, thus ensuring that the conversation could rise above the cautious platitudes that strangers exchange. In this case, everybody knew one another, except for Sister Maria-Fiore dei Fiori di Montagna, who, although she did not know everybody, was rapidly being known herself as a star in the Edinburgh firmament: a major dinner party, hosted in Heriot Row by Felicitas Macfie, had introduced her to a number of Edinburgh people who had been enchanted by the nun and her arresting aphorisms. Her success was remarkable: an introduction at this party to Hugh Andrew, the publisher, had already brought an invitation for her to edit a small collection of outstanding aphorisms, and she had also been requested to participate in a Radio Four discussion panel chaired by James

Naughtie. She had readily and courteously accepted these invitations, pointing out to Antonia that 'if we are invited to do something, then that is because some other person wants us to do something'. Antonia had agreed that this was, indeed, the case and had suggested that this observation be added to the list of those that would in due course appear in print.

Some of the other guests who were there as friends of Domenica or Angus, or of both, also knew Bertie, and had brought him a present. Judith McClure and Roger Collins, for instance, were old friends of Domenica, but were also fond of Bertie, on whose behalf they had looked after Cyril when Angus was away on his honeymoon. Mary and Philip Contini, the proprietors of Valvona & Crolla, the deli-catessen in which Bertie loved to inspect beautifully packaged boxes of Panforte di Siena, had been invited too and had brought Bertie a present of a large *panforte*. James Holloway, once again a neighbour of Matthew and Elspeth, was there, as he always came to Domenica's par-ties, as did Dilly and Derek Emslie and Maryla and Edward Green.

At an early stage in the party, James found himself talking to Matthew and Elspeth about their move to the house in the Pentlands that they had just bought from the Duke of Johannesburg.

'We'll miss you in India Street,' he said. 'I know the Linklaters have just moved in, which is nice, but it won't be the same without you and all those triplets of yours.'

'And our au pair,' said Elspeth. 'And our au pair's au pair.'

James laughed. 'That girl! What's she called? Birgitte? I saw her in Kay's Bar, you know. With Bruce.'

Matthew smiled. 'Yes, they've met up. I wondered whether I should warn her, so to speak, but then I realised that you can't warn people about other people. They don't listen.'

'They seem to be getting on very well,' said Elspeth. 'Even if he looks a bit odd at present – he's shaved off an eyebrow.'

'No,' said Matthew. 'That was a waxing accident.' He paused. 'But I must say matters have been much improved by her taking up with him. She's a little less ...'

'Strident?' offered Elspeth.

'Exactly.'

'Mind you,' said Elspeth, 'I think he might have found his match. Bruce is all bluster – narcissistic bluster. She's taking him in hand and making him do her bidding – or so Anna tells me. She says that Birgitte has decided that she wants to marry a Scotsman, and Bruce, it seems, is her choice. Apparently she always gets her way; he won't stand a chance.'

Matthew grinned. 'The end of Bruce's bachelor days – what a thought.'

The conversation turned to the new house. James asked whether they would have to do much to it, and Matthew replied that they had already been there with their architect, but that all alterations would be organic.

'I'm so relieved,' he said. 'I've at last found an architect who knows all about Christopher Alexander and his theory of natural order. When you look at what has been done to parts of this city by some architects ...'

Elspeth pulled a face. 'But you can't look at it – that's the problem. You can't look at what they've done because it's so ... so ...' She searched for the right adjective.

'So brutal,' offered Matthew.

'Yes. Brutal. And banal. Their buildings don't talk to their surroundings. Those great glass façades that kill the space they occupy, that are completely at odds with the buildings all around them.'

'Ego statements,' said Matthew. 'If you look at Professor Alexander's book, *The Nature of Order*, you see pictures printed side by side. One will be of a crass creation of modernist architecture, the other of a small-scale, sympathetic building. Then he asks: which one is alive? And of course you know exactly what he means. Some spaces and buildings just live – they just live. Others are dead. Look at Princes Street. Bits of it are lifeless – killed stone dead by buildings that have no relief in them – big flat expanses, with no human nooks and crannies, no play of light and shade.'

Elspeth reached out and laid a hand on his forearm, as if to comfort him. James lowered his eyes; he knew exactly how Matthew felt.

Matthew took a sip of wine. 'This city still has its beauty. But it is a fragile beauty, and that depends so much on one thing leading to another. One street leads into another; one view merges into another; one space draws attention to another space next door, and so on. Interrupt that flow and you destroy the beauty.'

'We can't let it happen,' said Elspeth.

'No,' said Matthew. 'We can't – not just for our sake but

for the sake of everyone who loves this place. And there are lots of them, you know. Lots of people all over the world.'

'How lucky is a city to be loved,' mused Elspeth. 'Just as we are lucky – ourselves – if we are loved.'

'Which you are,' said Matthew, taking her hand. 'And look over there, look at Pat with that new man of hers. Look at them.'

'Love,' said Elspeth. 'It's written all over them. And Pat deserves it, I think.'

James looked thoughtful. 'Is love a matter of desert?'

Matthew smiled. 'Dessert is the final and sweetest course,' he said. 'Only given to those who have earned it. That's what I was taught as a child.'

75. Be Kind

The raw carrots that Irene had envisaged being served at Bertie's party were not on the menu for the lunch party that day. Nor were they disguised as crudités – false colours under which carrots frequently aspire to travel; they were simply absent. Rather, there were Italian sausages, haggis parcels (haggis concealed in filo pastry), and quantities of smoked salmon. The juvenile palate was catered for through the provision of lashings of ice cream topped with chocolate sauce and a large, sickly cake, dyed green and orange. This was consumed with gusto by the children, particularly by Tofu, who ate six slices, and was copiously sick (in green and orange). Ulysses was sick too, as was Ranald Braveheart Macpherson –

315

in his case from sheer excitement. It was, everybody agreed, a great success.

The conversation was good, as it always was at Domenica's parties. Sister Maria-Fiore dei Fiori di Montagna excelled herself, coming up with observations on more or less the entire range of subjects discussed, including opera. 'The important thing to remember about opera,' she observed to Roger Collins, 'is that it is sung.'

Roger considered this for a moment before saying that he thought this was undoubtedly true.

'I'm glad you agree with me,' said Sister Maria-Fiore dei Fiori di Montagna.

Other subjects were subjected to similar analysis, and while this was happening the children went out into Drummond Place Gardens. Finlay, Big Lou's foster child, got on very well with Bertie, who felt that he had, in Finlay, found another true friend and ally. Sensing this, Tofu challenged Finlay by attempting to push him over, but was himself gently but firmly thrown to the ground by Finlay, who uttered the additional verbal warning: 'Watch your step, Fish Paste.' Ranald Braveheart Macpherson, who had lived so long under Tofu's heel, was particularly pleased by this exchange.

They went back inside for Irn Bru, and shortly afterwards Angus, having been asked to deliver his usual poem, stood up and smiled at Bertie. 'This time, it's for you, Bertie. It's a poem for your birthday. Turning seven is not easy – and you have accomplished it at last – and with such grace.'

Bertie inclined his head modestly as the poem began ...

Of the tendency, Angus said, of things to get better
Dogs and the optimistic are usually convinced;
Others, perhaps, are more cautious:
When I was your age I remember
Thinking that most of life's problems
Would be over by the next day;
I still think that, I suppose,
And am often pleasantly surprised
To discover that it is occasionally true;
Thinking something, you see,
Can make it happen, or so we believe,
Though how that works, I doubt
If I shall ever find out.
From your perspective, where you are
Is probably the only place
It is possible to be; some time soon
You will discover that we can, if lucky,
Decide who we shall become.
A word of warning here:
Of all the tempting roles
You will be offered, being yourself
Is unquestionably the safest,
Will bring the most applause
Will make you feel best;
Greasepaint, dear Bertie, is greasy:
Leave it to the actors;
The most comfortable face to wear,
You'll find, is your own.
So what do I wish for you?

Freedom? I imagine
You know all about that
Even if so far you've had
To contemplate it from a distance.
I could think of other things;
I might wish, for example,
That you should be whatever
You fervently want to be: a sailor,
A fireman, an explorer?
You may live, you know,
To seventy-seven and beyond:
What, I wonder, will Scotland
Be like seven decades from now?
I'll never know, but what I wish
Is that some of it will be left for you,
Some of the things we've loved.
Happy birthday, then, Bertie:
Be strong, be thoughtful;
Don't be afraid to cry, when necessary:
In operas, as in life, it is the strong
Who are always the first to weep.
Be kind, which you already are,
Even to those who deserve it least;
Kindness, you see, Bertie, is a sort of love,
That is something I have learned,
And you'll learn too if you listen
To the teacher we all should trust:
The human heart, my dear, the human heart,
Where kindness makes its home.

When Angus finished there was silence. Silence, like space in a great painting, can be so eloquent, can be so very important, can be the bit we remember.

THE IMPORTANCE OF BEING SEVEN

A 44 Scotland Street novel

Alexander McCall Smith

Despite inhabiting a great city renowned for its impeccable restraint,
the extended family of 44 Scotland Street is trembling on the brink
of reckless self-indulgence. Matthew and Elspeth receive startling – and
expensive – news on a visit to the Infirmary, Angus and Domenica are
contemplating an Italian *ménage à trois*, and even Big Lou is overheard
discussing cosmetic surgery. But when Bertie Pollock – six years old
and impatient to be seven – mislays his meddling mother Irene
one afternoon, a valuable lesson is learned: that
wish-fulfilment is a dangerous business.

Warm-hearted, wise and very funny, *The Importance of Being Seven*
brings us fresh and delightful insights into philosophy and
fraternity among Edinburgh's most lovable residents.

Abacus
978 0 349 12316 5

BERTIE PLAYS THE BLUES

A 44 Scotland Street novel

Alexander McCall Smith

Even down to its well-set Georgian townhouses, Edinburgh is a
hymn to measure and harmony. But on Scotland Street, domestic
accord is in short supply. Matthew and Elspeth welcome three new
arrivals, though the joys of multiple parenthood are somewhat lost
due to sleep deprivation and the difficulties of telling their brood
apart. Angus and Domenica are to marry, and Domenica has
ambitious and disturbing plans for their living arrangements,
especially when it appears that Antonia, in Italy recuperating
from Stendhal Syndrome, may not return. And little Bertie,
feeling blue, puts himself up for adoption on eBay.

Can Edinburgh's most deliciously dysfunctional residents
forsake discord and learn to dance to the same happy tune?

Abacus
978 0 349 00032 9

SUNSHINE ON SCOTLAND STREET

A 44 Scotland Street novel

Alexander McCall Smith

Scotland Street witnesses the wedding of the century, of Angus Lordie
to Domenica Macdonald, but as the newlyweds depart on honeymoon
Edinburgh is in disarray. Recovering from the trauma of being best
man, Matthew is taken up by a Dane called Bo, while Cyril eludes his
dog-sitter and embarks on a most unlikely odyssey. Narcissist Bruce
meets his match in the form of a sinister doppelgänger; Bertie, set up
by his mother for fresh embarrassment at school, yearns for freedom;
and Big Lou goes viral. But the residents of Scotland Street rally,
and order – and Cyril – is restored through the combined effects
of understanding, kindness and, most of all, friendship.

Abacus
978 0 349 13916 6

CORDUROY MANSIONS

Alexander McCall Smith

Welcome to Corduroy Mansions in Pimlico: comfortably
and genteelly weathered, it is home to a delightfully
eccentric cast of Londoners.

At the top lives William, with a faithful ex-vegetarian dog named
Freddie de la Hay and an indolent son who he hopes will soon fly
the nest. Four young women share the first-floor flat, including
twinset-and-pearls Caroline, Dee, vitamin addict and avid subscriber
to *Anti-oxidant News*, and Jenny, a put-upon PA. And round the
corner resides Oedipus Snark MP, who has succeeded in offending
everyone he knows, and many others besides. But what dark
revenge is being plotted by his mother, Berthea Snark,
and by his girlfriend, Barbara Ragg . . . ?

'A page-turner with many happy endings. Perfect'
Daily Express

Abacus
978 0 349 12239 7

THE DOG WHO CAME IN FROM THE COLD

A Corduroy Mansions novel

Alexander McCall Smith

At Corduroy Mansions, strange doings are afoot, mostly in the name
of love. Lonely William French and his faithful canine Freddie are
recruited to the service of MI6 by a beguiling lady operative; Caroline
finds her suitor James mysteriously lacking; and Barbara Ragg is
tempted to the Highlands by blossoming romance. Meanwhile,
psychiatrist Berthea Snark is called away to protect her
credulous brother from a band of New Age fraudsters.

Hilarious and affectionate, *The Dog Who Came in from the Cold*
joins Alexander McCall Smith's London tribe of misfits and
hopefuls in a new set of adventures in life, love and philosophy.

Abacus
978 0 349 12321 9